D1529027

Cover photography: Wander Aguiar

Cover design: Popkitty Designs

Get your freebie!

Don't miss your chance to read *Island Captive* for free, just for signing up to my newsletter! Get your freebie here: https://BookHip.com/QGLGGJ

Chapter One

Keenan

I watch from where I sit on the craggy cliffs of Ballyhock to the waves crashing on the beach. Strong. Powerful. Deadly. A combination so familiar to me it brings me comfort. It's two hours before my alarm goes off, but when Seamus McCarthy calls a meeting, it doesn't matter where you are or what you're doing, the men of The Clan answer.

I suspect I know why he's calling a meeting today, but I also know my father well enough not to presume. One of our largest shipments of illegal arms will arrive in our secured port next week, and over the next month, we'll oversee distribution from the home that sits on the cliff behind me. Last week, we also sealed a multi-million-dollar deal that will put us in good stead until my father retires, when I assume the throne. But something isn't right with our upcoming transactions. Then again, when dealing with the illicit trade we orchestrate, it rarely is. As a high-ranking man of The Clan, I've learned to pivot and react. My instincts are primed.

The sun rises in early May at precisely 5:52 a.m., and it's rare I get to watch it. So this morning, in the small quiet interim before daybreak and our meeting, I came to the cliff's edge. I've traveled the world for my family's business, from the highest ranges of the Alps to the depths of the shores of the Dead Sea, the vast expanse of the Serengeti, and the top of the Eiffel Tower. But here, right here atop the cliffs of Ballyhock, paces from the door to my childhood home, overlooking the Irish Sea, is where I like to be. They say the souls of our ancestors pace these shores, and sometimes, early in the morning, I almost imagine I can see them, the beautiful, brutal Celts and Vikings, fearless and brave.

A brisk wind picks up, and I wrap my jacket closer to my body. I've put on my gym clothes to hit the workout room after our meeting if time permits. We'll see. My father may have other ideas.

I hear footsteps approach before I see the owner.

"What's the story, Keenan?"

Boner sits on the flat rock beside me, rests his arms on his bent knees, and takes a swig from a flask. Tall and lanky, his lean body never stills, even in sleep. Always tapping, rocking, moving from side to side, Boner has the energy of an eight-week-old golden retriever. My younger cousin, we've known each other since birth, both raised in The Clan. He's like a brother to me.

"Eh, nothing," I tell him, waving off an offer from the flask. "You out of your mind? He'll knock you upside the head, and you know it."

If my father catches him drinking this early in the day, when he's got a full day of work ahead of him, heads will roll.

"Ah, that's right," he says, grinning at me and flashing perfect white teeth, his words exaggerated and barely intelligible. "You drink that energy shite before you go work on yer manly *physique*. And anyway, get off your high horse. Nolan's more banjaxed than I am."

I clench my jaw and grunt to myself. *Fuck*. Nolan, the youngest in The Clan and my baby brother, bewitched my mother with his blond hair and green eyes straight outta the womb. Shielded by my mother's protective arms, the boy's never felt my father's belt nor mine, and it shows. I regret not making him toe the line more when he was younger.

"Course he is," I mutter. "Both of you ought to know better."

"Ah, come off it, Keenan," Boner says good-naturedly. "You know better than I the Irish do best with a bit of drink no matter the time of day."

I can toss them back with the best of them, but there's a time and place to get plastered, and minutes before we find out the latest update of the status of our very livelihood, isn't it. I get to my feet, scowling. "Let's go."

Though he's my cousin, and I'm only a little older than I am, Boner nods and gets to his feet. As heir to the throne and Clan Captain, I'm above him in rank. He and the others defer to me.

He mutters something that sounds a lot like "needs to get laid" under his breath as we walk up the stone pathway to the house.

"What's that?" I ask.

"Eh, nothing," he says, grinning at me.

"Wasn't nothing."

"You heard me."

"Say it to my face, motherfucker," I suggest good-naturedly. He's a pain in the arse, but I love the son of a bitch.

"I *said,*" he says loudly. "You need to get fuckin' *laid.* How long's it been since the bitch left you?"

I feel my eyes narrow as we continue to walk to the house. "Left *me*? You know's well as I do, I broke up with her." I won't even say her name. She's dead to me. I can abide many things, but lying and cheating are two things I won't.

"How long?" he presses.

It's been three months, two weeks, and five fucking days.

"Few months," I say.

He shakes his head. "Christ, Keenan," he mutters. "Come with me to the club tonight, and we'll get you right fixed."

I snort. "All set there."

I've no interest in visiting the seedy club Nolan and Boner frequent. I went once, and it was enough for me.

Boner shakes his head. "You've only been to the ante-room, Keenan," he says with a knowing waggle of his eyebrows. "You've never been *past* there. Not to where the *real* crowd gathers."

"All set," I repeat, though I don't admit my curiosity's piqued.

The rocky pathway leading to the family estate is paved with large, roughly hewn granite, the steep incline part of our design to keep our home and head-quarters private. Thirty-five stones in the pathway, which I count every time I walk to the cliffs that over-look the bay, lead to a thick, wrought-iron gate, the entrance to our house. With twelve bedrooms, five reception rooms, one massive kitchen, a finished base-ment with our workout rooms, library, and private interrogation rooms, the estate my father inherited from his father is worth an estimated eleven million euros. The men in The Clan outside our family tree live within a mile of our estate, all property owned by the brotherhood, but my brothers and I reside here.

When I marry—a requirement before I assume the throne as Clan Chief—I'll inherit the entire third floor, and my mother and father will retire to the east wing, as my father's parents did before them.

When I marry. For fuck's *sake*. The requirement hangs over my head like the sharpened edge of an execution-er's blade. No wedding, no rightful inheritance. And I can't even think of such a thing, not when my ex-girl-friend's betrayal's still fresh on my mind.

I wave my I.D. at the large, heavy black gate that borders our house, and with a click and whirr, the gates open. When my great grandfather bought this house, he kept the original Tuscan structure in place. The millionaire who had it built hailed from Tuscany, Italy, and to this day, the original Tuscan-inspired garden is kept in perfect shape. Lined with willow trees and bordered with well-trimmed hedges, benches and archways made from stone lend a majestic, age-old air. In May, the flowers are in full bloom, lilacs, irises, and the exotic violet hawthorn, the combined fragrances enchanting. The low murmur of the fountain my mother had built soothes me when I'm riled up or troubled. I've washed blood-soaked hands in that fountain, and I laid my head on the cold stones that surround it when Riley, my father's youngest brother and my favorite uncle, was buried.

We walk past the garden, and I listen to Boner yammer on about the club and the pretty little Welsh blonde he spanked, tied up, and banged last night, but when he reaches for his flask again, I yank it out of his hand and decidedly shove it in my pocket.

"Keenan, for fuck's—"

"You can have it after the meeting," I tell him. "No more fucking around, Boner. This is serious business, and you aren't going into this half-arsed, you hear?"

Though he clenches his jaw, he doesn't respond, and finally reluctantly nods. I'm saving him from punishment ordered by my father and saving myself from having to administer it. We trot up the large stairs to the front door, but before we can open it, the massive entryway door swings open, and Nolan stands in the doorway, grinning.

"Fancy meetin' you two here," he says in a high-pitched falsetto. "We won't be needin' any of yer wares today."

He pretends to shut the door, but I shove past him and enter the house. He says something under his breath to

6

Boner, and I swear Boner says something about me getting laid again. For once in my life, I fucking hope my father assigns me to issue a beating after this meeting. I'm so wound up. I could use a good fucking fight.

"Keenan." I'm so in my head, I don't notice Father Finn standing in the darkened doorway to our meeting room. He's wearing his collar, and his black priest's clothes are neatly pressed, the overhead light gleaming on his shiny black shoes. Though he's dressed for the day, his eyes are tired. It seems Boner isn't the only one who's pulled an all-nighter.

"Father."

Though Father Finn's my father's younger brother, I've never called him uncle. My mother taught me at a young age that a man of the cloth, even kin, is to be addressed as Father. It doesn't surprise me to see him here. He's as much a part of the McCarthy family as my father is, and he's privy to much, though not all, of what we do. It troubles him, though, as he's never reconciled his loyalty to the church and to our family.

Shorter than I am, he's balding, with curls of gray at his temples and in his beard. The only resemblance between the two of us are the McCarthy family green eyes.

Vicar of Holy Family, the church that stands behind my family's estate, Father Finn's association with the McCarthy Clan is only referenced by the locals in hushed conversation. Officially, he's only my uncle. Privately, he's our most trusted advisor. If Father Finn's come to this meeting, he's got news for us.

He holds the door open to my father's office, and when I enter I see my father's already sitting at the table.

He's only called the inner circle this morning, those related by blood: Nolan and Cormac, my brothers, Boner, Father Finn, and me. If necessary, we'll call the rest of The Clan to council after our first meeting.

"Boys," my father says, nodding to Nolan, Boner, and me in greeting.

My father sits at the head of the table, his back ramrod straight, the tips of his fingers pressed together as if in prayer. At sixty-three years old, he's only two years away from retirement as Chief, though he keeps himself in prime physical shape. With salt and pepper hair at his temples, he hasn't gone quite as gray as his younger brother. He jokes it's mam that keeps him young, and I think there's a note of truth in it. My mother is ten years his junior, and they've been wed since their arranged marriage thirty-three years ago. I was their firstborn, Cormac the second, and Nolan the third, though my father's made mention of several girls born before me that never made it past infancy. My mother won't talk of them, though. I wonder if the little graves that lie in the graveyard at Holy Family are the reason for the lines around my mother's bright gray eyes. I may never know.

I take my seat beside my father, and pierce Nolan and Boner with stern looks. Boner's fucking right. Nolan's eyes are bloodshot and glassy, and I notice he wobbles a little when he sits at the table. Irishmen are no strangers to drink, and we're no exception, but I worry Nolan's gone to the extreme. I make a mental note to talk to him about this later. I won't tolerate him fucking up our jobs because he can't stay sober. I watch him slump to the table and clear my throat. His eyes come to mine. I shake my head and straighten my shoulders. Nodding, he sits up straighter.

Cormac, the middle brother, sits to my left and notices everything. Six foot five, he's the giant of our group, and, appropriately, our head bonebreaker. With a mop of curly, dark brown hair and a heavy beard, he looks older than his twenty-five years.

He nods to me and I to him. We'll talk about our concerns about Nolan later, not in the presence of our father. Or any of the others, really.

"Thank you for coming so early, boys," my father begins, scrubbing a hand across his forehead. I notice a tremor in his hand I've never noticed before and stifle a sigh. He's getting older.

"It came to my attention early this morning that Father Finn has something to relay to us of importance." He fixes Boner and Nolan with an unwavering look. "And since some of you haven't gone to bed yet, I figured we should strike while the iron's hot, so to speak."

I can't help but smirk when Nolan and Boner squirm. When Boner's father passed, one of the few gone rogue in our company, my father took Boner under his wing and treated him as one of his own. I love the motherfucker like a brother myself. Though he's got a touch of the class clown in him, he's as loyal as they come and as quick with a knife draw as any I've seen, his aim at the shooting range spot-on. He's an asset to The Clan in every way. When he's fucking sober, anyway.

Now, under both my gaze and my father's, he squirms a little. My father keeps tabs on everyone here, Boner no exception.

"I think it best I let the Father speak for himself, since he needs to leave early to celebrate mass." None of us so much as blink, the Father's duties as commonplace as a shopping list. We're used to the juxtaposition of his duties to God's people and to us. We have long since accepted it as a way of life. He has a certain code he doesn't break, though, and out of respect for him, we keep many of the inner workings of The Clan from him. We give generously to the church, and though God himself may not see our donations as any sort of indulgence, the people of Holy Family and Ballyhock certainly do.

Father Finn sits on my father's left, his heavy gray brows drawn together.

"Thank you, Seamus." He and my mother are the only ones who call my dad his Christian name. Finn speaks in a soft, gentle tone laced with steel: a man of God tied by blood to the Irish mob.

My father nods and sits back, his gaze fixed on his younger brother.

Father clears his throat. "I have news regarding the... arms deal you've been working on for some time."

My father doesn't blink, and I don't make eye contact with any of my brothers. We've never discussed our occupations with Father so out in the open like this, but like our father, he sees all. The church he oversees is sandwiched between our mansion that overlooks the bay to the east, and Ballyhock's armory to the west. Still, his blatant naming of our most lucrative endeavor is unprecedented.

Though we dabble in many things, we have two main sources of income in The McCarthy Clan: arms trafficking and loansharking. Though neither are legal, Father Finn's insisted we keep out of the heavier sources of income our rival clan, the Martins from the south, dabble in. They're known for extortion, heroin imports and far more contracted hits than we've ever done. Rivals since before my parents married, we've held truce ever since my father took the throne. Both his father and our rival's former chief were murdered by the American mafia; the dual murders formed a truce we've upheld since then.

"Go on," my father says.

Father Finn clears his throat a second time. "There's no need to pretend I don't know where you're planning to get your bread and butter," he says in his soft voice. "Especially since I've advised you from the beginning."

My father nods, and a muscle ticks in his jaw. His brother takes his time when relaying information, and my father's not a patient man. "Go on," my father repeats, his tone harder this time.

"The Martins are behind the theft of your most recent acquisitions," he says sadly, as he knows theft from The Clan is an act of war. "Their theft is only the beginning, however. It was a plot to undermine you. They fully plan on sub-contracting your arms trafficking by summer. They have a connection nearby that's given them inside information, and I know where that inside information came from."

Boner cracks his knuckles, ready to fight. Nolan's suddenly sober, and I can feel Cormac's large, muscled body tense beside me. My own stomach clenches in anticipation. They're preparing to throw the gauntlet, which would bring our decades-long truce to a decided and violent end.

"Where would that be?" I ask.

Finn clears his throat again. "I'm not at liberty to give you all the details I know," he begins.

Boner glares at him. "Why the fuck not? Are you fucking kidding me?"

The Father holds up a hand, begging patience.

"Enough, Boner," I order. There's an unwritten rule in my family that we don't press the Father for information he doesn't offer. I suspect he occasionally relays information granted him in the privacy of the confessional, something he'd consider gravely sinful. Father Finn is a complex man. We take the information he gives us and piece the rest together ourselves.

"I can give you some, however," the Father continues. "I believe you'll find what you need at the lighthouse."

I feel my own brows pull together in confusion.

"The lighthouse?" Nolan asks. "Home of the old mentaller who kicked it?"

"Jack Anderson," the Father says tightly.

The eccentric old man, the lighthouse keeper, took a heart attack last month, leaving Ballyhock without a keeper. Someone spotted his body on the front green of the lighthouse and went to investigate. He was already dead.

Since the lighthouses are now operated digitally, no longer in need of a keeper, the town hasn't hired a replacement. Most lighthouse keepers around these parts are kept on more for the sake of nostalgia than necessity.

The man we're talking of, who lived in the lighthouse to the north of our estate, *was* out of his mind. He would come into town only a few times a year to buy his stores, then live off the dry goods he kept at his place. He had no contact with the outside world except for this foray into town and the library, and when he came, he reminded one of a mad scientist. Hailing from America, he looked a bit like an older, heavier version of Einstein with his wild, unkempt white hair and tattered clothing. He muttered curse words under his breath, walked with a manky old walking stick, and little children would scatter away from him when he came near. He always carried a large bag over his shoulder, filled with books he'd replenish at the library.

Father Finn doesn't reply to Nolan at first, holding his gaze. "Aren't we all a little mental, then, Nolan?" he asks quietly. Nolan looks away uncomfortably.

"Suppose," he finally mutters.

The Father sighs. "That's all I can tell you, lads. It's enough to go on. If you're to secure your arms deals, and solidify the financial wellbeing of The Clan, and most importantly, keep the peace here in Ballyhock, then I advise you to go at once to the lighthouse." He gets to his feet, and my father shakes his hand. I get to my feet, too, but it isn't to shake his hand. I've got questions.

"Was the lighthouse keeper involved?" I ask. "Was he mates with our rivals? What can we possibly find at the lighthouse?"

Inside the lighthouse? I've never even thought of there being anything inside the small lighthouse. There had to be, though. The old man lived there for as long as I can remember. There's no house on property save a tiny shed that couldn't hold more than a hedge trimmer.

My father holds a hand up to me, and Cormac mutters beside me, "Easy, Keenan."

Father Finn's just dropped the biggest bomb he's given us yet, and they expect me just to sit and nod obediently?

"You know more, Father," I say to him. "So much more."

Father Finn won't meet my eyes, but as he goes to leave, he speaks over his shoulder. "Go to the lighthouse, Keenan. You'll find what you need there."

Chapter Two

It's been thirty-four days since my father passed away.

Perhaps thirty-five.

I pinch the bridge of my nose and close my eyes, feeling a little queasy when nausea gnaws at my stomach. I step down the small ladder that brings me to the main floor of the lighthouse, and the largest room of the home I've never left, holding tightly to the rails so I don't fall.

I'm out of my mind *starving.*

Maybe he had food stores he didn't tell me about.

Maybe there's money somewhere in this tiny home, something hidden that he put away for my well-being.

Maybe...

But I've been going crazy trying to find anything at all that would help me survive, and I'm scraping the barrel at this point. If things were normal... if people could be trusted... I'd go into the town center. I'm taking my life into my hands doing that, though, if I'm to believe what my father told me since I was a child.

Even if it wasn't dangerous... what would they think of me when they saw me? I know what they'd see *physically*. A tall, thin girl with raven black hair down to her bottom, dressed in her mother's old clothes. Barefoot. My mother was smaller than I am, and I've long since outgrown her shoes. It made me sad when I did for two reasons: it gets cold in the lighthouse at night in the winter, and wearing her clothing and shoes were the only contact I had with her.

My mother died when she gave birth to me.

According to my father, no one even knew she was pregnant, and no one knows of my existence. I prefer it that way. Or at least, I used to.

Now is another story.

Though I've had no contact with the outside world beyond the small confines of this lighthouse, I've spent the past two decades reading anything and everything I could get my hands on. My mother was an avid reader, or so he told me, but after I went through all of her books, I needed more. My father would get me books from the library when he bought our groceries.

When I was a little girl, I used to beg him to take me with him into town. After reading *Little Women*, I longed to meet the acquaintance of another little girl, at the very least.

"It's too dangerous," he'd tell me. "You're much safer here with me."

He never told me what the danger was.

But I know now that if I stay here much longer, I'm going to die. I have no food left.

I'm so hungry, I can't even sleep anymore. When I lie down, the hunger eats at me like moths to clothing, and I imagine my starvation has pushed me to desperation. I'd give anything for a slice of bread or scraps from a table.

My father hadn't planned on dying.

And though I've torn this place apart looking for hidden stores of food, I know it's no use. It's such a small place anyway.

I've found other things, though. Curious things. Books and notes, a diary of sorts with strange things written in its pages. A metal box I can't find the key to.

But no food. And no money.

If I were to walk into town, where would I go? How would I get there? Would my bare feet hold up to the two-mile trek? In the stories I've read, churches will often take in the hungry, and feed them. Or perhaps a kindly widow would. Or... something. I can see the spire to the church behind the mansion that overlooks the cliffs. I'd have to get past the mansion to get to the church, and what if no one at the church could help me? Maybe the rich people at the mansion could spare some food.

Surely someone has food they're willing to give me. Maybe I can find some if I forage behind restaurants, or... something.

I sit on the little loveseat on the bottom floor. In front of me is the white circular staircase that leads to the second floor, a spiral gateway to the rooms above. There's the base floor with our plumbing and tiny kitchen, the second floor where we keep our books and my little bed, and the floor above which functioned as my father's bedroom. He slept on the top floor on the sofa so that he could access the topmost floor where the light was kept. He said that he didn't want an extra bed in the house, for if anyone ever came by unannounced, they wouldn't suspect anything amiss.

About a week ago, the water started acting weirdly, though, and I'm not sure why. And a few days after that, someone came by. I hid on the bottom floor, the way my father taught me to, in the tiny closet behind the stairs.

It's strange being nonexistent.

I saw them before coming up the walkway from the basement level, and I barely made it to the closet before they entered. I could see just a sliver from my hiding place. Two men. One in a pressed policeman's uniform, the other wearing black pants and a striped shirt.

"Could give it over to the town's property," Striped Shirt said meditatively.

Give what over?

"Right," the police officer said. I couldn't see what he was doing, but I heard him pick up the cup of tea I left on the little table. I closed my eyes tightly. Would they know someone was here?

"'Tis cold," he said. "But doesn't look days old, does it?"

My heartbeat quickened, when I heard footsteps approaching the closet.

"Eh, I imagine the fresh air from the ocean changes the climate in here," Striped Shirt said. "Locked up tighter than a drum. Who'd come here?"

I held my breath until they left.

Now, I pace the bottom floor, kneading my hands on my belly. I can sneak out. I have to. I'll have to leave, though, I've literally never left this little haven I call home. I can walk out into the garden when night falls, then go into town…

But what then? How will I see at night? And what if someone sees *me*?

No. That's a terrible idea. Not only would that mean waiting all day, I wouldn't have enough light to see where I need to go. And darkness scares me.

My only other choice is to stay here and starve to death. I shake my head and peer out the tiny window on the bottom floor.

Would he have kept anything in the shed? I wasn't even allowed to go out that far, but now it seems I have no choice. It's worth looking, at least.

My hand trembling, I unfasten the latch that leads outside and formulate a plan. I'll go to the shed and stay there, investigating to see what I can find. I'll look at anything and everything, and if I don't find either money or food, I'll… I'll do something else.

What else? I have no idea.

But first, the shed.

I walk to the top floor, far away from the windows so no one who happens by could see me, as if my vantage point from here will help me make a solid plan. I haven't been up here in years, even after I saw them come and take my father. I crept down to the first floor and could hear them loud and clear through the window.

"Dead," one officer said. "Looks like a heart attack."

It killed me to see his body taken away. I have no idea where they took him, or what they did after that. My father always told me, no matter what, not to leave the lighthouse. That they'd find me. That my life would be forfeit.

They.

They.

If only I knew who they were.

I suspected, when I grew to be a young teen, that my father had some type of mental illness that made him suspect anything and everything. It didn't seem normal that I was tucked away like this, with no contact with the outside world. From my reading, I knew of such things as schools and villages and shopping areas. Neighbors and officers, political officials, and… friends.

But they're foreign concepts to me. My only contact was my father, my only companions my books.

I haven't even spoken a word out loud since he died. Even when he was alive, words were minimal, conversation sparse. Today's the first time I speak aloud.

"How could you?" I whisper to the sun. *"Why?"*

How could he leave me like this? Starving, without a crust to put in my belly or a penny in my pocket?

How could he have left me so isolated from anyone and everything that I'm bereft with his passing?

How?

I shake my head and straighten my shoulders. That's it. I'm going. I'm going to the shed to see what I can find, and if I can't find anything of use, I'm going into town. It doesn't matter if they hurt me. I'm already dying a slow death here.

So, with determination, I walk back down the stairs to the first floor, moving quickly so I don't lose my resolve. I turn the latch, careful to check to be sure my father's ring of keys sits in my pocket still. I open the door, take a deep breath, and step outside.

It's funny what people take for granted. The way they fall to sleep, their breathing slowing and bodies stilling. The way their heart beats, pumping blood through their veins. The way they blink, and swallow, how our limbs move in rhythm when we walk, sit, or stand.

I wonder if people take the outdoors for granted. When they step foot outside their doors, do they ever think of those who haven't? Who can't? Of those who've never seen the light of day?

Or am I the only who never has?

Gingerly, I step on the wobbly stone step that leads to the lighthouse. I half expect someone or something to come and attack me, he had me that riled up about danger outside these walls. Not surprisingly... no one does. Nothing happens.

A gentle breeze kicks up, and though it feels vaguely familiar—I do sit by open windows and let the wind rustle my hair and kiss my bare arms—it's still wholly different. Kept hidden away behind the walls of my tiny home, I've never felt the wide-open expanse of the entire world around me. For a moment, I can't breathe, I'm so giddy with the freedom this affords.

Oh, my, the sky is deep and breathtaking, blue sky as far as the eye can see. I swivel around to look behind me and cast a glance at the tumultuous ocean behind me. Waves crash on the shore, and I take in a breath. The magnificent blue of the ocean looks so much more vivid from here, like gems cast in spotlight. Glimmering. Shining. Radiant. I inhale deeply, salty air hitting my lungs, and open my arms wide before me. The world outside those walls is so vast. So beautiful. So endless.

Why did I wait so long to do this?

I close my eyes. It's sunny and warm, with a delicate breeze that rustles my skirt and hair. I feel the kiss of warmth on my cheeks, and spin around slowly. Living so close to the ocean means we frequently get frigid air, and this winter was brutally cold, but today is near perfect. Like a little slice of heaven. I almost forget how starving I am, and my lightheadedness clears just a little.

The stones feel cool under my bare feet as I walk toward the shed. There's a spring in my step now that I've gotten some fresh air. I don't know why my father never let me out. It's glorious out here.

When I reach the shed, the nervousness I felt earlier returns. I don't much like creepy, crawly things, and I hope spiders and the like don't come flying out at me. What if there's a... person? Someone ready to hurt me, like father promised?

But I've already combed the entirety of the inside of the lighthouse. This is my last possible chance to find anything.

I go to turn the handle, but find it locked. I frown. Why would he lock it? Then I remember the keyring in my pocket and take it out. I look back at the shed. There isn't just one, but a series of locks barricading this door. What on earth was he hiding in here that was of so much importance that he had to lock it up so tightly? Even our home wasn't quite this secured.

I fumble with the locks and try various keys. It's clumsy business, because I've only ever read about unlocking doors in books before. Finding the small keys to fit the right locks on the door is slow, tedious work. Finally, the last lock falls open, and I pull the door outward, bracing myself for a bat or spider or something to come flying out at me.

Fortunately, there's nothing but dank, musty air. With a deep breath, I step inside.

Chapter Three

Keenan

I don't know what I'll find at the lighthouse, but I'm familiar enough with Father Finn's knowing look that I decide to prioritize my visit. I take Cormac with me. Though I can hold my own in fist-to-fist combat, it doesn't hurt to have his hulking presence with me.

"You sure you don't want a third?" Nolan asked, his frown making him look a bit pouty. At twenty-one years old, he's not a lad anymore, though I can't help but think of him as the baby in the family. When I was his age, I'd already sealed the deal on multiple loans, had half a million dollars socked away in savings, and contracted my first hit. But even though Nolan's a man now, at twenty-one years old, it's hard for me to see Nolan as anything more than my knock-kneed teenaged brother.

"You sober yourself up," I order, fixing him with a serious look. "I don't need you to work with us today, but you need to be sober at the weekend."

He frowns. "Why?"

Why? My palm itches to smack some sense into him. Of all the fucking cheek...

"Because I said so," I answer curtly. Christ, I sound like my father. But as his superior, I don't feel the need to explain myself to him.

His green eyes flash at me like a bolt of lightning before he checks himself.

"You'll fit those shoes well, Keenan," he says tightly. I don't need to ask him which shoes. I take a step toward him, but Cormac grabs the back of my shirt and holds me back while Nolan stalks off.

"Not worth it, brother," Cormac says, shaking his head.

"The boy needs a proper beating," I say between clenched teeth. "Never had one, and he's gotten too fuckin' big for his britches, he has."

"Not gonna deny it," Cormac says with a sigh, as if it pains him to say it. We both know mam spoiled him rotten, and the future of our organization lies in our hands. Lack of discipline and focus will be Nolan's downfall. "But we have a job to do."

That we do.

"I'd honestly like his help," I confess to Cormac, as we exit the house and head to the garage. "But for this particular job, it's best it's just the two of us."

"Agreed."

We walk in silence until we get to the garage. I click the lock on one of the cars in our fleet, choosing a

Jaguar because I need a sleek, quiet ride. I slide into the driver's seat as Cormac folds his massive body into the passenger seat to my left.

"What do you reckon we'll find there?" he asks.

"No feckin' clue," I mutter. "I wish to God Father Finn wasn't so tightlipped. He says just enough to cause vague suspicion, but not enough to go on."

"Not exactly," Cormac says. "To be fair, he often tells us things way before anyone else knows. And if word ever got out he was confiding in us, that source would dry up faster than a bitch's pussy."

"Fine," I mutter on a snort. I can always count on Cormac for his colorful use of irreverent, descriptive language. "I know, I know." Always the diplomat, Cormac."

We drive down the driveway and exit the estate, and I bang a left at the fork in the road. The road to the right will take us deeper into Ballyhock, toward the church and armory, but to the left takes us to the shore. Drive too far, and we'd head straight into the ocean.

"Might help to have at least an idea of what we're looking for," Cormac begins.

"We'll know when we see it," I respond. "And I'll tell you."

He snorts. "You'll tell me? Maybe I'll be the one that notes it first and tells *you*."

I huff out a laugh. "Bullshite, but fair game, then."

We took our time this morning, finishing our meeting. By the time we reach the path that leads to the light-house and park the car it's early afternoon. There's no paved road we can drive to the entrance, so we need to go the rest of the way on foot. I lock the car and pocket the key, eyeing the lighthouse ahead of us with suspicion.

What the hell *will* we find that has anything at all to do with The Clan? It's odd, because we've never had any affiliation with the lighthouse keeper. None that I'm aware of, anyway. He kept to himself and was off his nut, and we have enough business to tend to without mingling with the local nutters.

"You notice anything strange?" Cormac asks, when we begin walking up the pathway to the entrance.

"Cormac, pretty much everything about this place is strange." Stepping foot on the property that leads to the lighthouse feels like taking a step back in time, with the weather-worn shutters by the tiny windows, the well-worn pathway.

"Right," he says, rolling his eyes. "But I mean more strange than usual."

I shrug. "I've always thought it odd this place didn't have a house. Where'd the old geezer sleep?"

Cormac shrugs. "Reckon he had a room inside. Some old lighthouses had limited space when built, so they don't have a house. The inside was the only home they had."

Not sure how I didn't know that, but I've never been what one might call a lighthouse expert.

"Right," I say with a nod. "But what would the old man have to do with what the Father said?"

"Not a feckin' clue."

We enter the lighthouse, surprised to find the entryway on the bottom floor open. I hit a switch on the wall, and the room illuminates. Frowning, I look at the details on the basement floor. I see nothing at all that would give us a clue. This floor has a toilet behind a door and a little kitchenette. It smells stale, as if no food's been prepared in some time, though it's neat and tidy. I look at Cormac and point to the spiral staircase. There's no fucking way he's going to hoist his massive body up that tiny staircase. He shakes his head, and I can't help but smirk.

"You keep watch down here, and I'll check upstairs." I'm a larger man myself, but thinner than Cormac.

He grunts, but it's really the only choice. The second floor has a small bookshelf and a tiny bed, neatly made with an ancient quilt that looks like it's about to fall apart. I look through every nook and cranny, frowning when I find a small closet with some women's garments in them. Did the lighthouse keeper have a wife? I'll have to ask my father. These clothes are old-fashioned, so they likely don't belong to anyone from the present day. But I didn't know Jack Anderson ever had a woman?

By the time I get to the top floor, I'm feeling frustrated.

"Y'all right up there, Keenan?" Cormac shouts from below.

"Yeah," I mutter. "Alright. You?'

"Fine down here. I did see a little something you ought to look at when you get down here, though."

"Be down directly."

The top floor has a small, dilapidated loveseat, a tiny table beside it, and little else. I look in the closet on this floor and find a handful of men's tattered clothing. I frown, looking at them. These must've belonged to the keeper.

The very top is where he did his work.

I peek around but see nothing out of the ordinary. I finally take my seat overlooking the ocean, giving myself the full vantage point he must've had. It isn't until I'm seated here that I blink in surprise.

I had no idea one could see so *much* from here. For Christ's sake, I want to kick my own arse for being so thick. The vastness of the ocean, the endless sky, the port of entry for every ship that comes our way, it's all clear as day up here, clearer than any other fucking vantage point in all of Ballyhock.

Wait a minute.

He could see every fucking ship that came into the harbor. Every transaction on the shore. In great detail.

Why hadn't I thought of this before? Our primary arms dealing means ship after ship dock right here, right under the watchful eye of the lighthouse keeper.

Is this what Father Finn wanted us to see? That we've been under the fucking *microscope* of a crazy old man for God-knows how long?

Jesus, Mary, and Joseph.

Of course, we've covered our tracks and don't do anything blatantly illegal without covering our arses, but we're well-known in Ballyhock. Anyone who'd watch us closely would get suspicious. Local law enforcement's under our pay, so they turn a blind eye, as long as we keep to our own code and morals. There's a fucking reporter who's kept her eyes on us. Has she been in touch with the keeper of the lighthouse? She's been trying to do an exposé on us for years.

I shake my head. Simply realizing the position of the lighthouse wasn't something worth calling a feckin' meeting at daybreak, for Christ's sake. And anyhow, the lighthouse keeper's dead. Anything he knew about us I'm thinking he took the grave.

I go back down the stairs.

"Find anything?" he asks.

I tell him about the vantage point at the top of the lighthouse.

"I wouldn't worry too much about that," he says with a shrug. "We've kept our noses and arses clean, yanno."

I nod, but don't reply. Something doesn't sit well with me. The Father sent us here to find something, and my gut says we haven't found it yet.

"You find anything?" I ask him.

"Wellll…" he says, his voice trailing off. "Not sure if it's worth noting?" he says, then he walks over to the bed. "But look here." He lifts the pillow. Beneath the white fabric lies a neatly folded old-fashioned nightgown. "You don't think… well, either the keeper kept his wife's nightie tucked under his bed, he wore it himself, and I wouldn't put it past him, he was that off his rocker," he suggests, his eyes twinkling, "or there's an option C."

"Which is?"

"There was or *is* a woman living here."

I snort. "Bollox," I say. "Ain't a woman here, Cormac, you know *that.*"

He shrugs. "Something to consider."

"I found nothing here," I tell him. "Nothing that's worth calling an inner circle meeting and sending us here, anyway. You?"

He shakes his head. "Naw."

"Back outside then," I say with a sigh. Perhaps I'll pay Father Finn a follow-up visit. Honest to Christ, if we don't find something soon, I'll have no choice.

We both look around closely as we exit the lighthouse, sure that we've missed a clue somewhere. Something, anything at all that could clue us in. I see nothing at first, but as we pass the small garden with overgrown shrubs, I hear a noise. I turn toward a dilapidated shed on the perimeter of the lighthouse.

"Did you hear something?" I ask Cormac. He shakes his head. I hold up a finger to my lips for him to be quiet as I turn toward the shed. I hear it again as we stand outside the door, a sort of rustling, followed by a humming. I look at him curiously.

We aren't alone.

What have we here?

I've learned to walk stealthily, so without a sound I approach the shed and stand outside the door. I notice when I draw close that the door is slightly ajar. What the hell? No one should be here.

The humming stops. I look back at Cormac. Wordlessly, he goes to the other side of the shed and crouches, prepared for an ambush or defense if we're attacked. I feel for the gun tucked into the waistband of my trousers. It's loaded and ready.

I hold up my fingers to Cormac.

One.

Two.

Three.

I yank the door open on three. I jump when I hear a decidedly feminine scream, and just in time duck when something shiny bears down on me. My instincts primed, I fall to the ground, grab her, and roll, bringing the woman down with me. In seconds, I have her wrists pinned above her head, the gardening trowel she tried to hit me with still firmly in her hand. I pinch between her thumb and pointer finger. Yelping, she drops the trowel.

"Son of a bitch," Cormac mutters as I get to my feet, dragging the girl with me. We can't see much of anything in the dark interior of the shed, so I drag her out into the open.

Jesus, she's a wild little thing, kicking and spitting at us like a feral cat. Her long, thick hair hangs down her back to her waist, and for a moment I wonder if she's playacting or some kind of an actress, because she looks as if she's stepped right out of another decade. Her clothes are faded and worn, and definitely out of fashion, her feet bare. But she wears no makeup, no jewelry. I hold her out in front of me so she can't hurt me and give her a little shake. I have no more freedom to observe or speculate, as the girl's still fighting to get away.

"Enough of that, now, lass," I say in what I hope's a calming voice. "We aren't here to hurt you now, see?"

"Liars!" she screams. "My father told me about men like you! That you'd come for me, that you'd hurt me!"

Her father? What's this, now?

Well, who knew? She has an American accent. What's an American girl doing traipsing around these parts?

"Stop fighting us, and it'll go better for you," Cormac says. Though I know he'd as soon cut off his own hand than strike a woman, he knows how to use his bulk and deep voice to intimidate. Standing in front of her with his arms crossed, he draws his brows together and glares at her. "Still, now, woman."

"Let. Me. *Go!*" she screams, then she twists so quickly out of my grasp she slips out and falls toward Cormac. I grab for her. In one swift move, she kicks Cormac right between the legs, and he falls to the ground, wheezing.

Aw, hell *no.* I've had enough of this.

I've got her back in my grip before she can do further damage, or worse, run. "Enough," I order, giving her a shake, and when that still doesn't still her, I spin her out and give her arse a good, hard slap. She gasps, and it seems a bit of the fight goes out of her.

"Enough with you," I tell her. "We've not come to do you harm, see. For Christ's sake, stop the attack, or we *will* be forced to hurt you."

33

Cormac's on his knees now, still wheezing, his face ruddy and contorted. She got him good right between the legs, the little vixen. Though I won't tolerate her cheek, I have to bite my tongue to keep myself from grinning. There's not much that would take a big man like Cormac to his knees, but she hit her mark.

I hold her back to my chest and wrap an arm around her front, holding her to me so tightly I feel her struggling for breath.

"That's a good lass," I say placatingly. I don't want her to know she affects me. I want her to realize she hasn't ruffled my feathers, that I'm in control. She smells clean and sweet, like garden wildflowers damp from rain, and even struggling, I'm vividly aware of her curves, her soft skin, her gentle feminine allure.

She's the most beautiful woman I've ever seen, nothing like the women at the pub or in our family, nothing at all like the brash girls I went to school with when I was a child. With her high cheeks and wide eyes framed in thick lashes, she looks almost otherworldly, as if she's got the blood of the fae in her veins.

"Let me *go!*" she screams.

"Well now," I say evenly. "I do that and you're apt to run, and we can't have that, can we? Hardly had a chance to get to know each other."

I look toward the shed and note a length of rope on the floor. Holding her tightly with my left arm, I leave Cormac gasping for breath, and walk her to the shed. I reach for the rope. I'm experienced enough in restraining a prisoner, that it's an easy matter to tie her hands behind her back and secure the rope tightly.

"Don't you *dare!*" she howls, hopping around on her bare feet to get out of my grip, but she can't get out of the bonds. I've no idea what we'll do with her, but I see no choice but to toss her in the back of the Jag and take her back for questioning. It's when I'm securing the final knot, my eyes adjusting to the dim light in the shed, that I see something that captures my attention.

What the hell is it? Since she's still kicking at me, I seat her firmly on the grass outside the shed, admittedly with a little more force than necessary. I've got to get the little hellcat under control. Her brows are drawn together, her cheeks flaming red. The girl's got fire licking through her limbs to defy two grown men as she has. Cormac's on his feet now, eyeing her warily.

It's rare Cormac gets angry, but he's full throttle now. He wags a finger in her direction. "You do a thing like that again, I'll break my 'no hittin' women' rule and redden yer arse properly," he mutters. At his threat, I look at him sharply.

No fucking way. The only person punishing this little vixen will be me, and with pleasure.

"Hell no, you won't."

Cormac looks at me in surprise but quickly nods, deferring. He knows.

I've put my hands on her. I'm heir to the throne. This victory prize belongs to *me,* and me alone.

"Cormac." I jerk my chin at him, and he looks my way, at the books stacked in my hands. "Look what I've got."

"Put those down!" she screams. "No! Don't you dare touch them. They don't belong to you!" Seems a gag would do well.

I ignore her and lift a record book, rifling through it. It takes me a moment to decipher what I'm reading, and when I do, my anger rises. As I look through the numbers and notes, my blood pumps hot and furious in my veins. I clench my hands so tightly on the book I'm looking at, my hands shake with fury.

"Fucking hell," I mutter. "For Christ's *sake.*"

She's got details on every fucking transaction The Clan has made in neat, handwritten rows.

The names of the men we've hired.

The payouts we've gotten for every arms sale we've made.

The names of every affiliate we've interacted with, and the list goes fucking on.

She's got every inside detail on every fucking transaction we've made going back to last year.

How could we have not known a spy was right under our very noses? What she's planning on doing with this information is a mystery to me, but it's no fucking good she has it.

Father Finn was right. She's a fucking danger to us.

We found what we needed at the lighthouse.

Jesus.

"We need to bring her back with us," I tell him. "This little lass has some explaining to do." She howls and rages like a feral kitten. I frown at her. The girl needs taming, and I'm happy to be the man for the job. "But for Christ's sake, let's gag her first."

Chapter Four

I can't believe I'm in the back of a car, bound like a hog-tied beast, and that they manhandled me. He hurt me. He *hurt* me. He had the nerve to strike me, and I think he bruised my chest with his iron grip. The ropes bite into my wrists, and if I move them in any way, the sting worsens, chafing my skin.

Where are they taking me? I'm already further away from home than I've ever been in my life. Though I know what a car is, of course, having read about them, I've certainly never been in one. It scares me a little, the way I'm being jostled around, and when we hit a particularly rough patch, my head slams against the car door.

I try to scream, but the gag they've got wrapped around my mouth prevents me. My eyes water, from both the pain and the utter helplessness I feel being taken away from everything that's familiar and comfortable in my life. I'm in danger. My father was right. The first day I ever set foot outside my home, and I'm taken hostage by two men.

They took my father's things with them, the metal boxes and reams of notes, though I don't have a clue what any of them are. Do they think I'm somehow responsible for them? God, *of course* they do. How could they not? They found me in possession of them.

Do the documents somehow pertain to the men that came? Is that why my father wanted to keep me safe, and why he kept the notes hidden in the garden shed?

When they take the gag off me, should I tell them those are my father's possessions?

Or is it better if they think they *are* mine? Would the knowledge give me better… what's the word… negotiating strategies?

I'm so outside my element, I'm not even sure what I think. It doesn't help I'm still famished, weakened and lightheaded.

"Christ, Keenan, where the fuck did she come from?" the big man in front asks under his breath, as if I won't hear him. So the driver's Keenan.

"Hell if I know," the one on the left says. I've never interacted with any man other than my father before, and it saddens me these two are bad men. I'd have liked my first interaction to be a good one, if I'm now alone in the world, and destined to be forced to deal with people. Who are these men? Criminals, likely, if I'm to judge by the ease with which they kidnapped me.

Where did they come from? Why? Though probably older than I am, I'd guess they're still young. And if I have to admit it, they're both highly attractive men, especially the one who carried me to the car.

The driver's tall and muscular, with a shock of dark brown hair, scruffy beard, and eyes as green as the Irish Sea, he looks ruggedly handsome. The other's attractive, too, but this one... if he weren't as evil as he is—any other time and place—that one would win my heart. His voice is deep and velvety, like thick hot cocoa, and he even smells... I don't know how to describe it. But the way he smells lingers in my nose and makes me feel oddly feminine.

But they're bad men. Evil. They're no heroes come to rescue me or... I don't know, whatever it is that men do with women. What do evil men like them do with girls like me? I don't know where they're taking me or what they'll do to me when we arrive, and my nerves are fraught with anticipation. Why me?

The two men are talking softly to themselves, not paying any attention to me. Within a few minutes, we're driving up a steep incline. My pulse races when I see an enormous house in front of us, large enough it could be a castle of sorts. I'm reminded of the fictional Palace of Justice of Notre Dame or a more gothic version of Camelot, the castles I've spent countless hours visiting in the pages of my books.

Keenan has something in his hand I can't quite see, and he waves it at a black rectangle on a post to the left. There's a beep, a tiny flash of red, and the gates slowly swing open. I gasp. It's like magic.

How'd he do that?

If I didn't have this gag, I'd ask him.

I feel my eyes widen in wonder as we drive toward the garage attached to the house. The estate's surrounded by the most beautiful garden. Thick willow trees bow as if on bended knee before royalty. Stone benches and archways lend an ancient air, beckoning fairies and sprites to come and play. Lilies and violets line the garden, and I'm enamored with the various shades of purple and yellow. Behind an archway graced with ivy, a fountain murmurs its secrets. All things I've only ever seen in books. It's overwhelming and wonderful.

I want to sit on a bed of moss by the fountain and breathe in the scent of flowers and trees. Though I know I'm in danger, a tiny flicker of hope blooms within me. I don't know what they have planned for me or what will happen next, but I'll make this place home.

I shake my head and focus back on the present. Has my isolation from others affected my logic and reason? Starved and lonely, am I still of sound mind? I have to keep my wits about me, no matter the circumstances.

But this… This place is enchanted, and I want to weave myself into its tapestry.

I suspected my father had a feeble hold on reason. Did I learn this as well?

We pull into a covered garage, and just that quickly, the brightness of a sunny day vanishes, as if to remind me not to get lost in my imagination.

I chant my internal monologue, repeating what I need to remember.

These men are not good men.

I'm in grave danger.

I make a vow to myself to observe anything and everything I can. I won't fight them, not now, not like I did when they captured me. We're on their land now, and I've no doubt I'm outnumbered. My suspicions are confirmed when several uniformed men approach the car.

Keenan and Cormac exit. Keenan hands one of the men a set of keys, and the possessions he stole from the shed. I don't even know what the items are, but they were my fathers, and it seems wrong that this man just marches in and takes them like a great big bully.

He's issuing orders left and right, and men are promptly moving to obey. "Alert my father that we need to speak to him promptly. He turns to Cormac. "Bring in Nolan and Boner."

They need more men to deal with me? I'm unarmed and ignorant. Why such a reaction?

What did my father *do*?

Cormac nods. Though Cormac's bigger, Keenan's in charge, then. But when Keenan opens my door and yanks me out, I'm reminded he isn't exactly little himself. Though I'm tall, I'm weakened from hunger and no match for this muscled, fierce man. He pulls me out of the car as if I'm a little doll, gripping my arm so painfully, I pull away instinctively in self-preservation. I can't speak because of the gag, but if I could, I'd have plenty to say. I kick my foot at his shin. It worked once before. He easily deflects my kicks and gives me a fierce shake.

"Don't you dare," he growls. "Unless you'd like to be properly punished before we've even entered." I shiver in fear. I'm outnumbered and in danger. It's a reminder of my decision to not fight, not this time, at least.

I walk quickly to keep up with his large strides, observing everything I can on my way. The garage houses rows of expensive-looking cars, well-cared for and in pristine condition. A small staircase leads up to a large door, and when we step into the house, there's a door to the left. I look quickly and surmise it's the kitchen, though of course I've never seen anything quite like it. My little kitchen at home could fit into the corner of that room and be swallowed whole. There are people bustling around in there, and several look curiously our way, but I'm quickly whisked away to the right.

We walk down a large, brightly lit hallway. I've read of places like this, with rooms upon rooms. How I'd love to explore this place without the watchful, angry eye of these men on me. It smells clean and welcoming, mild notes of cinnamon and nutmeg in the air. At the end of the hallway, we step through a doorway that opens to a large, airy entryway. A massive, intricately-carved doorway stands slightly ajar. Everything here is whites and ivory, blinding and beautiful. I look up, the ceiling so high I couldn't touch it if I stood on the topmost rung of a ladder.

I take this all in in seconds, as Keenan drags me to a doorway in the hall, and before I know what's going on, we're descending a flight of stairs. I stumble, weak from hunger and dazed from the sudden turn of events, but he quickly turns, lifts me in his arms, and carries me down the rest of the stairs. For one split second, my hands encircle his neck instinctively, and I gasp from the nearness and raw, masculine power that radiates off him in waves. I swallow hard, but before I can even form a cohesive thought, he tosses me back to my feet and continues his rapid march to wherever his destination is.

I hear voices before I see them, and when he drags me into a room, I nearly black out from the fear that hits me in the chest.

We aren't alone. There are men here. Lots of them. Scary, muscled, terrifying men, and their eyes are on *me*.

This room is nothing like upstairs. It's windowless and dark, the only light cast from overhead lighting. I look around wildly, panic gripping my chest. The stark barrenness of this room incites even more fear. It isn't just what I see. It's what I don't. There's no natural light, no fresh air. No sounds echo beyond the walls of this room. Whereas upstairs smells homey and welcoming, this room smells sterile and cold, like fear and desperation. I don't need them to tell me they do wicked, evil things in this room.

The men watch me, their gazes predatory and calculating, and I shiver when I realize my predicament. I'm one helpless female in a sea of dangerous, evil men. This room is a makeshift prison, and I wonder if it harkens back to a medieval dungeon of sorts. The rest of the house looks modern and sleek, but they've left this room untouched.

One man, easily the oldest of them all, with gray in his hair and beard, sits at a plain black table, his eyes fixed on me unblinkingly.

"I see you found what Father Finn referenced?"

The men around him chuckle nervously, as if trying to placate him and unsure of what he'll do next.

"Seems like it," Keenan says with a mirthless smile. He yanks a straight-backed wooden chair from the table where the older man sits and pushes me to sitting. I bow my head and stare at my hands, because I don't want to see them looking at me. I hate it here. I hate these men. I don't want to give them the satisfaction of eye contact.

"Tell me, son," the older man says. I look up quickly, my plan to look away forgotten that quickly. The older man is Keenan's father. Are the others his brothers?

"We went to the lighthouse as we discussed, though nothing there clued us in," he begins. I clench my palms. Who do they think they are, trespassing on my property without my permission? And what do they mean, nothing clued them in?

"Saw signs there was more than one person living there, though," he says. "I noted that the vantage point of the lighthouse gives full visibility to the ports and harbor."

What does that matter?

The older man nods wordlessly, and Keenan continues.

They recount what happened, and I watch, still gagged and humiliated, as they relay what they did while on my property. Tears well in my eyes I can't wipe away, for these men have been cruel. They trespassed on my property, violated my privacy, and took me against my will. What will they do next?

"Well done, Cormac," the man says, without taking his eyes off Keenan. Cormac doesn't respond, and Keenan continues.

"When we got outside, we heard a little noise in the garden shed. We investigated and found the girl hidden in the shed. When we opened the door, she attacked us, so we had no choice but to restrain her."

"Define attacked," the man says.

"She tried to hit me with a trowel and kneed Cormac in the bollox," Keenan says. The two men on either side of the older man, the leader of this group, snicker, but one stern look from their leader, and they quickly sober.

"Did you punish her?"

My pulse races, and I feel my entire body grow cold and still. I try to swallow but my throat won't work. Punish me? For what?

Keenan shakes his head. "Not yet, sir."

My heart taps a crazy, erratic beat in my chest. Not yet?

The older man grows impossibly sterner, his brows drawn tightly together, his lips curving downward. I shudder. He's terrifying. "Not yet? Explain yourself."

He's expected to have already done so? Why?

"What we found her in possession of required immediate attention, sir." His jaw tightens, gaze unwavering.
"But I won't neglect her punishment."

He plans on punishing me, then?

"Good," his father says. "You don't need me to remind
you how essential it is you establish immediate
respect. The girl will learn her place, and swiftly. No
one raises a hand to the heir to the throne. No one."

Heir to the throne?

"Absolutely."

"You'll give her her first lesson before the sun sets, or
you'll answer to me."

Keenan's gaze doesn't waver. "Yes, sir. You have my
word, sir."

"Now show me what you found."

They lay the items they took of my father's on the
table in front of them. I'm so angry at them for taking
his things, for violating him and me this way. I try to
protest, I try to grab them, but my protests are muffled
behind the gag, the bonds holding fast. Tears of frustration and anger trail down my cheeks. My nose
tingles, and the lump in my throat wells while I cry in
silent misery. The weight of grief I feel from my
father's death seems heavier to bear because of what
they've done.

How could he have left me like this? Defenseless, and
in possession of something as volatile as these things
appear to be?

"What are they?" the older man asks Keenan.

"Every fucking transaction we've made since last year. Names of who we've hired, payouts made and received, every single one of our arms contacts."

The small group of men curses. One mutters, "She's a motherfucking spy?"

"Obviously, ya wanker," one says, and then the older man holds up a hand for silence. He turns his impenetrable gaze to mine.

"Remove her gag. Give her a chance to explain herself."

I wonder even now if I should tell them the truth, but it seems disrespectful to the memory of my father to tell them anything. They've already taken me here and have no qualms about hurting me. Why would they believe me?

Keenan stalks to me, his face set in granite, and yanks a sharp blade from his boot. I blink and try to back away as he approaches me, but I can't. Is he going to cut me? Right now, right here, in front of all of them? The bounds keep me tightly secured, and the men surround me.

The *bullies*. The *cowards*. As if a girl like me, unarmed, could do a thing to defend herself?

When Keenan reaches me, he yanks me over to him, tugs my head and pulls my face against his shoulder. I'm frozen in fear, cringing in anticipation of sharp pain, when I feel the cold metal of the blade grace my scalp. The gag falls free.

I exhale in relief, stumbling when he releases me, but a firm grip on my elbow steadies me. Keenan holds me in front of the men.

"What have you to say for yourself?" he asks.

I open my mouth to respond but can't speak. I'm frozen in terror, and I don't know what I want to say. I swallow hard, and shake my head, but he won't tolerate that response. He reaches for my hair, wraps it around his hand, and before I know what's happening, tugs my head back so hard, I scream out loud, my scalp throbbing in pain.

"Answer. Me."

"I don't know," I wail. I've never told a lie in my life, but he leaves me no choice. I won't betray my father, I won't defile his name or the memory of him to these men, but I can't give them any information, either.

"You lie," Keenan says, his eyes narrowing on me. "You're lying."

"I don't know what they are," I protest, tears of frustration and anger falling down my cheeks. "I don't know where they came from."

"Then *why* did we find you in possession of them?"

"I don't know, you *brute*. Let me go!" I wriggle and writhe, trying to get away.

The older man crosses the room in one swift stride, and raises his hand to strike me, when Keenan moves so fast, I stumble to the floor. I hear a smack of flesh-on-flesh, and I look up just in time to see Keenan's hand on the man's wrist, the two of them eyeing one another in a silent battle of wills. Keenan's eyes flash, and the older man looks at him with widened eyes, as if he's surprised by Keenan's reaction. The room goes completely still.

"*I* will interrogate her," Keenan says with quiet but steely determination. "*My way*. And privately. You have my word."

The other man doesn't speak at first. No one does. It occurs to me this might be the first time Keenan's ever engaged in a power struggle with his father. They stare for long minutes. I'm holding my breath, watching this silent battle of wills. Finally, the older man nods, and I swear I see his shoulders drop a tiny bit.

"Do it," he says. "Or I will see it done properly." But his words have lost a bit of the edge they held before, as if this final promise is his last hold-out.

Keenan's grip doesn't loosen, and when he speaks, it's through clenched teeth. "That won't be necessary."

The older man swallows, though his eyes are narrowed and stern. "I'll trust you, son. I'll expect answers this evening."

Keenan finally nods, and it seems both are making a concession. I'm confused yet enthralled at the same time. Keenan finally releases the older man, and immediately turns to me.

He lifts me roughly under the armpits and drags me to my feet.

Keenan turns to the room, and his words take on a note of authority. "No one interrupts me. No one calls me. I want no contact until you hear from me first."

Chapter Five

Keenan

No one defies Seamus McCarthy.

No one raises a hand to Seamus McCarthy.

I just did both, and I fucking won. The realization brings both relief and a sort of weary sadness. My father's going to eventually concede the throne to me, and I know what happened in the interrogation room was his first concession.

His first ever?

But hell, when I saw him raise his hand to strike the girl, I reacted so quickly I didn't think before I did. I knew if he struck her, I'd kill him. I'd fucking kill him. And I can't let that happen.

Still, I leave the room with my head held high. Soon, so soon it feels as if it could be tomorrow, I'll assume the leadership role in The Clan. And I need the men in rank below me to respect me. Today, I won the battle of wills with my father. One brief moment in time, but it was a defining moment no less.

I love my father. Though stern and immovable, he's loyal to his very core, always fair, and the bravest man I know. I learned to respect both him and my mam from a very young age, and I was brought up with firm expectations, rules, and consequences. I knew when I fucked up, I'd earn certain and severe punishment. I learned quickly not to fuck up. Still, my father was a fair man and still is.

But no one in The Clan defies Seamus McCarthy.

And I just did.

But now that I've taken a stand, there's no question I need to prove my worth. I can't falter now. He's given me a job, and by damn I'm going to do it properly.

My father devotes himself to his family with everything in him. Mam worships the ground he walks on, and he's good to her. The only time his stern demeanor softens is when he's in her presence. The two can read each other so well, as a lad I vowed one day when I married, I'd cultivate a relationship like theirs.

They're a unified front, so entwined it's hard to see where one begins and the other ends. I can still hear her gentle voice admonishing me, "Obey your father, son." She's always upheld his authority, demanding obedience from me, my brothers, and every member of The Clan. My Clan brothers see her as their mother, and all treat her with the utmost respect.

I'll need her help with the girl I've taken as mine.

I take the girl by the arm and march her along with me in silence. We have much to discuss, but I have no interest in doing so until I have complete privacy. We're a good distance away from my room on the second floor, but I don't want to speak to anyone right now, so we walk with purposeful steps. She walks beside me in silence, and at one point, she stumbles. I slow my steps, frowning at her. I want to know why she's shown signs of weakness. Is it fear? Or something else?

Our servants are attentive as I walk with her beside me, and some raise eyebrows when I walk past my office and to the large, gleaming stairway that leads to the second floor. I've never taken a woman into our home. Not once. Men of The Clan don't date casually. We're no celibates, but we know where to find women, how to keep our interactions with them private, and how to prevent any ties from forming. Unions within The Clan are often arranged, as any possible union must be approved to solidify or strengthen us. So if a woman's brought home, she's done so as a kind of entry into courtship. You don't introduce a woman you don't wish to marry to The Clan.

Unless she's your prisoner, and we've had precious few of the female variety.

Finally, we get to my room. For safety purposes, each bedroom on the second floor has been protected with a variety of safety measures. The windows are kept locked, steel bars securing the outside. Security cameras are trained on every exit and entry into this house, the windows no exception. We've installed bright floodlights at the entrances and exits, and thorn bushes line the entire perimeter of our house.

I dismiss the men who work for us as my bodyguards. Standing at attention outside my bedroom, they're dressed in the suits we require, but I know beneath their jackets they wear harnesses and holsters. I dismiss them for now. I want privacy.

I open the door quickly, and drag her in behind me, before I shut and lock it.

I've got her alone now. My pulse quickens. I'm hyper aware that she's my charge, and I have full clearance to do anything I want to her.

Anything.

I swallow hard, tempering my need to master this beautiful, tenacious, headstrong girl. Christ but she's gorgeous. My methods of interrogation won't be the same as I'd use on a man.

She looks about my room with wide, curious eyes. If she's been as sheltered as I suspect, I bet she's likely never seen anything like this. My room is one of the larger ones, with a private bath, a king-sized bed, a small desk and chair, and ample room to move around. I can see the housekeepers have been in today. My beds made, the pillows fluffed, and there are still lines in the carpet where they've run the Hoover.

I leave her restraints on, lead her to the upholstered chair next at the foot of my bed, and push her to sitting.

I could take a stern approach with her. My father expects me to punish her, and I know why, of course. But her wide eyes tell me she's fearful. I'm tempted to coerce her. Intimidate her. Dominate her. Time will tell which methods she responds best to. It might help if I pretend I'm the good guy.

"Now, lass," I begin, pulling the chair from my desk and straddling it in front of her. "We talk."

She stares at me, and I can't quite read her expression. She's fearful, I've no doubt, I can tell by the way she swallows hard, her eyes wide, giving her away. But it seems she's also curious, and I suspect the girl's got questions herself. She looks away and tucks her head to her chest, as if to shield herself from me, and a raw, primal urge rises within me.

No one will touch her. No one will harm her.

I'll have the truth from her.

But this woman is *mine.*

The first woman that's ever been taken to my private quarters. The first I've taken prisoner. The first I've shielded from my father's wrath.

Mine.

I observe her without attempting to hide it. As mine, she'll learn to withstand my scrutiny.

She wears faded, dated clothing, a tattered dress that may have been white once but now is yellowed with age and wear. Is the woman eccentric, or something else? Her long, thick black hair hangs all the way to her waist.

"He's your father," she states plainly. It takes me by surprise. I don't expect it to be the first thing she says.

"Who?" I ask. I'm curious how she'll describe my dad.

"The older, stern man downstairs."

Older and stern. Accurate.

"The man who tried to strike me, before you stopped him."

She noted that. I nod. "Aye."

"Why did you stop him from hitting me?" she asks, her brow furrowed in confusion.

"I'm the one that'll ask questions first, lass," I tell her. She doesn't control this. I'm also not sure I want to tell her why I stopped him. If she gets it in her head that she isn't to fear me, or that I've got a weakness for her, it could complicate things.

She sits up straighter and holds my gaze. "Alright, then. Let's have it."

"Your name."

"Caitlin."

"Spell it."

"C-A-I-T-L-I-N."

Caitlin. An Irish name, then. Though she's American, and her father was, too, I wonder. Why is her Christian name Irish, and why does she live here?

"You mentioned Jimmy Anderson, the lighthouse keeper, was your father."

She nods but doesn't reply.

"Why does no one in Ballyhock know of your existence, Caitlin?"

Something flashes in her eyes, something I can't quite decipher. She swallows but doesn't break eye contact. "My father kept me hidden," she finally says.

"How so?"

She blinks, just once, swallows hard, then continues. "He said beyond the walls of the lighthouse were men who'd hurt me." Her voice hardens, along with her eyes. "Apparently, he was right."

I grip her arm. Threatening.

"Stick to the questions, lass," I order, my voice sharpening. I've brought her up here for a reason. She doesn't respond. "Now tell me how he kept you hidden."

"Until today, I've never stepped foot outside the lighthouse."

Is the girl out of her mind? Is she *sane*?

"Excuse me?"

She clears her throat. "I said, I've never stepped foot outside the lighthouse before today."

How is that possible? She's no child. Is she lying?

"Tell the truth," I admonish harshly.

She blinks at me in surprise. This either *is* the truth, or she's a very good liar.

"I did," she insists.

"*Never* left?"

"How many times are you going to make me repeat myself?" she asks.

I'll have none of her cheek.

"Listen well, lass," I say, my voice etched with warning. "You'll speak to me with respect."

She swallows hard. "Or you'll punish me," she says softly. She's a bright one.

I don't deny it. She needs to know where we stand. I came between her and my father's punishing hand today, but he isn't the one she needs to fear now.

"You'll be expected to obey me," I tell her. "Now answer the question."

She sighs, and I can tell she's warring within herself, wondering what I'll do and what I expect of her.

"No," she finally says with a sigh. "As I said, I've never left the lighthouse. It was the only safe place I had."

Though it seems nearly impossible that in a modern age she's been sheltered to such extremes, such a reclusive life isn't unheard of. And her father was most definitely eccentric and reclusive himself.

"No education?" I ask her.

She lifts her chin, and with a tone that's adorably haughty, she replies. "I learned to read at the age of four, and my father educated me thoroughly."

Well, then.

"So you've had book learning?"

"Of course I have. My father was a brilliant man, and he taught me himself."

I nod.

"Tell me the extent of your education," I demand. I'm not sure why I'm so fixated on this, but I'm filled with a burning need to know everything there is about her. Everything.

She shrugs. "He taught me algebra and trigonometry and calculus. I'm fluent in Latin and French. I've read the works of the masters, both British and American literature as well as the works of Shakespeare. I've studied the art and music of the greats."

I blink in surprise. It appears she certainly has had proper schooling.

It's time to move onto more pressing questions. I'll get to the records she held at a later date, but one thing's become clear to me. If her father was as educated as she gives him credit, it's quite possible the records belonged to him, and not her.

We'll get to that.

"You've stumbled several times since I've taken you with me," I state. "Tell me why."

Her face pales, and she licks her lips. "I haven't eaten any food in several days."

Jesus, Mary, and Joseph.

I don't realize I'm on my feet until I see her shrink back, looking up at me.

Christ, why didn't I notice before? Her eyes are a bit sunken, her skin so pale she looks like a newly-hatched sprite.

"Why haven't you eaten?" I demand harshly. I'm not angry with her, but I'm furious I've a woman in front of me literally starving to death.

Her gaze hardens. "I'd think it obvious. I had no food."

"The old man left you with nothing to eat?"

"Not nothing," she says. "But if you recall, he died last month. We had stores put aside, but I've eaten every bit of them. It was why I visited the garden shed to begin with. I wondered if he'd left anything there."

"Did he?"

"No...no food." She bites her lip, as if she's said too much.

No food. Are the records his then?

Still holding her gaze, I take my mobile out of my pocket, and make a quick call. Douglas, one of our servants, answers.

"Yes, sir?"

"I want a tray of food brought to my room within five minutes."

We've a kitchen that rivals the best restaurants in all of Ireland. They'll bring food, and promptly.

"Five minutes, sir?"

"Waste no time. I don't care what it is. Cut slabs of bread and cheese if necessary, but food and water's to be delivered as fast as you can."

"Yes, sir. Of course, sir."

She looks down when I hang up the phone, capturing her lips between her teeth. Fucking hell, I can't believe the lass is literally starving.

It angers me her father left her bereft, and that right here, in one of the most wealthy villages in all of Ireland, the lass is starving to death under our very noses. What possessed him to keep her apart from the rest of the world? Was he as insane as we all gave him credit?

I will not question her further until she's eaten.

Next, I call Sebastian, our clan's private doctor. We don't risk notice of the authorities when injured. Sebastian treats us promptly and thoroughly.

"Yes, sir?"

"How might one go about feeding someone who's been starving?"

"Well," he says thoughtfully. I can picture him stroking his chin. It's not a common question, I'd think, but at the same time, he's used to answering anything and everything from us. Waking in the middle of the night to tend to gunshot wounds or lacerations will do that to someone, I suppose.

"I'd go slowly, and introduce small, manageable meals that are nutritionally dense." I nod, even though he can't see me. "Of course, be sure hydration is prioritized as well. How long has said person been starving?"

"A few days."

"Then it's likely the same as coming off a fast," he says. "Was it likely he or she was malnourished before there was no food at all?"

"Highly likely."

"Then we'll want to get some vitamins in and good, nourishing food."

"Aye. I've ordered food brought for now, but I want you to call the kitchen and tell them to prepare what you think best for this evening and tell them I gave the order."

"Yes, sir."

"Thank you."

A knock comes at the door, and I quickly retrieve the food.

I hang up the phone and turn to her. But she doesn't care about my conversation. Her eyes are riveted on the tray in my hand, piled with the food I ordered.

"Oh, my," she whispers, licking her lips. "Oh, that looks so good."

"I'm going to unfasten your cuffs so you can eat. Don't you dare do anything stupid, or I'll punish you. *Firmly.*"

She nods. I release her hands.

She wrings her hands in front of her as if she's afraid I might turn and run with the tray. I slide it onto my desk.

"Come," I order, crooking a finger at her. She stands on wobbly legs and makes her way to my desk. I lift the heavy chair and bring it with her, setting the chair in front of the desk. "Eat. Slowly. Drink some water as well. Have you had anything to drink?"

She shrugs. "A bit. After a time, it gets difficult to drink when you're so hungry, though."

Fair enough. I lean against the desk and watch her as she sits gracefully onto the chair. Even held prisoner, under my watchful eye, starving and afraid, she holds herself with the elegance of royalty.

She reaches for a slice of bread, but when she lifts the knife to butter it, her hand shakes. The knife clatters back to the tray.

"Give it here," I say gruffly. She doesn't protest as I take the knife and smear a thick layer of butter over the crusty bread. I hand her the bread. "Eat slowly."

She doesn't need to be told twice. I watch as her lips close around the bread, her eyelids flutter shut, and she moans out loud. "Mmmm," she moans, the sound so guttural and hoarse, it's damn near sexual. My mind is spinning with a world of possibilities.

If what she's telling me is true, she's never been outside. Never left her house. The world of men is completely foreign to her, for better or for worse. God almighty, the power that gives me…

"Drink, lass," I order, after she's eaten half a slice of bread. She looks at me in surprise. "Drink," I repeat, jerking my head at the large pitcher of water. But I'm a wanker, not realizing the damn thing's too heavy for her to lift in her weakened state. She goes to lift the heavy pitcher, wrist trembling.

"Give me that," I say gruffly, taking it from her grip. "You'll spill that everywhere." Either she knows obedience is wise, or she knows her limits, but she quickly concedes.

I don't really care about her spilling anything. The housekeepers come several times a day, and a little water spill never hurt anyone. I do, however, value her obedience and submission. I'm watching her with a careful eye. I pour her a tall glass of water before I hand it to her.

"Good girl," I approve, when she takes large gulps. Not meeting my eyes, she puts it back on the tray, then returns to the bread.

"Finish that," I tell her, waving my finger to the bread. "Do your best."

She obeys, then follows the bread with a slice of cheese.

"This tastes so good," she says in a little voice. "Thank you."

I nod. She can thank me if she chooses, but I didn't feed her out of the kindness of my heart. I need the girl strengthened for what lies ahead.

Next, she eats from a small bowl of fruit, taking small bites and chewing carefully, before washing her food down with more water. A little color comes back in her cheeks as she eats.

She's a stunner, this one, simple and outlandish though she might be. Her high cheekbones are pale pink, highlighting her eyes. They're a pretty blue, framed with thick lashes. There's something special about this girl. I want to pull her to me and hold her close, shield her from any harm that may come her way. I blink in surprise and turn away. Has she bewitched me that I think strange thoughts around her? I don't feel this way around women, and certainly none who are potential spies, or threats to The Clan.

And even if the circumstances were normal, I can't have her. She's an American, and Clan rules specifically state we're to marry Irish.

Marry? What the ever-loving Christ's come over me that I even think of such a thing?

My father's words come back to me with the force of a hurricane.

First, I'll show her who's in control here. She opens her mouth to take another bite when I hold up my hand. "That's enough. Put that down, now. No more until later."

Her lips are poised to take a bite. She looks up at me in surprise,

"Excuse me?" Her voice registers something beyond surprise. Irritation? Anger?

"I said, you've had enough to eat. No more until I permit it."

Frowning, she places the food back on the plate. Still frowning, she stares at me in unabashed curiosity.

It occurs to me she doesn't know the rules of etiquette. She doesn't know how she's to behave or how to respond. She doesn't know how to socialize, or the unwritten rules of behavior. She's never known the companionship of anyone save her father.

If she were mine... if I were to truly keep this woman as my very own... I'd introduce her to everything. I swallow hard.

Everything.

And with that knowledge, I make up my mind.

Caitlin belongs to me, only me and no other, no matter the circumstance. I found her. I saw her first.

She's mine.

Chapter Six

My belly isn't empty for the first time in a month. I'm pleasantly satisfied with the simple fare, and after the day's events, I feel as if I need a nap to sleep the food off. I drink the water easily, and could eat more food without question, but Keenan takes it away from me.

He's watching me with a look I can't quite decipher. The green of his eyes, the same as his father has, and a few of the other men present today, makes him look a little less the fierce warrior I assume he is, or he appears to me. He has the eyes of an angel, a beatific vision. But this man is not an angel. Maybe he's a demon, then. One of the fallen.

Given what I've seen of him thus far, it seems like a distinct possibility.

I want more of the food before me, but he takes the tray away, and I know without him telling me this is a sort of test. He wants to test my obedience. Though I'm ignorant to the ways of the world, I'm not ignorant to the ways of men. I'm far too well read for that.

His father thought I should be punished, and for whatever reason he's chosen, Keenan hasn't punished me. Instead, he's asked me a few questions and fed me. What, then, *is* the man's plan with me?

So I play the cards he deals me and don't continue eating. Clearly, given the way he ordered food as if sent from heaven above in the hands of a winged messenger, there's plenty to eat around here. I'll find my way down to the kitchen if I have to.

I take another sip of water and sit back in my chair.

A stream of light illuminates his features for a moment as he watches me. I look to the window, uncomfortable under his penetrating glare. For the first time, I notice there are bars on the window. *Bars.* Thick, black, impenetrable bars. I rise to my feet, panic welling in my chest.

"This is a prison," I whisper, my throat feeling as if someone's wrapped a hand around it. "You pretended it was a bedroom with your pretty bed and luxurious carpet." I back away from him toward the bed, afraid of what will happen next. "But you tricked me. I'm in a prison."

His brow furrows and his lips turn down as he studies me. "No," he says thoughtfully. "The bars on the window are to keep people out, not to keep the occupants inside." His gaze swings to the window, then back to me. "But you're most definitely my prisoner. Does this surprise you?"

I'm not sure how to answer. Yes and no, I suppose. I knew I wasn't free to go. It wasn't until I saw the bars on the window that I panicked.

I clear my throat. "No."

"Now that we've taken care of the business of feeding you, it's essential we establish some ground rules," he says, a note of steel in his voice.

"Is it?" I ask, not able to mask the note of petulance in my voice.

"It is," he says, his voice hardening.

"Have at it, then. Rules and all that."

To my surprise, he walks to me, takes my hand, and yanks me to my feet. Placing one hand on my lower back, he pulls me to him so that I'm flush against him. I begin to tremble. I've not been touched like this by a man before, and it frightens me a little. And why is my body doing strange, wonderful, terrible things to me? A rush of heat flares in my body, my throat suddenly dry. He smells the way I'd imagine a waterfall would, strong and clean and powerful. His hand is warm, and I feel it straight through the thin fabric of my dress. My heartbeat quickens, and my palms feel weirdly damp. I've read of these things before, and if I didn't know any better, I'd think I were attracted to him. But how could I be? He's been nothing but mean.

His deep, rough voice, laced with his brogue, washes over me as he warns me. "When you speak to me, you'll speak respectfully. None of this 'yes' and 'no.' It's 'yes, sir,' and 'no, sir.'"

And odd rule, but I've noticed the men he speaks to calls him sir and it was how he himself addressed his father. He's an authority figure, then, just like his father.

"Yes, sir," I say, though I barely keep my tone cordial. He's a bully. "How long am I to be here? I want to go home." I was starving to death and lonely, but anything would be better than being here under his thumb.

I want to either pull closer to him or push away, but instead, I'm just frozen in place.

His brows rise for a barely noticeable fraction of a second before he draws them together again. "Are you really that naïve?"

Is he asking a question, or does he really mean that?

"I don't know how to answer that," I say, shaking my head. "Do you expect me to?" He runs his hand from my lower back upward, stroking as he maintains eye contact.

"You were caught in possession of notes, details, and data that mark you as a spy. Spying on The Clan is punishable by death. You raised your hand to me and tried to kick me, which earns additional punishment. You aren't going home, Caitlin. You've escaped with your life by sheer luck."

I feel cold and warm and a little dizzy.

They think I'm a spy? I'm not going home?

It doesn't matter that I wouldn't even know what to do with myself if I *did* go home. I have no food in the house, no contact with the outside world, and the home I lived in really was not much better than where

I am now. If I'm honest, this place is far more comfortable.

But I'm not safe here.

"I'm to deal with you, but first we need to deal with practicalities. You'll not present in front of my brothers looking like *that*."

My throat tightens and my nose tingles, and for one brief moment, I'm glad I haven't been around other people before now. People can be cruel.

"Mam, I need you," Keenan says into his phone.

Mam? He called his mother?

"Aye. Can you come to my room?" He listens. "Of course. Yes. Thank you."

"My mother will be coming here directly," he says. "I'm hoping she can sort your clothing." He releases me and walks away.

I look down at myself as if seeing for the first time. My cheeks flame with embarrassment, and I suddenly don't want his mother seeing me dressed like this.

Since I was old enough to wear my mother's clothes, it's all I've ever worn. I hadn't given them too much thought until he scorned me so fiercely. I swallow hard and turn away from him, not answering.

"Caitlin, look at me." His voice has returned to steel, as he stands in front of me with his arms crossed. "We must—"

A knock sounds at the door, and he crosses the room quickly, holding a finger up for me to stay where I am. As if there's anywhere to go.

He seems as surprised as I am when he opens the door, and it isn't his mother on the other side, but someone who looks like a paler, younger version of himself, with the same green eyes, but blond hair. This one *does* look like an angel.

"Well, well, well," the young man says, he's quite a bit younger than Keenan. "What have we here?"

"Oh come off it, Nolan," Keenan says, his bright green eyes darkening. "Get out. I told you *no one* comes here. Mam's coming to help me clothe her."

They're brothers, then. He did mention brothers, but I wasn't sure if he meant that in a figurative sort of way or not.

The man called Nolan looks sharply back at me. "Aw, feck. Ye got my hopes up. Thought I missed the fact she wasn't clothed."

Keenan crosses the room and reaches for him. He looks ready to throttle him, bright splotches of red on his cheeks, and his eyes narrowed on his brother. "You watch your mouth," he fumes.

Oh, my. Are they... are they fighting over me? I freeze, a little afraid of watching them...beat each other up or something.

Someone clears her throat in the doorway.

I look to the doorway to find a stunning woman leaning her hip casually against the doorframe. "Really, Keenan, must you?"

She's got similar facial features to her sons, even and symmetrical, though the angles of her face are gentler, more feminine. Her long, sandy-brown hair hangs just to her shoulders in waves. Dressed in a V-neck black sweater and jeans that hug her curves, it's hard to believe this woman ever gave birth. The only clue to me that she's older than she appears are the soft, gentle lines on either side of her eyes.

"Of all the cheek—" Keenan begins, shaking Nolan.

"Let him go," she says, her melodic tone gentle yet firm. "Please. You'll frighten the girl."

Keenan releases Nolan, who takes a few steps away as if to distance himself from his overbearing brother. "Seems that's what dad's ordered him to do," Nolan says casually.

Her lips tighten, but she doesn't respond for long minutes. Finally, she nods and looks to Keenan. "Is that right, son?"

Keenan meets her gaze. "Aye."

"We ought to be going, then," Nolan says, heading to the doorway, when his brother grabs him by the back of the shirt, drags him back, and pushes him to sitting in one of the vacant chairs.

"Oh, no, you don't. Sit."

Nolan looks at me sheepishly, flashing me a grin. I give him the tiniest smile back. I like him. It seems I may have a friend in this, if he doesn't get whisked away from me or murdered in his sleep by Keenan.

The woman crosses the room, but when her eyes come to my clothing, she freezes. I feel the heat return to my cheeks. Do I really look that bad? She pauses, unable to mask her surprise, before she schools her features, shakes her head, and continues walking to me. She reaches her hand out to me.

"Maeve McCarthy," she says. *Maeve.* I've never heard such a pretty name.

I don't know how to respond. It seems odd, really. I don't know what her purpose is here, or what's expected.

I clear my throat. "My name is Caitlin," I say awkwardly. Was that right? Is that how people respond?

"Oh," she says softly, and her voice gentles. "I'd chosen the name Caitlin."

"Excuse me?"

She shakes her head. "Eh, never mind that now. I once chose the name, for if I'd ever had a girl." She rolls her eyes and laughs, though she looks more like she's going to cry than laugh. "But wouldn't you know, as luck would have it, I got boys. All boys. Punishment for my sins, you see."

I can't help but smile in response.

Nolan snorts. "Reward for something good ya did, I'd say."

"Nolan, out," Keenan orders. "I need privacy."

Nolan gets to his feet and yawns, stretching his arms up over his head. "Suit yourself," he says, but it looks as if he only feigns nonchalance. He is indeed afraid of Keenan, and frankly, I don't blame him.

She comes to me and takes my hands, eyeing me up and down. "You're about five foot four, no?" She murmurs to herself. "Fifty-five kilos, give or take."

I shrug. "I... I have no idea."

She puts her hands on my shoulders and gives me a wide-eyed stare before responding. "Reeallllly. Not know?"

I shake my head. She looks back down at my dress and absentmindedly fingers the fabric. It troubles her, somehow. But before she can respond, she sighs. "Right, then."

Maeve walks around the room, picking things up and straightening the bed as if tidying it, though it already seems immaculate.

"Get to it, then, Keenan," she says. "What do you need from me?"

I blink in surprise, thinking she's rude, but he doesn't even flinch. Something troubles her. Something about me.

"Clothing," Keenan says. "I want her out of these old things and into something fresh, clean, and appropriate."

"Aye," she says, taking his perfectly fluffy pillows off the bed and fluffing them before returning them. "Naturally. When?"

"Before dinner, please," he says. "Will you get them for me?"

She turns and faces him but won't look at me. "Of course," she says. "Anything in particular?"

He shrugs, then looks back in my general direction, his eyes traveling from the top of my head to the tips of my toes before responding. He shrugs. "Nothing too... modern. Sleek. I kind of like the look of her in a dress, and for the love of God, nothing revealing."

I don't like how they're talking about me as if I'm not standing right here before them. It feels weird.

"Certainly" she says. She turns from me and leaves, without even casting a backward glance my way, and I'm left with a sadness that feels heavy on my chest. What did I do? I'd hoped for a friend in her, or... something.

It's confusing, all of this interaction with other people. I've never spoken so much in my life, and it's exhausting.

Keenan's walking to a large closet, bigger than my room at home. "I mean to find if you're telling me the truth, Caitlin."

"Of course I am," I tell him. "What use would it be to lie?"

He turns to face me, a length of rope in his hands. For some reason, the combination of the rope in his hands and the way he's eyeing me makes me shiver. "Not much use if I caught you in a lie," he says truthfully. "Doesn't mean you won't try it. But I've work to do and can't trust you. Give me your wrists."

Panic wells in me at the sight of the rope. He restrained me once, and I hoped he wouldn't again. I hated being restrained.

"Why?" I ask, but it's the wrong response. With a firm set of his jaw, he spins me around and cracks his hand against my backside. I gasp in pain and move to get away from him when a second hard blow follows the first. My cheeks flame with embarrassment. I'm humiliated at being punished like this.

"Stop!" I say, but he lands one final smack of his palm against my ass before he spins me back around to face him.

"I should punish you properly," he says. "Give me cheek like that again, and I will."

It's not lost on me that his father demanded just this, that he punish me. Is this what he has in mind?

"I don't know what you want from me," I protest.

He spins me around he grabs my chin so roughly, his fingers hurt. I wonder if he leaves marks. "Obedience," he says tightly. "Submission. I've given you more leeway that I should have. But I have my reasons. And your warnings are up, Caitlin. Now give me your wrists, or I will punish you properly."

With tears in my eyes, I obey. I hate him. *Hate* him. I was hidden away, apart from others, and my first interaction with people outside the confines of my home has destroyed my faith in humanity. My father had good reason to be hidden away like he was. Good reason. I swallow the lump in my throat and ignore the way my nose tingles while he ties a knot around my wrists.

"Good girl," he says. "Now, you'll wait on the side of the bed while I get ready." His voice drips with conde-scension, as if he thinks I'm only a child who needs correcting.

I scowl at him. I hate that this is my first interaction with the outside world, and he's taught me hate.

"I don't like that look on your face," he corrects. "Wipe it."

I hate him. *I hate him.*

It's almost like I hear an audible snap in my brain, like my resolve's been tied with string that can't bear any more weight.

"You're no better than your father," I snap, flouncing onto the bed. I don't curse, I will not, but I want to hurt him. "You're a jerk, just like him. I've done nothing wrong. Nothing, and yet you arrogant, domineering—" I'm so angry, hot, fat tears well in my eyes and I can't speak anymore.

The way his eyes flash at me, I know I've said the wrong thing. "I'll show you no better than my father," he says, his jaw as hard as granite as he reaches for me, flips me over, and presses me onto my belly. I roll, trying to get away from him, as panic floods me. He's going to hurt me. I can see it in his eyes.

He didn't save me from his father. He kept me for himself.

He pushes me into the bed so hard I can barely breathe. I turn my head and gasp for breath. He's got only one hand on me, but he's so strong I can't get away. My bound hands press into my chest. I hear a jingle of metal and a whirr. I flail in confusion and fear when the first searing strike hits me.

I howl in pain when a line of fire ignites across my thigh. "Stop!" I gasp, the pain's too much, but he doesn't heed my words. Still holding me down, he lashes me again, this time striking my backside. I gasp on a dry sob, wriggling to try to get away, but the harder I fight, the harder he pushes me. He strikes me again and again, until my world is throbbing pain and I'm choking on my tears.

"No more of your cheek. You'll watch that tongue of yours."

"Okay, *okay*. Stop, please!" I beg. "Please."

"That's for raising your hand to me," he says, before he gives me another wicked lash of pain, followed by two more in rapid succession. I sob.

"That's for your cheek, and *that*," he says, underscoring his lecture with harsh strokes that take my breath away, "Is for good measure."

"Please," I sob, my voice cracking.

"Let's be sure I've done a proper job," he says tightly. "Do you have anything else to say about spying? For whom did you work?"

"No one!" I cry. I don't tell him I didn't spy. I can't disrespect my father like that. He isn't here anymore to defend himself.

"You're lying," he snaps, lashing me again and again, until I feel my whole world is pain. I shake my head, refusing to contradict him but tempted to stop the punishment. He continues in silence, but I won't speak.

Finally, when I'm convinced I can't possibly take another moment, he pauses.

"I'll get the truth from you, lass. Will you behave your-self?" he admonishes, his tone cutting, lacerating my heart. If I thought I'd see any mercy at his hands, I was wrong.

"Yes," I say, though I'm still not even sure what "behave" means. "Yes. Please, stop hurting me."

He releases me, and I cry softly into the soft, satiny sheets. Whatever he struck me with clatters to the floor, but I don't know what it is, and I don't care.

He isn't done with me. Rolling me over onto my back, he drags me to my feet by my bound hands and pulls me to his chest. "My father ordered you punished," he says, his voice angry and fierce, and it might be my imagination, but it seems there's a note of regret in his tone. "I wanted to give you the benefit of the doubt. But if I show up with you unrepentant and defiant, he'll punish you far worse. Is that what you want, Caitlin? A man like my father meting out your discipline?"

I shake my head. I don't know what his father is capable of, but I can only imagine.

"No," I whisper, then quickly correct my response, a note of defeat in my voice that makes my shoulders droop. "No, sir."

His response takes me by surprise. Grasping the back of my head, he pulls me to him and kisses my forehead with a ferocity that belies the tender gesture. "Good girl," he whispers. "Good girl."

Chapter Seven

Keenan

I t's with great regret I stop myself from punishing her further. Keeping a watchful eye on the pretty lass with tear-stained cheeks, I thread my belt back in my trousers and watch her. She sits on the bed, her eyes on me warily, taking in every detail.

If I'm to believe what she says, the girl is innocent to the ways of the world and may not even know who The Clan is. All the more reason for the punishment I just administered. She's ignorant to the ways of organized crime, of criminals like us. And the sooner she sees how much danger she's in, the better.

We make our own rules. We adhere to a code. We obey the chain of command, and anyone who doesn't suffers the consequences.

Still, I couldn't help but give her some small measure of comfort after I punished her. Given that she's innocent and naïve, perhaps she didn't notice how punishing her affected me, how aroused it made me. It wasn't the first time I've whipped a woman, and it won't be the last. And if I'm honest, I liked it.

No.

I fucking loved it.

The way she squirmed and screamed. The power that rushed through me, pinning her to the bed and administering deliberate pain.

Jesus, Mary, and Joseph, I'm hard as fucking granite after that.

The girl's a virgin, I've no doubt, and it makes it that much harder to abstain. I've never had a virgin, and the thought of me being her first… Christ, I can't think like that.

"I've business to tend to," I tell her. "You'll stay here and wait for your clothing. When mam arrives, allow her to help you dress, and be ready for this evening's dinner. But before we go, I need to be sure you're prepared, Caitlin."

She looks up at me with those wide blue eyes, beads of tears still clinging to her eyelashes like tiny crystals. I swallow hard. There's something about her that's fetching, that makes me regret being the cause of those tears.

"What?" she says. I'm glad to see her tone's softened, that her punishment did something to mitigate her cheek.

"I'll give you one chance to speak truth before I take you before my father."

She blinks but doesn't reply.

"I need to know why you were in possession of materials suitable for a spy," I tell her. "My men will want to know." I speak earnestly, for this is important. If I can't prove she's innocent, her life is forfeit.

"I don't know," she says, shaking her head. "I truly don't."

"Were they your father's, then?" I ask.

Her brow furrows. "If they were, it is news to me," she says sadly. "I can't imagine he'd be a spy. I truly can't."

"Are you?" I ask her bluntly.

She looks at me as if I just asked her if she's ever visited the moon. "Do I look like a spy?"

I feel my jaw harden. She still doesn't get it.

"Answer. The. Question."

Of course she doesn't, but I never met a spy who did.

She stills, and squirms on the bed, likely mulling over the punishment I inflicted.

"I am not a spy. I lived the life of a recluse, until you robbed me of that and took me. I don't even know who you are, much less what you do. I don't know who owned the books in that shed, and the most logical explanation is yes, they belonged to my father. Why would he spy on you? I don't know."

She speaks the truth.

"Those were good answers," I tell her. "I have work to do before this evening. I'll be back. My men will be outside this door and mam will be back soon. You're to

81

call her Maeve, her Christian name, and do what she says. I trust her."

She doesn't respond, her eyes fixed on the window behind me.

"Did you hear me?" I ask sharply.

She starts, then drags her eyes back to mine. "Yes, of course," she says.

I nod, and for the first time, something in me loosens looking at her.

She could be the one.

The moment the words hit the periphery of my consciousness, I shove them away. I'm not the type to fall for sentimental notions. Nolan's the romantic; I'm the practical one. Men in our Clan don't marry for love but convenience, to solidify and strengthen our bonds, or to form alliances. Love can form, of course. Of this I'm certain. One only has to see the way mam looks to my dad with stars in her eyes, and the way he softens when she's near. But love is an ethereal emotion for which I have no time or patience.

And it's stupid to even entertain the thought of anything between me and Caitlin. She's my captive, and I'm to question her.

But what will become of her after tonight?

I don't like leaving her in the room. Though I know no one can penetrate the layers of protection that surround our estate, it troubles me. I call my men back to their positions outside my door, and when they arrive, it still doesn't put me at ease.

I want to be the one to protect her.

My phone rings as I exit my room, and I answer on the second ring. It's Carson, our Clan secretary and bookkeeper.

"Yes?"

"Keenan, are you on your way into the office?"

I grunt into the phone. "Yeah. Why?"

"I heard you had company, and wanted to be sure we were still meeting," he says. "I'll meet you there."

We disconnect the call. Word gets out quicker than wildfire in The Clan.

I usually prefer to drive myself into the office, but today I'm distracted. I call a driver, and within minutes, I'm in the backseat of one of our vehicles, scrolling through my phone and heading in. I have business to attend to, and want it done quickly and efficiently.

I could call off the meeting I have today, but I want to see how she handles my absence. I also want to be sure I've taken care of everything I need to, so I'm free to deal with Caitlin.

As Captain of the Clan, I oversee the finishing school we host at Saint Albert's. Every one of us was trained there; every one of our fresh recruits attends St. Albert's before they're initiated. The vast majority of the boys who train there are blood-relations, with few exceptions. Carson was one such exception.

Carson's mother, an English woman by birth, worked for my family all her life. She'd barely graduated University when she became a widow, left with Carson, then just a baby. She told my father she trusted him to help raise her son to be successful. My father, as Clan Chief, suggested he board at St. Albert's, the finest educational institution near us. At the time, it was merely a temporary, pragmatic decision. He had no intention of initiating Carson into The Clan. But the rest of us felt he'd become like a brother.

He lived in our home. Knew our ways. He was as much a member of our family as Nolan or Cormac. And his mother gave her blessing for full initiation before she died.

My father broke law and tradition with his induction, but Carson's brilliance and unparalleled logical mind are decided assets to our brotherhood. We had enough who could break bones and fulfill hired hits. We had muscle and brawn and leadership. We were in need of someone to keep our books and organize the business side of things.

Carson upholds the code of Clan brotherhood with the best of them, and my father's never regretted his decision.

Though there are many clans through Ireland, some rivals and some neutral, ours stands as one of the strongest. I've no doubt it's due in no small part to the finishing school we fund. Unlike our rivals and peers, the men of our brotherhood are trained at a young age in obedience, fortitude, and logic. By the time they're ready to graduate, they've been taught loyalty and our code of conduct as well. Men don't bite the hand that feeds them.

I look over today's agenda: review Clan finances, review the summaries given us from Malachy, the overseer of St. Albert's. Introduce the imprisonment and capture of Caitlin.

When I arrive in my office, my secretary sits at her desk, piles of paperwork stacked in neat piles. Though I've got an office at the house, there are times I need to conduct business elsewhere, to keep up appearances. I like to come here a few times a week.

"Catrina, I have a job for you," I tell her. She's young and put together, a petite blonde well-dressed in a skirt and jacket, eager to please, and though I've always found her pretty, it occurs to me she doesn't hold a candle to Caitlin's radiance.

What is wrong with me?

"Yessir?"

"Find out anything and everything you can about Jack Anderson, the lighthouse keeper. History, parentage, if he was married to anyone. Get in touch with Brady and tell him I want a full report as soon as possible."

"Yessir. Of course, sir. Several of your men are awaiting your arrival in your office."

Brady, one of several private detectives we have on staff, is prompt and efficient. I'll have what I need.

We've assumed Anderson was an eccentric old man, when he may have been a spy right under our very noses. Madness is a well-fitting disguise.

"Thank you."

I enter my office to find Carson and Malachy sitting amiably beside each other. They've known each other for years, as Carson and I were under Malachy's tutelage when we were in school together.

"Gentlemen," I say in greeting. Both men get to their feet to greet me, but I gesture for them to sit. All of the men in our Clan function as brothers, but the chain of command holds weight, and all know to show respect to those higher in rank. I've been Malachy's and Carson's superior for several years now.

"What's the story, Keenan?" Carson says amiably. He takes his laptop out of his bag and balances it on his knee. Though Carson's trained with all of us, rising to peak physical shape, he's the more studious of the lot. With his wire-rimmed glasses perched on his nose, we've always called him The Clan professor.

"Got a lass in my keeping," I tell him. "You've heard this?"

"I have," he says with a knowing smile. "A gorgeous lass, no less."

Something in me tightens.

That she is and hell if any of them come near her...

"Do tell," Malachy says, leaning back in his chair and crossing one ankle on his knee. Several years younger than my father, Malachy's my father's best mate and cousin. Malachy never married but has dedicated his life to the raising of the boys of The Clan into men. He's tall and muscled like all of us, and he's an expert in the study of *ealaíona comhraic*, Irish martial arts, encompassing everything from boxing to wrestling and stick fighting. We've all been properly trained.

Malachy's iron-gray hair is cut short, his jaw clean-shaven, his eyes as steely gray as his hair. Rumor has it his father's father's father hailed from Germany, and he's suited for training The Clan because of his family's Spartan rules and principles. It's why he's never married, he says. No woman would tolerate his regimen and monk-like existence. Though he rules with an iron fist and kept all of us in line with uncompromising discipline, Malachy is a second father to us all.

I sit behind my desk and loosen my tie.

"Pour us a drink, will you, Malachy?" Christ, I need one.

Malachy grins and goes to the sideboard I keep in my office, pouring a generous amount of Jameson in tumblers. I don't speak again until the hot, fiery liquid hits my veins. I sigh. I needed that. I clear my throat and begin.

"This morning we had early council. Father Finn had news to relay."

Malachy snorts. "Course he did," he says. "Always the fly on the wall of the confessional, eh?"

"Aye," I say with a smile. "That he is."

I fill them in.

"You left the lass in your room?" Malachy asks curiously. "You trust her?"

I'm not sure how to answer the question. Do I? There's something so winsome and wholesome about her, I can't deny that a part of me wants to trust her. Do I think she spied on my family? I have to assume she did until we can prove otherwise, though I think it far more likely her father was the one to blame. So I don't answer him. "I left her bound and under orders not to leave the room. My men are on guard, and mam's on her way to help dress her."

"Dress her?" Carson asks curiously.

"She came dressed in old, tattered clothing," I say, shaking my head. I don't tell them she's a recluse, never having left her home. It sounds too odd, too preposterous.

And it's something I want to keep to myself.

Like her.

A dark, almost perverted sense of ownership pervades me when I think of her locked up in my room. Innocent. Virginal. Fully dependent on me.

"How very interesting," Malachy says, his eyes twinkling.

"What?" I ask. He looks as if he knows something.

"First pretty young thing we take into our custody since you've come of age and you've ditched the bitch who held you by the bollox, and the new girl's privately held in your chambers, eh?"

I narrow my eyes at him but bite my tongue. He's baiting me, and I know it.

Though I'm above him in rank now, memories die hard. I've been the recipient of more than one thorough discipline session at Malachy's hands, and I still respect the man.

"Keep his history out of it, Malachy," Carson says quietly. "Leave off. Keenan's too dedicated to fidelity to've taken a woman when he was committed to another one, and you know it."

I give Carson a quick, thankful glance.

"I'm not here to discuss the girl," I say, changing the subject. "I've got others researching her father's history, and still others fingerprinting what she had in her possession. Let's hear what's going on, and be quick about it. Carson, you first." I ignore Malachy's snicker.

Carson's concentrating on the computer before him. "All's well, captain," he says. "Our investments in The Cask have tripled since last spring." Cask Whiskey's profitability's increased by twenty percent, and we're one of the first to invest heavily. "Our sources on the Isle of Man confirm the arrangement we've made for our dealing next month. Spain is strong, as well as our alliances."

Alliances are code for paid hits. We don't speak of them aloud unless in the vault-like interrogation room.

"Good," I say. "I'd like it so the arms trade increases three-fold by this time next year." I clear my throat. "And I'd like to see us eliminate alliances completely."

Malachy raises a brow. "Lofty goals, Keenan."

I turn to him. "We can do it. Anyway, it's safer," I tell him. "More reliable. And I have it on good authority there will be a stronger need for South African dealings in the coming years. If we've formed strong alliances and solidified our contacts, we'll be set financially for the next decade."

Malachy nods, accepting this.

Contracted hits are part and parcel for any organized crime group, but they aren't necessary. Given how lucrative our arms dealings have been, we can eliminate the riskiest of our income streams.

"Word on the school, next," I say, moving our meeting along at a breakneck speed. I want to get back to Caitlin. Christ, the woman affects me. I have to keep a close handle on my logic and reason. I can't have her swaying me from my job.

Malachy grins. "Our boys are thriving," he says. "Young Grady made star quarterback last term. Big, strapping lad. Lachlan's done well, raising his marks." Grady and Lachlan will graduate soon, steps away from formal induction into our brotherhood.

"No more write-ups?" I ask. Lachlan has a history of a hair-trigger temper the boy would do well to quell.

Malachy grimaces. "Four instead of eight."

I frown. "Still too high," I say. "I want to see him personally at the weekend."

Malachy nods. "It's fair," he says. "I'll not tell them you're coming. You'll see them at their most candid."

I nod. I'll arrange it so Caitlin can accompany me on this trip. I wonder how the boys will react to her.

He gives me the update on the rest of the boys, the staff changes, and the dedicated curriculum they've instilled with focus on martial arts. The faculty's made up of Clan affiliates, as well as the wives, sisters, and cousins of our members.

"You've got marks for me to look at?" Malachy nods. The marks include both academics and additional skills the boys are taught. They're kept in peak physical shape and trained like the soldiers they're meant to be.

"What shall we do about teacher retention?" I ask.

"I'd recommend a solid bonus and raise," Malachy says.

"Note that," I tell Carson, who nods and makes note. We discuss a few more items on the agenda, when my phone rings. It's my father.

"Got to answer this," I say. "It's dad."

I answer.

"Keenan."

"Yes, sir. What is it?"

"What did she tell you?" I clench my jaw. I told him I'd question her and answer him this evening, but he's obsessed. He wants answers now.

"My gut says she's an innocent in this. She found the records in the shed on her property, and insists she knows nothing about her father's affiliation with any of this."

"She's lying."

Heat flares across my chest at his accusation. I made the very same accusation to her myself today, but I can't abide it coming from anyone else but me.

"I'm not sure she is," I tell him.

"What sort of tactics did you use?"

My body tightens. We had a battle of wills this afternoon, and I'm holding my ground. "Do you trust me to do this right?" I ask him.

He pauses and doesn't answer at first.

"Do you?" I insist, my voice growing steely. My father's never been one to micromanage any one of us, and I can't have him starting now.

"Of course I do."

"Then please, let's keep this as we had it this morning. I'll interrogate the way I see fit and update you this evening."

I swear I can hear him grind his jaw on the other side of the phone. "Fair enough," he says. "You're usually bang on, so I trust you here. Do what you have to. I want to know tonight. Something's afoul, Keenan."

"Don't need to tell me that," I say grimly, with an air of resignation. "I agree. Trust me, and I'll find out what I need to."

"Right."

He hangs up the phone, and I look up to see Carson and Malachy looking at me curiously.

"What?"

"The girl's got you addled," Malachy says, shaking his head.

"She most certainly does not, ya wanker," I say, my temperature rising.

"Most certainly does," Carson says, his brows raised in surprise. "You haven't even questioned her yet?"

"I have," I protest, but I know what they mean. Have I tortured her, demanding answers? No. But they don't know what I do, that she's never been in the company of men. Her innocence paints her expression. I'm not sure she'd know how to lie if she tried.

Christ. I have to answer to my men tonight, and they'll expect answers.

She's had enough time alone and with mam. I'm going home.

"I'm going back to my place," I say, rising. "If there's anything else you need from me, you know where to find me."

On the way out, Catrina stops me. "You'll have a full report this week, sir," she says. "I've been promised."

I nod. "Thank you."

I'm going back to Caitlin.

Chapter Eight

CAITLIN

I sit on the bed, my wrists still bound, trying to observe anything and everything I can until it bores me. I manage to wriggle off the bed and walk about the room, noting as many details as I can.

There's a small bookshelf filled with books, though they look like they've never been opened. If I didn't have my wrists bound, I'd peruse them. I hope I get a chance before they send me home.

There's a massive bathroom, with a large, round, circular tub in it, an intricate vanity and mirror, and an enormous shower. Our tiny bathroom consisted of a stall shower and tiny toilet, the mirror old and streaked, so I could hardly see myself.

But this one... this one takes my breath away. I stand in front of it, staring at my reflection. I'm tall and thin, and it shocks to see the tattered, threadbare clothing that clings to me in the bright overhead light. Clearly too small, clearly outdated, and practically disintegrating.

And for the first time in my life, I'm ashamed of how I look. Keenan looked so fine when he was preparing to leave, so put-together, wearing a suit and tie and shoes that shone, reflecting the overhead lighting. And I look like a street urchin. Like an overgrown child.

I hope Maeve comes quickly. I want out of these old clothes.

I close my eyes and press my forehead against the cool, pristine tile.

Why did you do this to me? I ask my father. *Were you hiding things?*

Why would it surprise me if he was hiding things?

He hid *me.*

I start when I hear a door open, my heart racing like butterfly wings against my chest. Someone comes into the room. Is it Maeve? Would she come in unannounced?

I don't want to be taken by surprise, or for anyone to think I'm hiding, so I turn the doorknob and exit the bathroom. I freeze in the doorway when I see Keenan's father walking into the bedroom. Involuntarily, I step back into the bathroom. He's a dangerous man, and I need to hide. But he's seen me, and I know it's foolish to think I can get away from him.

"There you are, lass," he says, and though his words are casual, his voice is hard. It makes my pulse quicken. "Come here."

I take one step forward and don't go any further. His eyes narrow, and he crooks his finger at me. "Closer."

Keenan won't like this. Not at all.

I swallow hard and obey. He nods. "Good. Seems he's training you well, then." His eyes roam over my body. "I see no marks, though," he says disapprovingly. I swallow hard.

"I've been punished, if that's what you wonder," I tell him, a note of anger evident in my tone. What does he wish to see? Bruises on my shoulders or neck? I shudder.

His eyes darken. "Show me."

Revulsion churns in my stomach, and my cheeks flame. It isn't right. No. Keenan won't like this. He'll lose his mind if he knows his father did this, that he violated me and came in here.

"I—I can't," I whisper, faltering. "I don't think Keenan would approve."

He stares at me, and I wonder how he'll react. I can't swallow or blink. I'm frozen in place, at this man's mercy, when the door opens again, and Maeve steps in.

"Oh, there y'are, Seamus," she says, beaming at him. "Came to visit the lass?"

She's laden with bags, and Seamus walks over to help her carry them. I release the breath I was holding. He takes them in hand, nodding.

"Aye," he says. "Looks like you've got an errand with her, then. I'll leave you."

Relief floods through me all at once.

I could kiss Maeve. To my surprise, when he draws near to him, she gets up on her tiptoes and kisses him full on the lips, then wraps her arms around his neck, as if she hasn't seen him in ages. He pulls her to him, bags and all, and stoops down, hugging her. He whispers something in her ear that makes her giggle.

"Go on with you, now," she says. "Out you go. We've got girl stuff to tend to." She winks at him.

He looks to me, puts the bags on the floor, and nods. "You answered well, lass," he says, before he turns and takes his leave.

What? He's pleased with my answer?

Was he testing me?

Maeve looks at me curiously, her head tipped to the side. "What was that about?" she asks. I tell her about the brief exchange. Her large, luminous eyes widen, and a soft smile spreads across her lips. "Sweet girl," she says. "You told the Chief his son wouldn't approve?" She breaks into a full on grin. "You've got spunk, I'll give you that. Now let's get you out of these clothes and prepared for dinner."

I'm still shaking, but I soon forget what's on my mind when I look at the piles of items she's dumping onto the bed. They're all so foreign to me. Why did she bring so much?

Talking to people drains you. I miss the isolation and solace of being alone, the quiet and peace of holding my own counsel. I stifle a yawn as she arranges things. I'm tired. So tired.

But before we get to the clothes, I have questions.

"Was he going to hurt me?" I ask her.

She straightens in surprise, looks to the door, then back to me. She mulls her response over before answering. "He might've," she says thoughtfully, and it's strange how the honest response doesn't seem to trouble her. "He's a stern man, Seamus. But if he's told Keenan that you're his charge, I can't imagine he would betray that."

"He asked me if Keenan punished me," I whisper.

She nods, then goes back to unpacking the bags. "He would, yes. What did you do to earn a punishment?"

She's asking me this as if it's normal and expected. I tell her, and her brows go up.

"Well," she says. "Did he punish you?"

I nod. He did. My cheeks flame. I'm suddenly embarrassed to be having this discussion, but she doesn't seem the least bit bothered.

"Then you've nothing to worry about," she says. "We have a code here, and you broke it. You didn't know, I understand. But that rarely impacts retribution or consequences. You'll see."

I have so many more questions I want to ask her, but she's got a job to do. She lifts my bound hands and unties the bounds with matter-of-fact efficiency.

"Now, pretty girl," she says. "Off with this tattered clothing."

"May I go to the bathroom and—"

98

"No," she orders, her voice harder now. "You're going to be put to the test, Caitlin," she says. "You've been taken prisoner by some of the most powerful men in all of Ireland. It's absolutely crucial you learn to endure whatever trial they put you through. You'll have to learn to swallow that pride." Her final words come as a blow, sharp as a whip. "Now off with your clothes."

She'd have to be fierce to be married to the likes of Seamus, to have raised a man like Keenan. Still, I'm a little taken aback.

I swallow hard but do what she says. My hands tremble, and I want to die, but she's my ally in this. I have to trust her.

She looks politely away while I undress, turning her back to me. "Now, on with your bra," she says. "And your knickers." She hands me pretty lace white things. I put them on, fumbling with the clasp on the bra, and she turns. "Holy Mother, have you never seen a bra before, lass?"

"Not one like this."

She purses her lips but asks no questions, and quickly helps me dress.

"Aye, I've still got a good eye," she says with a smile. "They fit you like a glove, they do," she says. She lays out several dresses on the bed, but points to the blue one on the far right. "That one," she says. "It'll go with your eyes, and he'll love it."

I don't really care which one. I just want her to pick one out and I want to be dressed. I lift my arms when she gestures for me to prepare, then the pretty, silky fabric glides over my body. I sigh involuntarily. I've never felt anything so soft and luxurious.

I spin with my arms outstretched.

I wonder at how much I've missed. I've never worn new clothes, never felt the soft luxury of silky fabric. And clothing is the simplest of luxuries. How much more does the world have to offer? "It's beautiful," I say in awe.

"As are you," she replies. "Now let's freshen you up." She leads me to the bathroom and lays all kinds of things I don't recognize on the counter. I imagine they're beauty products, cosmetics and the like.

"Something tells me you're not familiar?" she asks, looking my way.

I shake my head and speak the truth. "I've never left the lighthouse. I—I've not been around people, much less used or owned things like that."

If she's surprised, she doesn't show it, and I realize she's likely learned the skill of schooling her features, living with men like these and being married to Seamus.

"Aye, he'll never let her go, then," she whispers to herself, then shakes her head when I give her a quizzical look. "Right, then," she says, as if what I told her was the most natural thing in the world. She gives me a lesson on washing up properly and taking good care of my skin, "though your skin's got a natural glow that'd be the envy of any woman," she admits. When I'm done, she spins me around to look at myself. I blink in surprise. I hardly look familiar. My eyes are brighter, my skin glows. My hair's piled onto my head, and a delicate silver necklace graces my neck.

Maeve's eyes grow a little wistful, and she speaks as if to herself. "You remind me so of someone I once knew. The resemblance is uncanny. But it's not possible."

I hear footsteps in the hall and look to the door just as Keenan enters. He looks more handsome than I even remembered, his hair tousled, his sleeves rolled up, revealing corded forearms. His eyes come immediately to me. He freezes.

"Holy Mother of God," he mutters.

Maeve smiles, gives me a quick hug, then turns to Keenan.

"I guess I did a right job of it, then, didn't I?" she asks. "See you at dinner, you two." She reaches for my hand and squeezes. "Stay brave, sweet Cait."

I like that. *Sweet Cait.*

Stay brave?

And then she's gone.

I never knew my mother, and for one brief moment, I'm filled with a sort of desperate longing. But I can't decipher the meaning of it. As soon as she's left the room, Keenan's crossing the room to me. I take a step back, afraid of what he'll do when he reaches me. He stands in front of me, tall and stern, his beautiful green eyes cloudy, before he takes my chin in his hand and holds my eyes to his.

"None of them will touch you," he whispers. "None of them."

I nod. I don't know why he's making this declaration or what he's anticipating they'll do.

"You've told me the truth, Caitlin," he says. "You know nothing of what you held."

"No, sir," I say, remembering my instructions from earlier.

He nods. "And when you say you've never left the lighthouse, you mean that?"

I nod.

"Then how is it you know anything at all? Explain."

"I've read a book a day for as long as I can remember. All sorts, all types. All I know has been gleaned from the pages of a book. Thousands upon thousands of books."

"Right, then." He looks at me again. "Fair enough. I must confess, your new clothing pleases me very much."

"I'm glad you like it. I like your mother."

"My mother's the absolute best," he agrees.

"She seemed to really be crazy about your father," I murmur. "When he came in the room, she—" His sharp tone interrupts me, and I stop speaking mid-sentence.

"Excuse me?" he asks in a deadly voice.

I can't reply. My mouth won't seem to work properly.

"I asked you a question," he says. "And I want an answer."

"He--he came in before your mother did," I stutter, speaking in a small voice. "He had some questions for me."

"Like what?" his voice is hard and demanding, and I try to take a step back from him but can't.

"He... he asked me to show that you punished me. He wanted to see marks."

Keenan curses so hard and angrily I close my eyes with the onslaught. "Son of a fucking bitch," he says. "Testing both me and you." Then he stills, bends to me, and holds my chin in his hand again. His fingers are rough, but his tone is gentle. "Did you show him?"

I shake my head. "I told him I didn't think you'd approve," I say. I don't know what he'll say to this, how he'll react, but what he does shocks me. He grins.

His face breaks into the most brilliant smile, and once more I'm reminded of an angel. My goodness.

"You passed the test, then, lass," he says. "Now let's see if you'll pass mine."

A test? I don't like that anyone's testing me.

He releases me, steps back toward his bed, and leans against it, folding his arms across his chest. "Go to my desk," he says, making a little twirly motion with his finger to indicate I'm to spin around. "Lift your dress and show me."

It feels as if something warm glides through me, even as my nerves are fraught.

"What?" I whisper.

He leans slightly forward, his voice dropping to a lower octave.

"Go to my desk," he repeats. "Lift your dress. And show me the marks I left from your belting."

Oh.

It was his belt, then. He struck me with his belt. And he wants to see the marks he's left.

I shiver. I passed the first test. Will I pass this one?

Why does he want to see? Is he proud of hurting me? Is a twisted, perverted part of him attracted to the marks he left? Or does he just wish to set me off kilter?

There are words for men like him, men that take pleasure in inflicting pain, but they escape me. I feel strangely lightheaded. A bit trembly. I do know I pleased him with how I answered his father, and it's crucial that I obey Keenan now.

So I do. I walk to the desk, and turn to face it, conscious of his eyes following my every move. I take the silky hem of my dress and raise it, lifting it so all he can see are my bare legs and the white lace of my undergarments. I feel as if time is suspended while I wait for his response.

"Mother*fucker*," he mutters. I hear him stepping toward me. I'm still holding my dress, my belly pressed against the cool, firm hardness of it, when I feel his warmth and presence behind me. I turn slightly to watch, then my body goes still when he drops to his knees.

His knees. This powerful, fearsome man kneels on the floor behind me, like a servant.

His large, warm hand caresses the white lace across my backside. I hold my breath when he grasps the elastic band and drags the lace downward, baring me. I begin to tremble. This isn't right, and yet a part of me would be woefully disappointed if he stopped now. My mouth is dry. I don't blink. Watching him. Waiting. His beautiful green eyes rove over my naked skin, and little goosebumps rise as if his very look caresses me.

"You bear my marks well," he says in a throaty, husky whisper. The lacy panties glide down my bare legs to my ankles. My shaking intensifies. He could hurt me right now. He could violate me. Yet I don't want him to stop.

He anchors his hands on my hips, his rough, calloused palms grazing the tender, soft skin. I freeze.

I should be embarrassed. I should want to cover myself in modesty or push him away. But I don't. I've lived a sheltered life, and yet here, with him, I'm somehow still sheltered. He's got me under his watchful eye, but there's more to it. The way he looks hungrily at me makes me feel… I don't know. It's all too foreign, too overwhelming.

But I know one thing. I don't want to hide from him. There's nothing short of adoration in those brilliant green eyes of his, and I want to keep that focus on *me.* The more he hungers for me, the more I want him to. It's all so new to me, so unexpected, I don't know how to react except to welcome him. I close my eyes and relax into his touch.

Leaning closer to me, he places gentle kisses to the stripes of red. His marks. The feel of his sensual mouth and the roughness of the whiskers send a tremor through my body. Heat pulses between my legs, warmth and pressure throbbing. I'm filled with the need to have him closer to me. My pulse races when he kisses every inch of my aching, throbbing skin.

"You've never been with a man, Caitlin."

He isn't asking a question but stating the obvious. I'm not sure why.

"Of course not."

He swallows, his Adam's apple bobbing.

"You will."

I want to. I don't know why or how, but I've tasted his bold, uncompromising possession… and I want more.

More.

He returns to kissing the marks he left, his mouth traveling upward until he reaches the valley at the small of my back. It tickles, so I can't help but giggle when he kisses me there.

"Does it tickle?" he asks, his voice husky and affected.

"Yes."

"Does this?" he asks, dragging his tongue along my naked skin. I close my eyes at the warm, sensual feel, and moan.

"No," I gasp. "Not that."

Then he stops. Pressing his forehead to the small of my back, he holds my hips in his hand and sighs.

"We have to go," he says. He rises to his feet, and I watch as his shield goes back up. The change in the expression on his face is palpable. Is this man such a chameleon, that he changes to suit who he has to be next? His jaw hardens and his eyes grow colder and distant again. He doesn't speak at first, adjusting his pants and flexing his shoulders. I watch his muscles ripple, and I'm reminded I'm in the presence of a powerful man.

"We will go to meet with my brothers now."

I don't even know what could have happened right then, what he could've done to me. I feel the loss of his heat and touch, but try not to show it. I have to be brave.

Stay brave, sweet Cait.

I'm terrified at the thought of entering a crowded room full of strangers. I don't want this. I want to be alone and solitary again.

"What will happen?" I ask.

He won't meet my eyes. "They'll ask questions, and I'll tell them what I found. No more, no less. Answer truthfully, and you've nothing to fear."

But I do. *I do.*

The look in his eyes makes one thing imminently clear: he's what I should fear the most.

Chapter Nine

Keenan

I don't like her being in the presence of my father and brothers. She's nervous and jittery, stuttering when she's asked a question. I remind myself that she's not been around others very often, and socializing like this is likely quite overwhelming. With my prompting, she answers quickly and honestly. My father seems satisfied. I don't mention that I know he paid her a visit.

"Bradley will have news tomorrow," I tell him, and we continue with business as usual. But I want her alone. I need her alone again. Caitlin is uncomfortable in the crowded room, and I want her taken back to quiet. I don't blame her. She's been alone for how long? And now she's thrust in the open, taken away from anything and anyone familiar. And she's still mourning the loss of her father. So before dessert is served, I excuse both of us.

Her father… something tells me there are clues I'll need to unearth.

She holds my hand when I take her back to my room, an act of trust. A small one.

"Your father didn't seem as—" her voice immediately trails off when she clamps her mouth.

"As what?" I ask her, ascending the large, carpeted staircase with her.

"Oh, nothing," she says, her cheeks flushing pink.

"It wasn't nothing," I admonish. "If you've something to say you shouldn't, then don't open your mouth to begin with. But since you did, you'll complete the thought. Now say it."

It's harsh, I know, but a lesson Malachy taught me at school and one I adhere by. Say what you mean and mean what you say.

"He didn't seem as mean," she says, flushing. "Am I allowed to say that?"

I school my features with effort. I want to laugh out loud. "No," I tell her. "You do need to watch what you say about him. He's different around my mam, though. Very different."

"I've noticed," she says quietly. "And I'm sorry."

"My father is a harsh, exacting man," I tell her when we reach the landing. "But he's fair and loyal, and no one is allowed to say a word against him. Including you."

She frowns and doesn't reply.

"Respond correctly, Caitlin," I instruct.

She looks at me with challenge in her eyes, and it surprises me at first that she doesn't do what I ask. She was docile as a lamb over dinner. Now she's choosing to be defiant?

I release her elbow, swing her out in front of me, and slam my palm against her arse. I won't allow her to look at me that way, to challenge me.

She yelps but tightens her jaw and doesn't speak.

"I said, respond correctly," I admonish.

"Yes, sir," she finally says tightly, yanking her arm from me.

"Did you forget what it felt like to be punished, Caitlin?" I ask her. "Would you like me to refresh your memory?"

I want her to give me a reason, so I can feel what it's like to wield my power over her once more.

Her eyes cloud, and she shakes her head. "No," she whispers, before she amends, "I'm sorry, sir."

I take her into my room and bring her to the side of the bed. "Off with your clothes," I tell her. "You've a nightgown hanging in the jacks. It's what you'll wear to bed when you sleep tonight."

"Jacks?"

"Bathroom," I growl impatiently.

She looks at the bathroom, then back to me, but doesn't argue. She prepares for bed in silence, and I watch every moment as she undresses herself. God, but she's gorgeous. I don't touch her, though. I don't make a move.

I strip my own clothes off and prepare for bed myself, when my phone rings.

Bradley. "Yeah?"

"I need a handwriting sample from Caitlin, please."

"Alright," I say. I take down the details he wants me to get and beckon her over to the desk. "Come here and write this." I point to the table.

She scowls but obeys. I take the scrap of paper, fold it, and place it on the bedside table.

"Now sleep," I order, folding down the blanket and pointing to the bed.

"Where... where will you sleep?"

I raise a brow to her. "In my *bed.*"

"And... and where will *I* sleep?"

I repeat, "In my bed."

She furrows her brows together. "Alright." She doesn't say anything else, but I can tell she wants to. She climbs under the covers, keeping herself at the very edge of the bed. I'm exhausted and don't fight this. When I'm ready, I climb into the other side of the bed and shut the lights.

"We've guards outside these doors and bars on the windows. Surveillance cameras over every inch of this property. So don't try it, Caitlin."

She doesn't respond. I soon realize it's because she's already fast asleep. I check my texts and finish my business, ignoring my conscience that plagues me for being an arsehole. I can't grow complacent or too soft with her, though. Finally, I place my phone on the bedside table. Soon, I join her in sleep.

I wake early in the morning when my phone buzzes. It's still dark outside the window. I glance at the time on my phone.

Six a.m. Who the fuck is calling me this early?

"Hello?"

"Sorry to wake you, sir. Did I call too early?"

"Wee bit, Bradley." I say gruffly, walking away from the bed so I don't wake Caitlin. If he's calling me this early, he must have news for me.

"You find something?"

"Lots, sir. You'll want to see this."

"Meet me in the foyer," I instruct. "When can you be here?"

"I'm outside your front door."

I disconnect the call and throw on a pair of joggers and a t-shirt. Caitlin stirs. I walk to her, lift the blanket, and tuck it in around her. I want to stay. I want to wake her with a kiss and show her the sweet, sweet secrets of her body. What I could do to her...

With reluctance, I leave. One of my guards is slouched over by the door. Feckin' *hell.*

I shove him, and he nearly topples over. "Sleeping on the job?" I ask curtly. "I've got a woman in there I want kept safe. Hey, you." I point to the second man who stands at attention. "You're in charge." I take the sleepy guard by the back of the shirt and shake him. "And you are dismissed."

"Sir!" he protests. "Please don't. I need this job!"

I narrow my eyes on him. "Then you should've taken said job seriously. Leave. Immediately."

I report that I've fired him to Carson. "Have Cormac escort him off the property," I tell him.

"What'd he do again?" Carson asks curiously.

"Fell asleep while keeping guard."

There's a pause. "You fired him over that?"

"Of course I did. What good is he asleep?"

"None," Carson concurs. "But, question, boss. Was Caitlin in the room? Was she the one he was meant to guard?"

"Shut it, Carson," I tell him. "Fire him. Have Cormac walk him out. Get his papers."

I'm fuming by the time I get down to the entrance and let Bradley in.

"So sorry to get you so early, boss," he says, stepping into the house. He's a short, stocky guy related to Sebastian, our doctor. Their family, like several others, has worked for ours for years.

"It's fine," I tell him. "Let's go to the office."

The office, one of the larger meeting spaces on this floor, is only a few paces from the main entrance. I sit at the chair behind the desk and welcome him in. "I want all the news you have."

"Can you tell me what she told you?" he asks, and the way he asks it makes me wonder if he suspects her of a lie. Goddammit, I hate the way it makes me feel when he asks that. I hate that she might've been lying. It isn't uncommon for prisoners, of course. But why do I feel as if I were betrayed by a good friend? She isn't my friend.

"She told me she's been kept in the lighthouse her whole life," I tell him. "Her father told her there was danger outside the lighthouse, and that if she left, she'd be killed."

He nods vigorously. "Good. *Good.* This is what I need to hear."

I scowl at him. "She says she was not in possession of the notes and papers and that she knew nothing about them."

"Also true," Bradley says, nodding his head. Okay, then. This is good. Maybe she didn't lie to me.

"She's been thoroughly educated, and she's well read. Her father taught her."

"The man who called himself her father," Bradley corrects.

I pause, leaning pack in the chair, and eye him curiously. Now that I didn't expect.

"Come again?"

"Jack Anderson was not her father," he says, shaking his head. "It wasn't possible. He was American, we know that, and I traced his roots back to Boston. He likely had an affiliation with the Boston Irish."

"So how does that possibly prevent him from being her biological father?" I ask.

"Because Jack Anderson was married once. To one of the Boston Irish. She died from ovarian cancer when she was thirty, and he had a vasectomy before she died."

Likely thought if she couldn't have children, he wouldn't either, I wonder. But then why did he tell Caitlin he was her father?

And who was her mother?

I shake my head. Bradley's raised more questions than he's answered.

"Did you check the fingerprints on the notes we have?" I ask him.

He nods, frowning. "Yes, and superficially it looks as if she could've taken the notes. But you don't pay me to do a superficial investigation."

"Certainly not," I tell him, and imagine reaching over the table and wrapping my hand around his neck. I don't like how long it's taking him to tell me this. "For fuck's sake, spit it out," I tell him.

"Please show me the writing sample you got."

I take the folded paper out of my pocket and lay it on the desk.

"Exactly what I expected," he says. "The notes are taken in a decidedly masculine slanted script. Hers is not at all like his. It's finer, more feminine."

"So what are you telling me?"

"Her prints are on the outside of the books only. You found them in her possession. Therefore, her prints, as well as some of yours and Cormac's are all over them.

But in the pages of the books? Nothing. Hers are absent. And that'd be impossible if she were the one taking notes."

"It was her father, then," I say with a nod. "Or Jack Anderson, I should say."

"Yes," Bradley says. "What was his affiliation with the Boston Irish? I don't know. But something tells me the clue will come if we find out who her mother was."

"And you've no answers for me on that count?"

He shakes his head. "None," he says. "How old is she?"

I shake my head. "I've no idea."

"Do you know her birthday? Where she might've been born?"

I shake my head. "Unfortunately not."

I stroke my chin. I want to find out everything I can about her. Who her real parents are. Why the man who called himself her father kept her so well hidden. Something tells me she fits into the picture of our puzzle, but I don't know how or why.

Bradley gets to his feet. "I'll tell you who to ask."

I scowl. "Father Finn?"

He nods, folding up his papers. "The very same. He's the one that'll know what to tell you. How did you even find out she was there?"

I growl and don't respond, making Bradley laugh out loud. "Naturally. Busybody priest, that's who."

"Thank you," I tell him, getting to my feet and escorting him out.

Caitlin isn't a traitor. She had no news of the notes we found, and no clue her father orchestrated the spying.

But why would he spy?

And who is she?

I'm relieved and at the same time, troubled. I need to know more about this mysterious girl. But until I do, I'm not letting her out of my sight.

When I open the door for Bradley, I see a figure roaming the garden outside the house. The morning still holds a bit of the chill of spring, but I step outside to get a closer look.

I recognize the long, wavy hair, and her posture, arms crossed over her chest as she walks. Mam.

Bradley goes to his car, and I shove my hands in my pockets, walking to the garden. Mam doesn't notice I'm there at first, and she startles when she turns and sees me.

"Keenan! I didn't see you coming, son," she says softly. She sits on one of the stone benches under a blooming arch. The sun's barely risen, the light of early morning filtering through patches of leaves.

"Sorry, mam," I tell her. "I saw someone out here and wanted to investigate."

She smiles and nods, and it seems her smile is a bit sad.

"Something troubling you?"

She shakes her head slightly. "Ah, only a bit," she whispers. "Just a bit."

Mam keeps her troubles away from us boys. The women of The Clan are expected to be strong and fearless. She doesn't like to show fear, and I don't blame her.

"It doesn't help anything," she says. "But goodness, the girl bears the resemblance of someone I knew."

I sit up straighter. "Does she, now?" I ask. "Can you tell me?"

She shakes her head. "It's silly. Just an old friend of mine. But it's strange, son. She bears her name as well. 'Tis like looking at a ghost, seeing that girl of yours."

A chill runs down my spine. This is something we need to pursue.

"Who was it?" I ask her. "Can you tell me?"

"Yes," she says. "But ye must not repeat it, son. Promise me that."

"I give you my word. But it's important you tell me, mam. Caitlin is innocent, I know that. But she was told her father kept her in the lighthouse to keep her safe. Though she may not be a threat to us, it's likely she's in grave danger."

My mother's eyes look sorrowful. "The Caitlin I knew was the daughter of Mack Martin."

Jesus, Mary, and Joseph.

Mack Martin.

The head chief of our rival clan.

"Was?"

My mother nods. "Yes. She left with someone she loved overseas. When she came back, she was a different woman. Changed. She wouldn't speak to me of what happened. And then one day, she left and didn't come back. We were told…" her voice trails off.

I wait for her to tell me.

"She'd taken her own life."

How is this possible? How could it be that the woman bears such a resemblance to Caitlin? Were they related?

"Good to know, mam. I've got some investigating to do."

I know who'll have the answers. I'll have to force Father Finn to fess up. I stand to leave, and she reaches for my hand.

"Be careful, Keenan. If she was hidden, I can imagine there was good reason. Take good care of her, son. And if she was indeed Caitlin's daughter… well, then she was right to be hidden."

If Caitlin is the granddaughter of Mack Martin, she ought to be hidden *now*.

I don't need to ask why. The Martins are a ruthless, barbarous lot.

My mother feels an obligation to watch out for Caitlin.

And hell. I do, too.

Chapter Ten

Caitlin

I wake with a yawn, stretching in the bed, when my body goes still.

I was so tired the night before, I fell asleep quickly, even with Keenan on the other side of the bed. He didn't touch me at all, and his bed was so large we might've been strangers.

Well. Okay, so, we are.

I look over to the side of the bed, at the rumpled sheets, and sit up. Where did he go? And why didn't I hear him? I suppose men like him learn to move discreetly.

I swing my legs over the side of the bed and stand, when I hear footsteps outside the hall. I freeze. I don't feel safe here, not yet, not when his father could walk in at any minute. But when the door opens, it's only Keenan that enters.

He's wearing a t-shirt and loose-fitting pants, when he enters the room.

"Good morning," I say.

He raises one eyebrow. "Morning, lass."

I like the way he says that. My father was American, and though I've lived here my whole life, the Irish accent is new to me.

"Where'd you go?"

He looks at me again, a quizzical expression on his face. "You're never to ask me that, Caitlin," he corrects sternly. "I've many errands to attend that don't involve you, and it's best you don't ask. Ever. Understood?"

I can hardly make a move without doing something wrong. I sigh.

He's walking toward me. I swallow hard.

Though I walk freely about this room, I'm still not free. I'm still his captive.

"Yes, sir." He walks past me toward the bathroom, and I feel oddly bereft.

"After I shower, you're to shower as well. I have an errand to run, and I don't want to leave you alone today."

I nod, but don't respond. He showers quickly, and a few moments later, returns to the room. "Off with you, now."

I do what he says, but it takes me a minute to figure out the elaborate shower in here. It's nothing at all like the one at home. I finally push a lever, and steaming hot water fills the tub. I gasp in surprise, stumble forward, and bash my head against the tile.

I'm such a klutz. I'm rubbing my head when I hear him behind me.

"You alright?" he asks. I nod, closing my eyes. I swallow hard so I don't cry.

"Konked yer head, then?" he says. Sometimes his accent thickens. I'm not sure why, but it does now.

I nod. Leaning down, he rubs his thumb over my sore forehead and gently kisses the tender spot. Before I can recover, he stands and reaches for the shower, framing my body in front of his as he instructs me. "Like this, lass." He turns the lever, and steaming hot liquid fills the shower.

"Be quick, now," he says.

He leaves the room. My heart smacks against my rib cage, my pulse racing at having been so near to him, so close. I shiver. He seems stoic and detached, save for the few moments he's lost absolute control.

And a little part of me… the cheeky little part, he's called it… wants to see him lose some of that control. I wonder if I can affect him. So instead of dressing back in my pajamas, I leave the bathroom just in my towel.

I walk in the room nervously, not sure how he'll react, but look away as if looking for clothing. He turns to see me walk in.

"Christ," he mutters. "Jesus *Christ.*"

I lower my eyes, not sure what I'm supposed to do now. This is about as brave as I get.

"Come here," he whispers, his voice choked and rugged. "Now."

I walk to him tentatively, though I'm eager to see what he'll do to me. There's a tenderness hidden deep within his stern exterior I want to unearth.

When I reach him, he touches the edge of my towel and tugs. I don't stop it as the damp fabric falls to the floor, and I stand in front of him naked. I'm shaking, unsure of what to expect, unsure what he'll do.

And I don't care.

I want him to touch me again.

I spent my life hidden behind the walls of what could've been a prison. I never saw the loveliness of the garden or bright sunshine. I never spoke with another person or walked the cobbled streets of our village. And I most certainly have never, ever been touched by a man.

I've experienced so little, I'm starving for human affection.

"You're fucking gorgeous," he grates against my ear, his lips grazing my lobe and sending a delicious shiver down my spine. "*Gorgeous.*"

I swallow hard. "It pleases me that I please you."

"Caitlin," he groans. "You shouldn't have said that."

"Said what?" I ask. "I only speak the truth."

"God, woman, don't I know it?" he whispers. When he pulls me to him, I feel his hardness between us, and I take an involuntary step back.

"Don't be frightened, lass," he whispers. "I'll not hurt you."

"That's a lie," I whisper back. "You're so capable of hurting me it frightens me."

"Does it?" he asks, and there's something like hunger in his eyes. The warm vibration of his voice tickles my ears, his whiskers grazing my skin. "A little fear can heighten an experience, though, as can a little pain."

My heart hammers, as he runs his hand up and down my back. How can a chaste touch like this ignite me? How does the threat of fear make me eager to hear more?

Weaving his fingers through my soaked hair, he massages my scalp. My head falls back and I sigh, it feels that good. "More," I whisper. "Mmm, I like that."

"Say please," he commands.

"Please, sir."

"The two magic words," he chuckles. "Not sure how much I could deny if those words are uttered in that pretty voice of yours."

He continues to massage my scalp, his mouth hovering over mine. I lean toward him and he pulls back, one corner of his lips quirking up. He's teasing me. He knows I want this, that I'm eager to feel what it's like to be kissed. And yet... what will I do when he grants me that wish?

His lips brush against my cheekbone, then lower to my jawline. My head still pulled back by his firm grip in my hair, he kisses everywhere but my lips. Both sides of my jaw. My nose. Each eyelid, one by one, then back to my neck, until I'm dying to feel his lips on mine.

His mouth comes back to my ear. "Do you want me to kiss you, pretty girl?"

I nod.

"Then say those magic words."

I've never touched liquor in my life, but I imagine this is what it feels like, as if I could float away, as if words escape me now and all I can do is feel.

"I… I…" I can't remember.

He pinches my naked backside, and I squeal, coming up on my toes. But he was right. A little pain *can* heighten things. As heat rushes to where he pinched, my body heats in turn. I shiver deliciously when he rubs his rough palm over the place he hurt.

I have one moment of clarity, and breathe out in a rush of words, "Please, sir."

"That's it, pretty lass. Just like that." He smells of woodsmoke and whiskey, so masculine my toes curl. Framing my face in his hands, he makes me feel as if nothing matters beyond this moment, this perfect moment in time before he kisses me. I close my eyes the second before his lips touch mine and sigh into him.

It's a gentle kiss, chaste and sweet, yet I'm so eager to feel this, an electric vibe snakes through me. I want more. So much more.

But too soon, he pulls away, tugs my head toward him, and tucks me against his chest.

"We've an errand, lass," he whispers. "There's so much more I wish to do to you. But if I start now, there won't be any turning back."

I nod, dazzled and bewildered by the too-short kiss. My mouth is dry, but there's a humming need he's stirred deep in my belly.

"Caitlin," he says, his voice choked, as if it pains him to say it. "Get dressed."

He turns away as if to give me privacy, but perhaps he means to collect himself. I walk on trembling legs to the dresser and tug a drawer open. I take out the first pair of panties and bra I see, when he grates out in a hoarse whisper, "No knickers."

I look at him curiously. "Say that again?"

"No. Knickers."

I stare at him.

"If you cover that arse of yours with knickers, I'll spank you before we go."

I drop the silky pair back in the drawer and bite my lip.

"Good girl."

I like how that makes me feel, all warm and soft and pleased.

He quickly tugs on clothes as I slide into another dress. "There's only dresses in these drawers," I say to him. "Am I to have no modern clothing like your mam?"

"Not on my watch," he says. "I like you dressed like that."

I smile. Well, then. That pleases me very much.

"May I ask what errand we're to run?" I ask.

"You'll see in a moment."

The air is thick with something, though I don't know how to describe it. I'm eager to come back here with him, though. Eager to be alone with him again. It's safe to say I affect him, and Lord knows he affects me, too.

"We'll get breakfast on the way back," he says.

"I'm still your prisoner?"

He doesn't reply at first, but after long minutes, he nods.

"You are."

Why did he hesitate?

I suppose I have to wait until he finds me innocent, then.

"Where will we get breakfast?" I ask him. "And how does one even 'get breakfast?' What does that mean?"

"Jesus," he mutters. "I forget how innocent and inexperienced y'are. We'll stop at the bakery, lass. I'll order for you, and we'll have a bite. It's time we see, anyway," he mutters, but he doesn't explain what he means.

He takes my hand and tugs me along with him. "Now, no more questions." But he doesn't have to tell me twice. I have enough to think about, I'm mulling it in my mind already.

His warm, strong hand feels surprisingly reassuring in mine, and the tingle I felt through my body returns. Is this what romance feels like? I wouldn't know. And why would I want anything romantic with a man like Keenan?

I'm lost in my thoughts while he leads me down the long hallway to the staircase. This place is so much larger than ours that it surprises me a little. How can people live in a place so vast?

"Don't you... well do you ever have a hard time finding someone you're looking for?" I ask him. "I mean, it's practically an entire village right here in this house, and you—ohhh. Oh, Keenan."

I pause, bringing my free hand to my mouth. At the very top of the stairs, I get a view for the very first time of the large, plate glass windows that line the entryway to the house. Their house—or mansion—is situated atop the cliffs that overlook the ocean. And from where I'm standing, I can see miles and miles of endless blue, white-caps, and waves.

He pauses with me, the two of us side by side looking out into the ocean.

"Beautiful, isn't it?" he says softly. "One of my favorite views in all the world. And to answer your question, no. I don't worry about finding anyone. When I want them, I snap my fingers and they come running or deal with the consequences."

I frown and look at him sharply, when I see his eyes are twinkling.

"You're teasing me, aren't you?" I say. "You are!"

He doesn't answer, but leads me down the large, carpeted stairway to where several men wait in the lobby.

I don't like this, being thrust into situations with so many others. Last night at dinner, my only consolation was that Keenan's mother was there, and I like her. I hated being near his father, and there were several others there as well. I breathe a sigh of relief when I see the jovial blond man in the group of severe-looking men below. But he doesn't look so jovial right now. They look serious, and stern, like modern-day soldiers prepared to go to war.

"What's the story, Keenan?" A tall guy with a shaved head asks, but his eyes are on me.

Keenan holds me closer.

"Off to the church," he says. "Need answers. And after, I'm taking Cait to get a bite to eat."

The men give him a curious look, but no one questions him.

Cait. It's the first time anyone's called me that. Why do I feel as if I'm not really his prisoner? Why do I feel I'm something... more?

The tall man's eyes widen. "Are ya, then?"

"She's never been," Keenan says. "But I want her kept safe, so she stays with me."

A big, burly man that looks quite a bit older than the rest guffaws. "As if she's safe with *you?*"

"Shut it, Tully," Keenan says severely. They're... teasing him about me. I don't really know why, or how that impacts things. I want to go back up to the room and hide away from all their prying eyes.

The burly, gruff man sobers. "Aye, boss."

"Spoke with Bradley this morning," Keenan says to a man with wire-rimmed glasses. "Clears the prints. But Finn has answers."

Nolan, the blond younger brother, snorts. "Course he does. And hell yeah, let's get some breakfast."

"Watch, Boner. You've got the eye." Keenan says to the man with the shaved head. "See if anyone notices when we come into the shop, yeah?"

I don't know what they're talking about, but the man he calls Boner nods his head. "Aye, boss."

He opens the door and the men file out ahead of us, beside us, and behind us. I feel as if I'm walking into battle, these soldiers, whoever they are, are ready to protect and defend.

They tease each other and make crude jokes as we walk along the stone pathway away from the ocean and into the village.

"Keenan, you missed yer brother last night," the burly man he called Tully says. "Right good thing Cormac took 'em in hand, or we might've had to bail 'em."

"Oh go on with ya now," Nolan says, and though he's laughing, his gaze comes quickly to Keenan. "Shut it, Tully."

"That right?" Keenan asks. I feel bad for the younger cheerful brother. Seems his older brother keeps a close eye on him. "Care to tell me what happened?"

We walk past a small patch of thorny bushes, and on instinct, he pulls me a little closer so they don't catch in my skirt.

"Not really," Nolan says, and the other men all laugh.

"Nolan," Keenan warns.

"Nolan got free with the drink is all," another says. I recognize him as the man that accompanied Keenan to the lighthouse.

"Got free with it?" Keenan asks.

"Y'all are a bunch of lazy louts," Nolan mutters. "I'm a grown man now. Not holdin' onto me mam's apron strings anymore."

"Grown man who's got the weight of responsibility on him," Keenan says.

Tully guffaws. "Nolan? Weight of responsibility? You mean the weight of a pretty lass straddling him, aye?"

The men laugh out loud, and my cheeks flush when I'm assaulted by a sudden vision of a naked woman atop Nolan. I look away.

But it made Keenan smile, anyway, and for the first time I notice he's got a dimple in his left cheek. He gives my hand a little squeeze.

"Now, lads, we're in the presence of a lady," Keenan says. I pull a little closer to him. I'm a lady, then.

We turn the corner around the garden. Behind the house lies a church, its steeple reaching heavenward, surrounded by a quaint garden of tombstones. The church graveyard. I want to go there. I want to explore every inch of it. I feel as if I've stepped into one of my novels, back to a simpler time, when I look upon the church and graveyard. A fog hangs heavy and thick in the air, preventing me from seeing further.

"What's past the church?" I ask Keenan.

"Cold Stone Castle and the Armory," Keenan says. "But after we've visited the church, I'll take you into town."

He's said as much, but it makes me nervous.

"Do we have to?"

"Yeah, we do," he says, but he doesn't tell me why.

Keenan and I lead the group of men to the steps that lead to a little house attached to the church.

"What's this?" I ask him.

"Rectory," he says, but that still doesn't mean anything to me.

"Does someone live there?" I ask.

"You really don't know, do you?"

I shrug. "Know what?"

"Who anyone else is," he says. "At all."

I swallow hard. "Guess not."

I haven't a clue what he's talking about. Should I?

"So you've never seen Father Finn?" he asks.

I shake my head. "No. As I've told you, the only person I've ever spoken to was my father."

"Right," he says, looking ahead, as if he doesn't want to make eye contact with me.

My heart's still hammering in my chest when we reach the doorway of the rectory, and Keenan knocks. After a moment, the door opens, and an older man with graying hair answers.

"Keenan," he says. "How are you, son?"

"Doing well, Father. Need to ask you a few questions."

The older man scowls at the small crowd of men. "You needed reinforcements to talk to your uncle, did you?"

But before Keenan responds, the man's gaze swings to me, and he gives a little start. "My God," he whispers, bringing his hand to his mouth.

"Dead ringer for her mother, is she, Father?" Keenan says.

My mother?

Chapter Eleven

Keenan

I didn't think we'd have to use our harsher methods on the Father. Though he's many flaws, dishonesty isn't one of them. I wanted to see what he'd do when he looked at Caitlin. If she's the spitting image of her mother like mam says, he won't be able to hide his shock.

"Come in, boys," Finn says, opening the door wide. "Dorothy's just pulled out some scones. Help yourself."

The men pile into the door and assemble in the Father's living room. They eat the scones on little glass plates, all on their best behavior. Father Finn looks older every time I see him, the worry lines around his brows deeper. He sighs, taking a seat beside me in a large, overstuffed chair.

"What do you need to know, Keenan?"

"Who her mother was," I tell him. "And what her story was."

Finn closes his eyes briefly, and in that moment, I see panic written in Caitlin's features.

"Me?" she whispers. "Are you asking for me?"

I nod.

"Her mother was Caitlin Martin," Father says. "I counseled her twenty-one years ago, when she came to me."

"Because she was pregnant," I say.

"Yes."

"Who was the father?"

He shakes his head. "I've no idea, Keenan. She wouldn't tell. She took it to the grave. But she told me, and I believed her, that if anyone heard of the babe's existence, it would mean war between the Clans."

"Jack Anderson was not her father, then," I say. I know this, but I want his confirmation.

Father sighs. "Jack Anderson never even knew her mother. Her mother died in childbirth, and back then the child would've gone to an orphanage. I didn't think her safe there." His eyes swing to Caitlin's, and he pats her hand gently, the worry lines around his eyes deepening.

Caitlin's eyes go to me, and I watch as her gaze clouds. It's the first she's heard that the man who called himself her father wasn't. Her eyes meet mine, and I give her hand a little squeeze. I hate that she has to find out this way, that the one truth in her life, her only constant, will be taken away from her like this.

"Why Anderson? Why'd you interfere?"

He looks back to me. "Because it wasn't safe if anyone knew she was alive, Keenan. Think on this, son. And Anderson owed me a favor."

Think on it I will.

"Why does mam seem to think her mother committed suicide? She had no idea her mate had a child."

Father Finn clears his throat. "It was an unfortunate rumor that was… started… so that no one would find out she was with child."

He lied then? He, or someone he knew, fabricated that lie. I ask him everything I can, until it's clear he's got nothing left to offer. He's told us everything we need to know.

"I'll be back, Father," I warn him. I would never raise a hand to him, and I don't mean to threaten physical harm. But I will have my questions answered.

At the doorway, he places his hand on my arm and speaks so low, only I will hear. "Take good care, Keenan. The girl will be sheltered and in danger. Take good care."

"You have my word."

We leave the rectory, and Boner scoffs a handful of scones on the way. Cormac's sober, and even Tully and Nolan are quiet. If Caitlin's existence will bring about trouble for The Clan, we all have to be on the same page.

What would've caused war between The Clans?

"What did you get out of that?" I ask my men as we assemble outside the rectory, heading down the cobblestone street that bears right and takes us into the heart of the village. I promised Caitlin we'd get breakfast, and I mean to keep my promise.

"Her mam must've been promised to someone powerful, for one," Boner says. "Her betrothed would've killed her if he'd found out she was pregnant with another's child."

"No doubt," I agree.

Christ, it's a problem. The Martins are our biggest rivals in all of Ballyhock. I'll have to investigate with my mother and father as well. I'll need to know the history of The Clans to get to the bottom of this.

"I can't believe it," Caitlin says, as we walk hand in hand.

"What's that?" I want to hear what she got from that.

"That he wasn't my real father."

"He raised you as his daughter, and that's all that matters, Caitlin."

"It isn't," she says. "What if my father's a monster? What if the man whose blood runs through my veins is a despicable, evil man?"

"Could be, lass," I tell her, as we approach the main street that brings us into Ballyhock centre. "But most men aren't pure evil or pure good. Most war with good and evil."

"I can't—I can't stand the thought, though," she says.

I lace my arm around her shoulders. "Listen to me, Caitlin," I say. "Men are complicated creatures. Some do evil things, yet their hearts aren't made of stone, see? They're loyal and fair to their core."

"Like your father," she says.

"Caitlin," I warn, when Boner's head whips back to look at us.

"Hush, woman," I order. "You'll not speak ill of my father."

She blinks in confusion. "Speak ill? I was only speaking the truth, though."

I feel my lips twitch. She's cute. "Aye," I say softly, so none of the others would hear. "Like my father."

She's quiet for a minute before she continues. "And like you."

I don't answer.

I take her into the Cottage Brew, the tiny coffee shack that sits on the adjacent cliff that juts out beyond The Clan estate. I hold the door open for her, and she steps inside, sunlight peeking through a cluster of clouds makes it look like she has a halo.

"You're looking at me funny," she says with a smile as we step inside, but before I respond, she takes in a deep, cleansing breath, her shoulders lifting before she releases the breath with a sigh of contentment.

"What is that?" she whispers. "Smells like honey and sunshine and the warmth of a hearth."

I love how she makes the simplest statement poetry.

"Miss Isobel's soda bread, and the finest tea this side of the Atlantic."

"Soda bread," she breathes. "I've been dying to try some."

"Not had *soda* bread?" I ask, bewildered.

She shrugs, while the men pile into the shop and head to the counter. Isobel, a petite, round woman with spectacles perched on her nose, ruddy cheeks, and a beaming smile, welcomes us in. We're neighbors, so we're her regulars, and like our alliance with the church, we see to it that Isobel is safe and secure.

"Ah, me boys," she says in her thick brogue. "What brings ye here?"

We order our food, and I observe the reactions of the customers in the shop. Many avert their eyes, for our reputation precedes us. We own most of this town, and keep the peace, but though our darker dealings aren't broadcast afar or widely spread, they know who we are.

Though some look at Caitlin with mild curiosity, none react with shock. None with even the faintest bit of recognition. Isobel's newer to this part of the country, so I don't expect her to show any. Still, the regulars here who knew Caitlin might've.

Caitlin takes a bite of the dense, mildly sweet bread, slathered with Isobel's creamy butter, and her eyes widen. She chews, swallows, and sighs. "That's delicious, Keenan. My, it's better than I even expected." She turns to Isobel and grins. "My compliments to the chef!"

Jesus, this girl's adorable.

When we're finished, her shoulders droop, and I can tell she's exhausted. She isn't used to socializing, and it drains her.

"Time to go home," I announce. I ask my men briefly if they've seen anything, but all concur. No one shows any signs of recognizing Caitlin. She asks what the other shops are, so I show her. I point out the other places along the street. There's the fish shop across from Cottage Brew, D'Agostino's down the road, The Blimey Pub, and Lickety Split Ice Cream Shoppe. The Cheeky Mackerel on the shore, Ballyhock library, and the Village Seamstress.

I want to take her everywhere. I want to sit beside her when she drinks her first pint, give her the first golden chip she's ever eaten, feed her the flaky, steaming hot fish straight from the fry basket at the Mackerel. I want to show her what the sunset looks like from the very top of Cold Stone Castle. I want to sneak her away to the highest of the mountain peaks in Dublin. I want to sit beside her when she dips her toes in the Irish Sea for the first time. I want to give her her first taste of champagne, her first moonlit walk, and so much more.

So much more.

She's so tired when we head back, I send her upstairs to rest with half a dozen men guarding her, Tully at the lead.

"Come with me?" she asks me.

"Can't, lass. I've got to work today. Wait for me, and rest. Spend some time looking over my bookshelves and entertaining yourself, and I'll take you to dinner tonight."

Taking her out to dinner will bring her in contact with a larger group of people and will give me a broader spectrum of people to observe.

"You take your captives to dinner?" she asks, her pretty, intelligent blue eyes teasing me. "Or just the pretty ones?"

"None of your cheek, lass," I say, wagging a finger at her.

She giggles when I swat my hand at her arse and miss by a mile. I'm smiling when I shut the door behind her and leave my men to guard her. Tully raises a brow to me.

"Captive indeed," he mutters, giving me a wink.

"Shut your pie hole," I mutter, but I'm still smiling when I get to my office. I finish my work in record time, and stand, ready to go home.

My first thought is of Caitlin. How is she feeling after what she learned today? How did she entertain herself? Is she waiting for me?

How will she respond when I give her more than the slightest hint of a kiss?

When I weigh her perfect breasts in my hand, and brush my thumbs across her nipples?

When I make her climax for the first time?

"You're a mile away."

I blink, turning to see mam by the door.

"Yeah," I say, with a shrug. "Thinking of work's all."

"The hell you are," she says with a laugh. "I know the look of a man who's got a pretty girl on his mind. Mind you, I learned how to put that look on a man's face when I was a lass myself."

I only grunt in reply, and don't give her the satisfaction of knowing she's right.

"I need to talk with you," I tell her. "But not now. Tonight?"

"Tonight," she agrees.

I skip the steps two at a time, ignoring mam's laughter and teasing behind me, and make it to my room in short time. My men are still standing out front, standing guard. I open the door, but when I enter, I don't see her.

"Caitlin?" I call. "Where are you?" My room is large, with several nooks and crannies, but the only place she could be is the jacks. Panic wells in my chest when I don't hear her.

"Caitlin?"

Did someone find their way in here? Is she alright?

"Caitlin!" I shout, trying to open the door, but it's shut fast, the lock secured. "Caitlin! Open the damn door," I say, pounding my fist on it. If she doesn't answer in five fucking seconds, I'm knocking this goddamn door down. I kick the door and shout again, hearing the door behind me open and my guards come in the room when I hear something clatter to the floor. A moment later, the door opens. She's got a towel wrapped around her, and behind her, a broken phone and headphones lie on the tile.

Christ, my heart's coming out of my throat. I shield her with my body. No other fucking bloke'll see her dressed—or *not* dressed, more like.

"Get out," I growl to the guards over my shoulder. They fairly run and slam the door before I kill them.

I turn to her, ready to spit fucking fire. "What the hell?" I ask her.

She's white as a sheet.

"What is it?" she asks. "Why are you so angry? What did I do?"

I gather her to me, my heart still thumping erratically in my chest. "Sweet girl," I whisper, caught between wanting to hold her to me and turn her over my knee for scaring me. "Good God, you scared me. Why didn't you answer me?"

"I couldn't hear you," she says. "Your mom taught me how to listen to music on headphones, and it's been one of the most amazing things I've ever *heard.* I can't believe I've gone this long and never even known what that sounded like. I... I had it turned up very loudly. It felt like I was *there.*" She sighs, looking at the floor. "It's broken now, though."

"I'll replace it."

"Why'd you panic so?"

How do I tell her? How do I explain that when you've seen death like me, both at your hands and before you, that when you've seen people you love and people you care about taken from your grasp before your very eyes, you don't take anything for granted?

Nothing.

"Glad you're alright," I tell her, not answering. I realize the towel she's got draped over her damp body is sliding down her body to the floor. She bites her lip and looks down but doesn't try to stop the slithering towel from sliding down her body.

Jesus.

I reach for the towel and tug the rest of it to the floor. She doesn't stop me.

"Come here," I murmur. "You scared me, lass."

Her eyes snap to mine.

I swallow hard. "You ought to be punished for frightening me like that."

Her eyes go from confusion to curiosity, then she freezes, and I watch her transformation, her look now lust-filled and curious.

"I did, didn't I?" she says.

"Yes, and I should punish you," I repeat. Christ, what I want to introduce her to. What I want to *do* to her. How I'd love to see her bucking beneath the onslaught of orgasm after orgasm I wring from her beautiful body. Moaning while I bring her to climax on my tongue. Writhing in restraints I keep tied about her body or squealing in pain before I bring her to utter bliss.

She bows her head, and her hair, still dry at the top but damp and curly at the bottom, all the way down her back. I sit on the edge of the large, circular tub, and take her hand.

"Why am I to punish you?" I ask, my voice thickening with lust. "What did you do?"

144

"I scared you." I hope she knows that this time, though I want to punish her, I'm so eager to feel her skin beneath my palm, that this punishment will bring her to the edge of climax. And yet, I'll expect her obedience and submission on every level. Her allowing me to protect her, instruct her, and yes, discipline her, will give me utter satisfaction.

"I don't know anything about this, Keenan," she says in a soft voice. "I don't understand it. I should fear you, but I only want to be near you."

I guide her over my knee, and run my hand over her beautiful, perfect backside.

"I feel it too, lass," I admit. "I do, too."

I position her so her naked body hangs over my lap, her hair like a veil that falls all around her. This moment is sacred, this togetherness hallowed. Somehow, I've been given the precious gift of this moment with her. I've been with women who fought this side of me. They said I was mental, perverted, and somehow equated my need to control sexual intimacy as part of my fucked-up nature. And hell. Maybe they aren't wrong.

I lift my hand and slam it against her upturned arse, watching my handprint bloom like pink lilies.

But I don't strike her again, not yet. I glide my hand along the pink prints until I get to her thighs, and gently part them. Without a word, I trail my hand up to the heated vee at the apex of her thighs. I want her to crave my touch. I want her panting with readiness, so eager for me to bring pleasure to her that she can't think of anything else.

I lower my voice. "Do you like being punished, lass?"

"No, sir," she whispers, shaking her head side to side so the silky sheet of her hair brushes my legs. I wrap the strands around my fist and hold her in position, then slam my palm on her arse again.

"Ow!" she squeaks. I respond with another measured spank.

Then another.

And another.

I spank her with leisurely, purposeful strokes, covering the sensual swell of her backside until she throbs in hues of pink.

I part her legs further, but don't touch where she aches for me.

I want her throbbing. Swollen. Ready to fly.

"I don't... Keenan..."

"When you're being punished, you'll never call me by name," I say sharply, punctuating my words with another firm smack.

"Yes, sir."

The perfume of her arousal permeates the intimate setting, intoxicating me.

I can't help but edge her just a bit more. I smack her upper thighs, just enough to bring the heat of a sting to the surface, before I skate my hand between her legs again, the top of my hand grazing the soft curlicues. My mouth is dry, my cock so hard it's throbbing and painful. I want her virgin cunt wrapped around my cock so badly I'm shaking.

With a sigh, I gently push her off my legs, then pull her in front of me so she's between my thighs. Mother*fucker*. Her full breasts are swollen, her nipples hard and erect. Before I know what I'm doing, I lean forward and grasp one of the firm buds between my lips and suck.

"Ohh," she sighs, her eyelids fluttering shut. "I... I don't... you thrill me," she finishes in a throaty whisper.

My lips tug upward.

You thrill me.

The single most erotic line a woman ever said to me. She speaks from her heart, overcome with desire.

I want her.

I need her.

I crave her.

My hand wraps around her slender waist as I suckle one nipple, then release it before I lave the second one. Her hands travel to my shoulders, bracing herself, and she trembles like shimmering starlight.

I sit back and let her breasts swing free. I hold her gaze with mine.

"Come here," I whisper, tracing her jaw with the tip of my finger.

"I'm here, sir."

"No. Closer," I order. "I don't want any distance between us."

In silence, she steps closer until she's flush against my legs and I can hear her soft breathing.

"What will you have me do, sir?"

I could demand she do anything in that moment. Fall to her knees and suck me off. Fondle the swollen, damp folds between her legs until she brings herself to climax between my knees. Kneel and present before me, ready for the kiss of pain and promise of pleasure.

I swallow hard, drunk on the power she gives me with those simple words, her freely given submission.

"Kiss me."

Chapter Twelve

I wondered what he'd have me do. What he'd ask of me. I wondered what he'd demand, but never imagined it would be a task so simple yet so hard to do.

Kiss me.

My body's on fire, and I don't know how I feel about this. You'd think being consumed by flames and heat and molten lava would be a bad thing. But it isn't. I crave more. I don't want to be quenched.

I'm tingling and shaking while I stand in front of him, my hands placed to steady myself on his shoulders.

"Kiss me."

But what if I don't know how? What if I don't know what I'm doing? Okay, there's no "what if." I definitely don't know what I'm doing.

"Why are you hesitating, lass?" Keenan says, his green eyes darkening, a note of correction in his voice I feel straight between my legs. He just put me over his lap and spanked me, heightened my awareness and arousal with expert strokes of his hand, made me starving for more without even touching where I need him to. There's something about the stern look he gives me and the promise of punishment, when laced with his masterful manipulation of my body, that heightens my body's response. He's like a magician or an expert hypnotist. One wave of his hand, one word from his mouth, and I respond.

"Because I don't know how, sir," I say as honestly as I can. For I do want to kiss him. I've felt his lips once before, and the idea of feeling them again sends shivers through me.

"You don't need to," he says simply. "All you need to do is what I ask." His voice deepens. "And I'm not going to ask you again."

I try to swallow but my mouth's too dry. There isn't anything to this, right? Just... touch his lips with mine and maybe then I'll know what to do. How to make him like it. It's vitally important to me that he likes it. That he likes me. Though I'm ignorant to the ways of the world, and don't even really know who he is, who the men he calls brother are, I know that a man like Keenan, so powerful and handsome, could have any woman he wants. And yet I'm the woman standing naked in front of him. That means something.

I don't want him to grow angry or disappointed, so I force myself into the unknown. I bend my head to his, my hands still anchored on his broad shoulders, and with the faintest touch like the flutter of angel's wings, I touch my lips to his. The way he groans into my mouth encourages me, so I lace my fingers behind his neck and gently part my lips. His hands span my lower back, pulling me closer. I could do something with my tongue, but I like it just like this, the sensual, soft feel of his lips while he holds me closer. We fuse together. I'm so close now there isn't an inch between us. I don't understand how or why, but with his lips on mine, the heat he sent vibrating through my body intensifies. A humming sensation ripples through me, and I finally realize I'm making a sort of moaning noise.

I pull away, confused at how I'm reacting like this.

"What is it, Caitlin?" he asks. "You were doing wonderfully."

My belly flips with his praise. "It's... a little overwhelming," I confess. "And I fear I won't please you."

"Not please me?" he says, as if I just suggested we fly to the moon. "Your very presence pleases me." He shakes his head. "A man like me craves the submission and trust of a woman, and you grant that to me without a second thought. And I didn't know how badly I craved your innocence until I tasted it."

My innocence? My submission and trust? I don't quite understand it all, but I do know that I please him. And I like that.

"It... it pleases me to please you." I shake my head and my cheeks heat with embarrassment. I didn't mean to sound so awkward and silly. "I mean I—" but I don't know what I mean, so I don't finish it. "Oh, bother."

He chuckles. "I think it's best if we—"

Something vibrates in his pocket. I watch a shutter go down over his face, the temporary glimmer at his own vulnerability gone.

Holding me with one palm on my lower back, he removes his phone with his free hand.

"What is it?" he snaps. Then he closes his eyes and mutters, "Christ. Yeah. I'll be right there."

My heart sinks. He's being called away again. Is nothing sacred for him? Must he always be on demand to fulfill the needs of his brothers, his group of men?

"I've got to go."

"Okay," I say, trying to be brave. I don't want him to go. I feel as if we've just popped the cork on a bottle of champagne, but he has to go before we've even sipped it. We were only just beginning. I'm sure of it.

"I'll be back, sweet girl. I have to be sure you're safe, so I still don't want you to leave this room. No dinner out this evening."

He's putting his shield up again. I can see it in his eyes.

"If it weren't the type of errand I need to run alone, I'd take you with me. I'm taking you with me to the school at the weekend." I have questions about that but know better than to ask. "I'll tell you more when I return," he says, as if he's read my mind and realizes I have questions I need answered.

"Okay," I say. There's so much more I want to say, but I don't know if it's my place.

Come back to me.

Stay safe.

I'll be waiting.

I'm confused about my feelings toward him and his evident feelings toward me. I thought I was a prisoner, but it seems we flirt with moving past that into this odd arrangement.

"You're a good lass," he says, leading me to the bed. "Now put some clothes on so none of my men see you. It'd be complicated having to kill one of my own."

I giggle, but he isn't smiling. Oh. Well, then. I quickly grab a dress, heeding his "no knickers" growl from where he's taking things out of his dresser. I look over my shoulder to see him sliding his arms into a black harness type thing, which he fastens in front before he takes a locked box out of his bottom drawer. Removing several guns, he slides them into the holsters. There are... many guns. He doesn't even think twice. He got a call, and now he's outfitting himself with weapons. I swallow hard. Keenan McCarthy is not a good man. Then why do I feel the way I do about him?

"What would you like to eat?"

I shrug. I have no idea. I grew up eating food that was served simply for the sake of filling my belly.

"Are your tastes so simple, sweet Cait?"

"Oh, I don't know," I say, with a smile, before I can censor my response. "I have a taste for you, and you're anything but simple."

He sobers, and a look crosses his eyes that I can't quite decipher. "We've the finest fish in all of Ireland, our greens grown right here on property. I'll order you dinner and dessert, and hopefully by the time you've finished, I'll be back."

He's wearing an overcoat now, a thick, heavy thing that covers the weapons he's hidden beneath it. His phone buzzes again. Cursing under his breath, he comes to me, weaves his fingers through my thick hair, and pulls my head back. When I open on a gasp, he captures my mouth with his, this kiss as different as the one I gave him as night to day. This is at once a capture and claim, but it ends as soon as it begins. "Be a good girl while I'm gone, and we will pick up where we left off when I return."

And then he's gone. A sort of sadness comes to me at his absence, one I don't understand. As I said to him, I've grown used to my own company. I'm not afraid of being alone. But we've started something we haven't finished, and I mean to see where that leads us.

Food is brought up directly. I enjoy the delicate, flaky fish, savory pile of wilted, buttered greens, and golden roasted potatoes on the side. I eat until my belly's full, but I've saved some room for the dessert, a pretty white cake topped with whipped cream and red berries.

There's an elegant glass of a light, golden liquid. Is it wine? I've never had any before. I take a tentative sip and nearly choke, sputtering and coughing. I'm glad Keenan isn't here to see that. Would he laugh at me? I place the glass back down. He can keep that for himself. I push the tray aside on the desk and stand, walking to one of the large windows with bars on it. I don't like the bars, because no matter what he's said, it feels like I'm imprisoned.

How long will I be held here? How long will I be his prisoner?

And why do I wish he won't let me go?

Chapter Thirteen

Keenan

I'm fucking done with contracted hits. Done.

And not just because tonight's yanked me out of a taste of perfection with Caitlin. Mack Martin's group is well known for contracted hits, but their work is sloppy and haphazard. Last year, one of his men performed half a dozen hits, a Clan record in Ireland, and the fucking wanker marked every one of them with a slash of blade on the back of his kills. The police found him on the seventh, and easily linked each one of the deaths he'd marked. The Martin's worked hard to ensure that none of the blame fell on them, but as insiders, we knew better.

"No more hits," I tell Carson. "For fuck's sake. The only hits we do from here on out are for retribution."

"Aye, boss," Carson says. "That's what this is, though."

Well that's a horse of another color.

"Not a contracted hit?" How'd I miss the details on that? Is the girl affecting me? Have I lost my focus?

"Nossir," he says, opening the driver's side door and sliding in. He clicks the locks so I can ride. "Patrick O'Conner's owed The Clan three million dollars since before the new year. Your father gave him until yesterday to pay, and Boner caught him trying to flee the country."

Son of a bitch. I should fucking know this.

"And why didn't you tell me this before?" I ask. I fucking hate being left out of important details. Carson's eyes widen, and he shakes his head.

"We did, Keenan. Yesterday."

Christ. The girl is affecting me.

I don't respond.

"Our plan?"

"Boner's got him in lockdown and Tully's prepared to finish the job."

"He's been punished?"

"Thoroughly. Begging for them to end him now."

I don't respond. I can envision already what's happened and what will. And it doesn't bother me. It should. It fucking should. No matter who I am or what I do, I won't allow myself to become immune to the brutality we inflict, we endure, and the lives we take. As Clan leader, when I rise to that role, I'll keep myself sharp.

We're off site tonight, and I almost wish we weren't, that we would do what we had to in the interrogation room, right here on our property. As soon as I'm able, I want to get back up to Caitlin. To touch her. Speak with her. And somehow, some way, be cleansed of tonight's deeds with her purity and simple candor.

Just yesterday, I wished I'd be sent on a mission of violence, one I could control and manipulate with my own bare hands, but this time I'm glad I'm only here as witness. I don't want to touch the unsullied girl with blood-stained fingers. Not tonight. Christ, not tonight.

We pull into the parking lot of an abandoned warehouse, one of the very few on the outskirts of Ballyhock, and in silence leave the vehicle. The gun I'm carrying has a silencer, and though I hope I don't have to use it tonight, I'm prepared. I pull on gloves, check my weapon, and march to where my men wait by the warehouse.

Tully and Boner are inside, but Nolan waits with a few of my other men by the door. Nolan's fucking sober this time, for once. He nods and opens the door. Though we do what we have to, not a one of us is immune to the taking of a life when necessary, and few of us like it.

"Keenan," Nolan acknowledges me as I pass.

"Any word?" I ask, code for asking if we're clear. No one's followed us, no one's tapped us, the man we'll execute tonight's not brought baggage with him.

"No word," Nolan confirms, walking in with me.

I enter the warehouse, my feet leaden. I never feel like this. I thought I'd grown immune to the taking of a life, even enjoyed the power and control fulfilling an assignment gave me. But tonight feels different.

Perhaps Caitlin's affected me in more ways than I've realized.

I hear the man's cries before I enter the room.

"Shut it," I snap. "You brought this on yourself, and I don't want to hear you blubbering like a fucking child."

I take it all in in seconds. The man on his knees, arms tied behind his back, his face beaten beyond recognition. Though his eyes are swollen shut, tears still manage to leak down his bloodied face. Tully's bare from the waist up, his muscles covered in a fine sheen, glistening under the overhead lighting. His clothes are neatly folded, tucked under Nolan's arm. He doesn't want to harm his clothing. His fists are covered in blood, his eyes cold and uncompromising. He nods to me without turning his head.

"Boss."

"You've something to say for yourself?" I ask the man in front of Tully. He only sobs louder.

I nod to Boner. With grim determination, his jaw locked, Boner removes his gun.

"Fucking silence it," I snap. Without his silencer, the gunshot could be heard for fucking miles. It's a rookie mistake, and he'll answer for that. His eyes snap to mine in wide-eyed surprise. He knows he fucked up.

Swallowing hard, he puts the silencer in place.

Tully stands to the left, prepared to mete out further punishment if I give the order. Boner sets his face to steel and cocks his pistol. Bile rises in my throat and my stomach clenches. I swallow hard, surprised by my reaction. I don't feel remorse when I make a kill or

159

witness one. Retribution is one of the most basic tenets of my brotherhood, an iron-clad law we don't compromise on. Then why now?

"You made your choice," Boner says to the man, as if to convince himself why he's carrying out this sentence. He goes to pull the trigger and a hawk screeches outside. Boner misses, his shot wedging into the ceiling.

"Get out of the way," I order Boner. You finish a kill with one bullet, or you fucked up. I'm out of patience. Without a backward glance, I reach for my gun, silencer in place, kneel before our hostage, and pull the trigger. My shot's certain, my mark is clear. Blood blooms on the side of his temple, and he falls to the ground.

"Need to cleanse my palate," Nolan says as we finish up cleaning the room and prepare to leave. I raise a brow at him.

"Oh?"

"Let's go to the club," Boner says.

I want to go home to Caitlin, but I need to reconnect with my men, and as Nolan says, cleanse my palate. I don't want to go back to her with the memory of vacant eyes and pools of blood. Not now. Not yet.

Why does this bother me so? I'm the first to take the assignment of a hit, and I don't waffle in the face of what needs to be done.

"This weekend, you'll come with me to St. Albert's," I tell Boner. He hangs his head and a muscle twitches in his jaw, but he doesn't say a word. He fucked up, and it's my job to mete out punishment. In our line of work, punishment for fucking up a job could be anything from physical labor, to a beating, to menial labor. I've chosen something in between. The weekend is his time to party with his friends, and he spends every waking minute at the club. He'll forfeit his weekend off to assist me at St. Albert's.

The men around me sober. Though Boner's like a brother to me, our ranking is clear as day. Stepping into the role of Clan Chief is a gradual process, one task to another, until my duties mirror my father's, as his duties mirrored *his* father's. When I rise to the role of Chief, we'll stand side by side on equal footing until he defers full leadership to me. The men below me know better than to talk back. Though I consider these men my brothers, the uncompromising hierarchy of power holds us together. The structure of The Clan is unchanged since its founding in the 1960s, and anyone who can't abide by our laws and principles isn't welcome among us. We know this. We were taught this from the cradle, the rules reinforced at St. Albert's.

"I'm sorry, Keenan," Boner says. I nod. Apology accepted.

"Come with me to the club, brother?" Boner asks tentatively. He wants to make amends. He wants us on good footing again. I want to go back to Caitlin. I long to see her sweet, innocent eyes looking up at me, to hear her gentle voice, to run my hands through her midnight length of silky hair. I swallow hard, surprised at the strength of my desire for her. But what I want isn't as important as bringing Boner back into the fold, for him to know he may've fucked up and I noticed, but he's still my brother.

"Aye," I tell him, earning a hoot from Tully and a fist pump from Nolan. My brother's eyes light up like Christmas candles, and I can't help but smile. I'm stern with him, I know, but I love the son of a bitch.

I look over the room. I called my men and ordered it cleaned thoroughly, the floor immaculate, the body disposed of. Tomorrow, word will get out unofficially about what happened tonight. Some will cross themselves and wish for deliverance, but most will nod their heads. We've sixty years of experience in Ballyhock, and those who know us know we're fair, we're just, but we're exacting. You don't borrow money from The Clan you can't repay.

Still, I wonder what Caitlin would say. Why does it bother me that I fear her response? I shake my head, physically casting off the niggling fears I carry, when our ride arrives.

"'Tis a good night, Keenan joins us on the lash," Nolan says as we pile into the car.

"We'll see 'tis a good night," Boner says. "See if he snogs someone, aye?"

Nolan snorts. "Snogs? See if he bangs one, more like."

"Not gonna happen, lads," Tully says, pulling a flask out of his pocket and taking a hearty swig. He hands it around, and I take a good pull myself. "Don't you got eyes in yer heads? Bejesus, he's got a sweet little flack waitin' for him at home."

"The prisoner?" Nolan asks. "Got a good eye full of her myself, and she—" he shuts his trap when I punch his arm. "Aw, I mean her eyes, brother, not her body." He rubs his arm and pouts.

"Y'all have been runnin' your gobs about this place for so long, I figure it's time I get a good look," I say. Boner grins. We're good. He'll pay his penalty at the weekend, but he knows I'm not holding a grudge. We can't, in the brotherhood. Have to have each other's backs.

We pull up to the club, and I don't miss the way people whisper when we arrive. Three large bouncers at the door let us in without carding us, and we're brought immediately into where I've been before, the main club entrance. I walk to a table and go to pull out a chair, when Nolan's hand comes to my arm and he stops me.

"Keenan, are you out of your fucking mind?" he says. "You don't sit in *here*, brother." He shakes his head and casts his eyes heavenward.

Boner said something of this before. I don't reply but cross my arms on my chest and look to Nolan for the lead. He leans in, whispering in my ear, "This is only the front, ya plonker. You're feckin' heir to the throne. You come with us."

There are dozens of people in here, throwing back drinks and cajoling one another. Several couples are groping and snogging, and one girl's sitting on the lap of a man who looks old enough to be her father. But Nolan and Boner lead us past the throng of people on the dance floor, past the dimly lit bar, past the waitresses that look longingly after Nolan. They stop when we reach a silver elevator with two large men guarding the door. Their clothing's black as midnight, matching the color of their skin, their eyes glittering with the promise of violence to anyone who dare step a toe out of line, but when they see Nolan and Boner coming, they smile.

"Where've you been, mate?" one asks. "Missed you at the weekend."

"Had some business to attend to," Nolan says, then he grabs my arm and yanks me over in front of him. "But I brought a guest tonight. My older brother."

The men incline their head in greeting. "Heir to the throne, aren't you?" one asks. I nod, not wanting to attract the attention of anyone else. Nolan beams with pride. "Best leader we've ever had," he says. "You boys treat him well, aye?"

My younger brother's proud of me. *Proud.*

"Certainly," the one on the left says. "Aye. This way, sir." He slides a card in a slot by the gleaming elevator door, and we step inside. The elevator quickly swoops downward, and when the doors open, I realize these two are right. This is nothing at all like I've seen above. Down here is another world altogether.

I step off the elevator and try to take it all in, but it's unlike anything I've seen before. The bar lines the left side, a gleaming affair lit with golden lights that high-light the bottles upon bottles of drinks and taps. Chandeliers hang from the ceiling in golden clusters, and circular glass high top tables welcome patrons to come and sit for a while. But it isn't the bar scene that catches my attention first.

A woman walks by on stilettos wearing *nothing* but the shoes. Her breasts hang free, full and beautiful, and her arse is utter perfection. I blink in surprise, when my eyes cast behind her to a couple on a golden leather loveseat. The woman's dressed in what appears to be pink latex, her hair plaited, and she's kneeling before the man. She's attached to him by a thin metal chain

164

around her neck that clips onto his belt, and he's spreading his legs for her to service him.

Jesus, Mary, and Joseph.

Light strings of melodic music plays in the background, and the air is thick with the smell of whiskey and sex. In the far corner of the room, I see various accoutrements lined up, and I'm familiar enough to know there are several spanking benches, a whipping post, and metal rings for restraints.

"Come with us, brother," Nolan says, leading me past the bar and to another room just off the main entrance. "We'll see you sorted." He beckons to three beautiful women dressed in violet dresses that barely cover tits to arse.

"Get me sorted?" I ask. "I don't want to be sorted. I came here for a drink, not an orgy."

Boner guffaws and slaps my back. "Need to get you *laid,* boss."

"Bite the back of my bollox," I mutter. "Screw off."

It only makes him laugh as the women approach us. "Give him the special," Nolan says, nodding to me, and two of the women make their way toward me.

I turn away. "I'm here for a drink."

Nolan sidles up to me. "Keenan," he says, as if he's trying to get me to see reason. "Honest to God, brother. You need a night off where you aren't bearing the weight of the world on your shoulders."

I don't contradict him. He's right, and I know it.

"Taste just a little," he says. "It feels fucking *good* to take control. Tie one of them up and use them. Wear her out. Trust me, that's why they're here."

The idea leaves a sour taste in my mouth, but not because I don't like what he's suggesting, that I'm not tempted by the idea of tying one of them up and using them well and good. All I can see in my mind's eye is the innocent look of the woman that waits for me. None of them is the woman I'm interested in.

"Drink only," I insist, taking my seat on one of the stools. "That'll do." I wave to the bartender. "Pint of the black stuff."

He shoves a frothy mug of Guinness my way, and I empty half of it one gulp, then sigh contentedly. Christ, but it's good. I polish it off and order a second. "Round on the house," I say, waving to my brothers. I don't want to be a wet blanket. I'll drink alongside them, I'll fucking drink them under the table, but I'm not touching any of the women.

I watch the scenes in front of me, and my mind begins to churn.

I want to bring her here.

I want to use her.

I want to tie her to one of those posts and mete out perfect punishment, to bring her to the edge of bliss before I release her into ecstasy.

Over.

And over.

And over.

Chapter Fourteen

CAITLIN

I wait for him until my eyelids droop, and the book I'm reading falls on my face.

"Ow," I mutter, glaring at the traitorous copy of *The Sun Also Rises* on my nose. It's a decent enough book, and I've read it before, but this time it's boring me. I place it on the bedside table when I hear footsteps outside the door, followed by the low murmur of voices. I sit up. Is he back? A moment later, the door swings open, and in the darkness, I see Keenan's silhouette enter the room.

"Keenan?" I call out, needing to hear the reassurance that it's him.

"Sir," he says. "You'll call me sir." His words are slurred, and he walks a bit off balance. Is he drunk? His voice is laced with danger, and though I find myself a little apprehensive, my pulse begins to quicken.

Sir.

"Yes, sir." I swallow hard. There's something seductive in the words of submission, something sacred in the acquiescence. I watch him amble toward me, and I wonder why I'm not frightened. He's a powerful, ruthless man, and I've no doubt he's done terrible, wicked things. But I'm not scared. Maybe I should be.

I left the window open, and a gentle breeze stirs the bedclothes. He looks toward the window, when the thinnest glimmer of moonlight casts across his features. His dark brown hair looks lighter in the moonlight, the green of his eyes mesmerizing. I swallow hard when his eyes swing toward me, his look voracious.

"Where were you?" I ask, but he holds up a finger to warn me and shakes his head.

"I told you not to ask that," he admonishes. "It's late, Caitlin. Do you want to be punished at this hour?" He's off kilter, as if he's looking for a reason to punish me.

I shake my head, watching him as he reaches me and kneels on the bed, his knee beside my body. "You ought to be punished."

"Why, sir?" I don't know why, but this feels like a form of foreplay. The low, seductive sound of his voice laced with anger and something else I can't quite put my finger on. He smells of whiskey and something else, something sweet and pungent like warmed honey. I note a smudge of pink on his cheek, and feel my body go still.

Is that lipstick? Did someone kiss him?

He stands, his large form looming over me, and shrugs out of his jacket. Tossing it to the chair behind him, he keeps his gaze on me. The harness comes next, as he lays one gun after another on the bedside table.

"Why spank you?" he asks, his voice smooth as silk with a note of danger. "You don't ask me questions, Caitlin."

"Are you drunk?" I ask before I can stop myself, before I've processed that he just asked me not to ask questions.

He shakes his head slowly from side to side. "You're a naughty little thing," he whispers. "Just begging for that spanking, aren't you?" He stands before me, wearing only his t-shirt, the fabric stretched across his biceps. I swear his arms are as thick as my thighs. I watch, enthralled, as he grabs the bottom of his shirt with both hands and yanks it up over his head. It's somehow arousing, just watching him remove his shirt.

Tossing the shirt behind him, he points to the headboard. "Turn around," he says, in the same deep, velvety voice, "and place your hands on the headboard."

My heartbeat quickens. Is he looking for a reason to punish me? Does he crave this? Or is there something else going on?

My eyes on his, I gently push down the bedding. I've worn a simple silky sheath nightie to bed, white as snow and sensually soft. I'm covered fully, but the delicate fabric clings to my curves, dips between the valley at my breasts, hangs at the gentle part of my thighs.

"Bloody hell," he whispers. "Christ, woman."

I don't respond, determined to do what he says. Rising to my knees, I turn my body to face the headboard. Still kneeling, I grasp the very edge.

And then I feel him beside me, his warm, reassuring body pressed up against mine. "Stay right there, lass," he whispers in my ear. "Stay. *Right. There.*"

I close my eyes. I'm going to do exactly what he says.

I hear him open the drawer beside the bed, hear him remove something, but I don't turn to look, for I don't want to bring on his displeasure. I want to please him. And I have to admit, I'm a little scared. But a part of me is neither scared nor eager to please. He has lipstick on his cheek, and I don't like that one bit.

Why don't I like that? Why does it trouble me?

Could I be jealous about my captor, so soon? Why? Why do I wish it were *my* lipstick on his cheek? He's a powerful man. Others obey his orders. What could he possibly want with a girl like me?

Cool metal against the silky nightie makes me shiver. I swallow, but don't speak, curious what he'll do next, when I feel the metal graze my neck.

"A naughty little girl ought to wear a collar," he says, clucking his tongue. "So she can be trained properly."

My mind is a jumble of thoughts.

What on earth is he doing?

What will he do next?

Why do I feel excited?

He clicks the collar in place, and I gasp at the weight of it. It's heavy and cold, and it's connected to something else. I look down when I hear the clink of metal.

It's… a chain?

There's another clink of metal, and he produces two thick metal bands he slides around my wrists.

I've read classic literature, and in those books… men don't hurt women. They don't abuse them and degrade them and… and spank them… and yet why do I feel so hyper aware of all things Keenan? His voice, his scent, the way his warm fingers graze my skin when he fastens the locks in place.

The feel of his mouth—oh, *God*—his mouth on my neck when I'm well and securely fastened to the bed with yet another chain. I shiver in delight, and there's a low pulsing between my legs, and deep in my belly. I swallow hard and close my eyes. I don't know why I feel this way, or how I can possibly control the erotic flare of heat that weaves through my body like a teeming river. He licks my neck and cups my bottom in his large hand, giving me a gentle squeeze.

"Do you need a spanking?" he whispers in my ear.

"I…" I don't know what to say. A spanking is a punishment, a humiliating one at that, and I've done nothing wrong. I don't think.

He slaps my backside and I straighten my back.

"Do you?"

I don't think twice before responding. "Yes, sir."

Yes, sir.

What is going on with my crazy mind? Am I addled? Insane? Somehow under the influence?

I feel a thin, sturdy something on my lower back, like he's tracing the edges of my curves with a stick. His hand wraps around my waist, a thin whistle of something cuts through the air, and I squeal when a line of fire cuts across my backside.

"Count," he says, his voice as sharp as whatever just struck me.

I inhale.

"One."

Another hard strike lines the lower curve of my backside, then another. It hurts, it hurts badly, but the sting quickly dissipates into heat that flares to my core.

"Two."

"Three."

When I get to five, my skin is throbbing, but the ache between my legs has only magnified even further.

He parts my legs with the same thin, supple rod he struck me with, and I quickly move my legs apart. The edge of the rod glides against the silky triangle of fabric between my legs. He's touching me *there*, and I might fly out of these shackles with the intensity of my need.

The friction he builds goes faster, and faster, until I'm whimpering with need and the pulsing between my legs is so intense, I can hardly breathe. He taps the rob, a quick swat between my legs. I gasp in pain.

Then he stops.

Stops.

I stifle a sob.

"Are you disappointed, lass?" he whispers in my ear. "You wish to come?"

I shake my head from side to side. I don't know what he means.

"I… I don't know," I falter.

"Jesus, Mary, and Joseph," he groans. "Christ Almighty, woman. You're so fu—you're so innocent it's intoxicating."

I don't understand what he means, what he wishes from me. And why did he stop himself from cursing?

I hear a clink and whirr and see him unfastening his zipper. He holds my gaze with determination as he removes his jeans.

"What are you doing?" I whisper.

"I want to mark you, lass," he whispers back. "I want to fuck that sweet, virgin cunt of yours until you scream my name."

I'm shaking with fear and anticipation, wondering what he'll possibly do next.

Seems he's forgotten his momentary desire not to curse, and as he speaks, I feel my cheeks flame with heat. His words are wicked and dirty, but somehow, I feel more powerful, more attractive, as if the very words he speaks are an aphrodisiac.

I've never done this before. I have no idea what to expect, and it makes me a little nervous. No. It makes me a *lot* nervous.

What will he do to me? Why do I want this man to do anything he wants?

"I want to be the first to make you feel *everything*," he whispers in my ear, his breath pungent with the sweet heat of liquor. *Is* he drunk?

Do I care?

I feel something both hard and soft at my back, and when I look down, I see him hard and erect, pressed up to my back. It doesn't scare me, though. I'm more curious than anything. I've been hidden away so long, I managed to convince myself I wasn't wanted by anyone. That I was an insignificant little creature, a forgotten soul that had no impact in the world in the least. But the way he's looking at me now, as if he owns me, the way he wants to own my body as well... I like it. It makes me feel special. Attractive. I'd even go so far as to say... sexy.

"Keenan..." my voice trails off when he wraps his hand around my throat and squeezes. I can't breathe, but it doesn't frighten me. He's in control. He wants to control this, too. He breathes warm air on my neck, rustling the tendrils of hair and making me shiver, and still, he holds his hand on my neck. I feel a little dizzy and lightheaded when he releases me, and as I gasp for breath, he sinks his teeth into the bare, tender skin at my shoulder, but like all things he does, this pain tempered with the promise of pleasure, my fear quickly dissipates.

"How did you learn such bravery, sweet Caitlin?" he whispers in my ear, then he mumbles in a foreign language, one that sounds so ancient it's as if he's drawn it straight from the past. I want to know this language that he speaks, to understand the hidden depths.

I don't respond. I don't know how to. It isn't that I'm intrinsically brave, or anything like that, really.

It's easy to be brave when I'm with him.

He slides a key to the cuffs at my wrists, but leaves the collar on my neck, then he moves at my back, stroking his hard length with one hand while holding my gaze with the other. My mouth goes dry, for I don't know how to handle this, what I should do. I'm holding my breath while he strokes harder and faster, his breathing becoming labored, and he manages to whisper, "Touch yourself."

I don't need to ask him to repeat himself, or what he means, my need for pleasure between my legs is all-consuming. With a trembling hand, I push down the silky edge of my undergarments, and slide my fingers to the slick, swollen folds. I gasp when I stroke up once.

"Work yourself," he whispers in my ear, closing his eyes as rubs his length on my bare back, and I know he's going to mark me, just like this. I marvel at how little I need to know and how natural this all feels.

It feels exquisite, putting pressure right there, building to something better than even this.

And then he's behind me, his swollen length against my back, pulsing and rocking while he moves my hand away and puts his own there instead. I brace myself on the headboard, breathless with the feel of his fingers working expertly, massaging and stroking and bringing me to where I've never been.

"I own this pussy," he growls in my ear. "I own your orgasms. I own your pleasure and pain."

He's stroking himself with one hand and working me with the other, until I'm keening with pleasure, my breath caught in my throat. With a guttural growl, he jerks, hot liquid splashing on my naked skin at the same time my pleasure reaches its pinnacle.

My pulse races and he groans against me, both of us writhing in ecstasy. Spasms of pleasure ripple through me, pulsing against his hand while I explode into blinding pleasure. I close my eyes, unable to look at anything or focus beyond the feel of his hands on me, the feel of my whole body teeming with utter bliss. His groans of pleasure echo my own, until we're panting and sated and a ridiculous mess.

"Stay there," he orders, his voice a harsh slap of reality after that little bit of heaven we tasted. I don't move, still panting with pleasure and surprise, not sure what just happened or what his purpose was. "Right there." I hold onto the headboard as he instructed, trembling from the aftershock of what just happened. He dresses beside the bed and pads off to the bathroom, returning a moment later with a small towel, a warm washcloth, and a clean nightgown. In silence, he cleans us up. I let him dress me, removing my hands from the headboard before he spins me around to look at him.

He drapes the new nightgown over my head and points to the bathroom. He looks suddenly weary, his beautiful, vibrant eyes sated but tired. "Get ready for bed," he instructs.

I walk quietly to the bathroom, disliking the separation from him. Something's missing, but I don't know what. Many things are missing, though. So many. I know we aren't following the rules, whatever those are. So I do what he says, rushing through brushing my teeth and washing my face, because I'm weirdly and inexplicably eager to get back to him. I stare at the ring of metal on my neck. Will he take it off?

I think he's asleep when I reach the bed. He's bare from the waist up, wearing nothing but a pair of boxers. I stare at him for a moment, surprised at how peaceful he looks like this, one arm up and over his shoulder, the marks of ink on his arms clearly visible, his eyes closed in slumber. My heart sinks a little. I don't want him to be asleep yet.

But when I step beside the bed, he opens one eyes. "You're like a little fairy," he says. "One of the fae."

I've read enough I know what he means, and it feels like a compliment?

"Oh? How so?"

He folds down a corner of the blanket and pats the bed. It's oddly welcoming and homey. I slide under the sheets beside him, roll over onto my side, and place my hands under my face. I watch him as he takes in every detail. He sits up, takes the same key that he used to unfasten the cuffs, and unlocks the cool metal collar. Placing it in the drawer beside him, he explains.

"In Irish mythology, the fae, the *aos sí,* live in underground fairy mounds. The good ones are called our good neighbors, as they dwell in fairy rings and bring peace and protection. They're mystical and powerful, spreading good will and cheer among those they encounter. And they are stunningly beautiful."

"I like that," I say, my hands still tucked under my cheek as I watch him. "I like that a lot. Especially the part about being stunningly beautiful."

He smiles, both sad and gently, his eyes crinkling a bit at the edges. "This feels like a stolen moment," he says. "A tryst between lovers."

Lovers.

"Does it?" I whisper. "And what does... what does a lover do after such a... tryst?"

"Kiss," he says, reaching for the back of my head and drawing me closer to him. I close my eyes seconds before his lips meet mine.

This. This was what our heated exchange was missing. The intimacy and connection of a moment shared. I sigh when his tongue gently slides past my lips, the heat and warmth of his kiss sending tingles of aware-ness and pleasure through my limbs.

He pulls his mouth off mine with reluctance, draws my head down, and kisses my forehead. "I'll sober in the morning and have to deal with the aftermath of my weakness," he whispers. "But tonight, just for tonight, let me hold you."

I don't know what he means, what he refers to, but when he reaches for me, I have no power to stop him. I want this. I want him. I want this togetherness. I didn't know I was lonely until he filled my world with his presence.

He draws me onto his chest and holds me, breathing in deeply, then exhaling as he tightens his grip around me. He doesn't release me but holds me for long minutes, then quickly reaches for the covers and tosses them on both of us.

"Sleep, little fae," he whispers.

So I let him. For tonight. Just for tonight… I let him hold me. I fall asleep to the sound of his slow, rhythmic breathing.

Chapter Fifteen

Keenan

I wake with the most beautiful woman I've ever laid eyes on sleeping beside me, curled up to my chest. Her long, long, black hair hangs down her back in waves of silk, and the purity of her expression gives me momentary pause.

What did I do last night? My head pounds from the drinks I had, my mouth as dry as cotton. *Motherfucker.* I haven't had a hangover since I was a fucking teenager. She barely stirs when I sit up and get out of bed. I tuck the blanket back in around her, a sort of pride or maybe joy filling me at the opportunity to take this tender moment of caring for her.

I've never cared for anyone before. I've protected them. I've defended them. I've learned and led, listened and spoken. But never have I taken care of anyone, not like this. When my brothers were little, I was off to

180

Saint Albert's, boarding with Malachy, and not brought back to be with them until I'd been trained in the way of The Clan.

I sit on the edge of the bed, cradling my head in my hands with a smashing headache, and reach for my phone.

"Pain relievers," I croak into the phone when Sebastian answers.

"Sending them up, captain," he says. "And drink what I send you as well."

He's no fool. He knows why I'm hungover and will help me relieve my misery.

I hang up the phone, when I feel gentle hands on my back.

"Are you okay, Keenan?"

"Hungover, lass, but I'll be fine."

"You said last night that you would be."

"Did I?"

I don't remember. Fucking hell.

"Yes," she says softly, looking up at me with those wide eyes that steal my heart with every flutter of her lashes. "You said you'd deal with the aftermath today. And here you are. I'm sorry, I wish I could help."

Is the girl that innocent that she thinks my headache is the aftermath I referred to? Jesus.

I get to my feet and head to the shower. "I'll have food sent up," I tell her. I want to crawl beneath the covers and hold her again, as if she's my talisman against the work that I do, the demons I wrestle. But I can't lose my edge, my focus.

"Get up and ready. You can shower after me."

I ignore the look of hurt on her face and get clean clothes from my dresser, when my phone rings.

"Yeah?"

"The body was disposed of, sir."

Tully.

"Well done, Tully. Any blowback?" I need to know if the man we killed last night was missed by anyone. If we should brace for retribution.

"Nossir. Seems some were happy to be rid of him, truth be told."

"Aye. Well done, you. We'll call a meeting later today to discuss what happened, and my plans for the school this afternoon."

"Yessir."

We disconnect the call, and I head to the shower. I take a steaming hot one, but even the scalding water isn't enough to cleanse me, to rid me of what haunts me. Angrily, I shut the water off and head back to the room. Caitlin's sitting at the desk, a book in hand, dressed in a dainty pink dress. She doesn't even look up when I enter the room.

I don't speak to her when I dress. I answer the door when our food and my medicine arrive, and point to the tray I slide in front of her.

"Eat," I order.

Without looking at me, she obeys. She butters her scone and eats it with her hot cup of tea, following it with a bowl of fruit, and eggs with sausage. Her eyes stay on her plate, as she effortlessly eats the entire meal, then pushes her tray to the side and picks up her book again.

"Caitlin." My voice is stern and sharp, but she doesn't flinch.

She looks back up to me. "What?"

My hands clench. "Is that the correct way to speak to me?"

Pursing her lips, she corrects herself. "No, sir. What is it, sir?"

"Why so narky, lass?"

"Narky, sir? I don't know what you mean."

"Cranky. Out of sorts." I know why, but I want to hear her say it. Women don't handle hot and cold well, and clearly, my little fae's no exception.

She shrugs. "I don't know what to tell you."

"The truth, please."

She hasn't learned the art of deception, or how to hide her feelings. She wears her heart on her shirtsleeve, her eyes mirrors to her soul as wide as the Irish Sea.

She takes in a deep breath, and to my horror, her lower lip trembles when she speaks. "Well…" she begins, exhaling on a sigh. "I don't like feeling like I'm someone special one minute, then nothing at all special the next. It's really as simple as that."

I blink. Though I expected truth, this still takes me by surprise.

"I see. And when you—" but I'm cut short when a knock comes at the door. I hold a finger up for her to wait a minute. She shrugs. Where else is she going to go? She picks up her book.

I answer the door to my mother standing there holding a bottle of Nurofen, a bottle of a sports drink, and an expression of utter disdain.

"Caught Sebastian on the way up," she says, her lips pursed. "And don't let yer father know you've been on the lash and got yourself hungover like a damn schoolboy."

My mother rarely lectures, but she's spot on this time. I grunt, take the meds down and swig the drink.

"Hello, Mrs. McCarthy," Caitlin says pleasantly.

My mom's eyes widen, and she smiles, walking into the room. "Hello, sweet Caitlin," she greets. "What's the story?"

Caitlin's brow furrows. "The story?"

My mother laughs out loud. "Means how are ya, lass."

"You Irish have many... peculiar expressions," Caitlin says.

"She don't know the half of it," I mutter, and mam smacks my arm.

"Keenan, you said you wanted to talk."

"In private," I tell her, ignoring the look of hurt on Caitlin's face. "Later this evening, aye?"

"Aye," my mother says.

She takes her leave and I depart with reluctance, kissing Caitlin's pretty cheek and giving her a few things to do in my absence. "Stay here until I return." She remains aloof and reserved. She doesn't look up from her book when I leave. It unsettles me.

The lass is innocent. But who is she? Why am I allowing this pure, unblemished woman, someone who could bring destruction to us all, to infiltrate my mind, and dare I say, my heart?

When I'm done with work, I see my mother by the garden, her favorite haunt. Perhaps we can talk earlier than this evening. But when I draw near, I hear a familiar laugh. I pause mid-step, the door to my car still open, when I hear it again.

Is that Caitlin? In the *garden*?

I slam the door to my car and march off to the garden. And there she is, picking flowers and gathering them to her breasts, her hair pinned back in plaits, adorned with flowers.

Christ.

For one brief moment I imagine her just like this, but she wears a dress of white, her pretty feet bedecked in delicate ballet slippers. She holds my arm as I march her down the aisle and take my vows before my brothers. Before everyone. I shake my head. I'm dreaming like a goddamn schoolboy.

"Keenan!" Mam greets as I draw near. "Fancy you coming home early."

"Didn't expect it then, did you?" I ask severely, my anger at having been disobeyed directed at both of them. The lass will be punished for this, and not the type of punishment that ends with her climaxing.

"Who gave you permission to set foot out of that room, Caitlin?"

"I did." I turn in surprise to see my father coming up behind me, his stern, immovable expression giving me pause. What the hell is this? I look into the eyes that mirror my own, trying to seek understanding.

"She had strict orders from me not to leave the room," I begin. "She was not to—"

"Keenan, listen to me." My father interrupts, his voice lowering as he approaches. He waves a hand at mam and Caitlin. "You girls carry on while I have a word with Keenan."

Caitlin's eyes briefly skirt to mine, then away again, as my mother gets her attention. She's troubled about her disobedience and worried about my reaction. Good.

"I've good reason, son, and I'm sorry if it seems I undermined you in any way."

Well, then. This is new. My father rarely apologizes, and certainly's never had any concern about undermining me. The time for me to take the throne is near. He's abdicating authority to me already, even on the day he's allowed her to defy me.

I stand and cross my arms, casting a glance from him back to Caitlin and mam.

"Alright," I tell him. "Let's hear it." My tone is brisk, but he looks at me almost placatingly, as if begging my forgiveness. Something in me softens toward him, at this hardened man who's taught me right from wrong. He's aging, and it shows.

"I questioned your mother today about what she knew," he begins, his voice low so only I can hear. "Came clear as day she knew Caitlin's mother. Finn's admitted he knew of the pregnancy and condoned the birth, aye?"

"Aye."

"And said that Caitlin's mother was thought to have killed herself."

I nod, agreeing again.

"I've asked your mother for more information, and Father Finn as well. I've spent the afternoon looking through records, piecing things together."

"What'd you find?"

"Caitlin Martin was betrothed to Ouen O'Gregor, in the north. Their marriage was to bring an alliance to two rival clans, but she went to Boston on college break, and lost contact with your mam. Word was that she'd killed herself, but we know now that wasn't the truth. She was pregnant, and Father Finn avoided war between The Clans by hiding the child."

If The Clans knew she'd been knocked up by another man other than her betrothed, there would've been hell to pay, no question.

"Caitlin. And why did Anderson spy on us, then?"

"My theory's that he did it to keep an alliance with the Martins. If they knew he had a girl that belonged to them by birth, related by blood, they'd kill her. Martin's another daughter of his own, now, and Caitlin's birth would complicate things."

I nod slowly. Christ, but it makes sense.

"So Anderson spied on us as a way to form a truce with the Martins. If he was their informant, he'd have some sway."

"Looks like."

I look at the girl, twirling violets in her hair with the innocence of a child.

"What the fuck am I to do with the girl, then?"

My father doesn't bat an eyelash. "Well isn't it obvious, son?" He shakes his head, as if he's given me a mathematical equation with an obvious answer. Two plus two is four.

"*Níl leigheas ar an ngrá ach pósadh,*" he says in guttural Gaelic. I frown at him. I know the expression well.

There is no cure for love other than marriage. The only way to solve the troubles of being in love is to marry someone.

In love? I'm not in love with the girl. I barely know her.

I look at him curiously.

He shakes his head. "Christ, Keenan. *Marry* the lass. If you're married, Martin can't touch her, even if he does find out who she is and how she got here."

He says it almost casually, as if he didn't just suggest changing the entire course of my life.

He scrubs a hand through his short gray hair, looking older than I've ever noticed before. "Keenan, you've taken her into our custody. If Martin catches wind, he'll consider this in act of war."

"Bloody hell." I shake my head. He's right. I can't believe I haven't thought of that myself. She's his blood relative, for Christ's sake, and my taking her here against her will *would* be an act of war, firing the first shot as it were.

But marry her?

"The girl isn't going to want any part of marrying me. For Christ's sake, she's an innocent."

"Son, in order for you to assume the throne as chief, you know you need to marry. Of that there's no question."

"Aye."

"Rules state she's to be of Irish descent, and that's also clear now. Her mother was Irish, she's of Irish descent."

We've detailed history of relations of mine as well, so I know there isn't a chance her mother hooked up with any of my own relatives either, thank Christ.

"Mother of God," I mutter. If I marry her, I'll be able to assume the throne as Clan leader. I'll protect her against any retaliation with the Martins. "If done right, we can actually form an alliance with the Martins over this."

"Aye."

I watch her walk in the garden, holding out a cluster of violets to my mother.

"Don't think too deeply on this, son. In our family and line of work, marriage for the sake of convenience is the norm."

"I know it." Christ, don't I. But how can I tell him what I fear? That touching a woman like her with my blood-stained hands, that defiling her, will be the very thing that damns my soul to hell? She's too good for the likes of me. Too fucking good.

"Think on it. Ask counsel of those you trust. Then do what you must."

Again, deferment to my authority where none existed before. A lump rises in my throat, and I swallow both pride and emotions when I nod.

"Aye."

"Go," my father says. "Make an honest woman out of her. And tell me what you need."

His phone rings, and he goes to answer it. I stand in the garden, looking at Caitlin and my mother, and for the first time in a long time, the first time in years, the first time in, *God*, ever? Hope rises in me.

Marry her.

My mother comes to me, but Caitlin holds back. She pretends to stoop to pick something up, but I know she's fearful of coming to me. She knows she disobeyed.

"Caitlin," I say sternly, crooking my finger at her. Now that I know she's to be mine, I feel the weight of responsibility on my shoulders. The obligation to ensure she obeys me, that she learns her rules of The Clan for her own safety. That she knows she's my very special girl, and that I'll not let a hair on her head be harmed. Her wide eyes look up at me with apprehension.

"Yes?" she asks, her gaze quickly flitting to my mother's, as if wondering if my mother can shield her from me. I feel a corner of my lips quirk up. How adorable. She absolutely cannot.

"Come here." My mother looks from Caitlin to me, then back again.

"Now, Keenan," she begins. "Your father and I—"

I hold up my hand for her to stop. "I know it," I say to her. "That doesn't change the fact that I gave her an instruction, and she's to obey me."

"It does, though, son," my mother begins. "Just listen to reason—"

"She's my charge," I say to my mother. "And as such, she'll do as I say."

It's essential I draw the boundaries where necessary and show myself to be a trustworthy, respectable, and honorable leader. "Now come here, lass."

Her eyes unwavering, she walks to me, her steps as light as feathers. When she reaches me, I slide my hand to the back of her neck and give her a gentle squeeze. I watch as her eyes flutter closed, she breathes in, then she lets her breath out again.

When she opens her eyes, the distance of this morning has fled. "Welcome home, Keenan," she says pleasantly, in her clear, lilting voice. She falters, as if she doesn't know what to say next, then, "You've lovely parents."

My mother grins, and I blink in surprise. "Do I? Don't believe anyone's ever called me dad lovely. Mam, yeah, but dad, now that's a new one."

Caitlin flushes madly and bites her lip. "Did I say something wrong?" she asks. "I don't know—"

I shake my head and take her hand. "No. You don't censor your speech and *most* of the time that's adorable."

My mother breathes out a sigh of relief, as if she's held her breath waiting for my response. "You talked to your father, then, son?"

I nod.

"I did. This weekend, Caitlin and I will travel to Saint Albert's. When we return, I want to make arrangements, but let me discuss them with the lass, yeah?"

My mother blinks, then beams at me. "Certainly. Oh, yes, certainly, Keenan."

Caitlin looks back and forth between the two of us, as if trying to decipher what we're talking about.

"*Níl leigheas ar an ngrá ach pósadh,*" my mother says, her eyes bright. I roll my eyes.

"You and dad are eerily alike, you know that?"

"I don't know what you're talking about," Caitlin says.

"I'll explain in private," I say to her.

But will I? What will I say to her? How will I propose? I don't have a romantic bone in my body. The only way of communicating is with orders and commands, and I could try to order the girl to marry me, but would that work?

"Okay," she says brightly. "In private, then."

Chapter Sixteen

CAITLIN

He holds me to his side with purpose, and I wonder if he'll punish me when he has me alone. He clearly enjoys the job, and at times he's given me reason to sort of enjoy it myself as well. Isn't that unusual, though? For someone to enjoy being punished? It's deviant behavior, I have no doubt, and I wonder if my naiveté is to blame. Does he take advantage of me?

Of course he does.

Then why does a part of me crave this? His stern correction and demeanor, the way he's utterly focused on only me.

When his father and mother came to me and instructed me to come with them, I protested at first.

"Keenan said not to leave," I told them, knowing full well I'm expected to obey him. They assured me it was fine, though. Maybe I shouldn't have believed them. I don't know what to expect when I return to the large house with him.

We go to the room, now fully lit with the midday sun, a tray of lunch foods waiting for us on the little desk. He strides into the room, sits at the chair, and tugs me onto his lap sideways, so my legs dangle from one side. He's large and sturdy beneath me, and the intimacy makes me feel small and quiet.

"Now, lass," he says, his voice gentler than I expected. I look at him expectantly, feeling only minor trepidation at what is to be my lecture, or… or something. He tucks me against one arm, and with his free hand, cups my jaw, coaxing my gaze to his. His warm, inviting scent, so masculine yet classy, makes me sigh into him.

"Caitlin, I know you were given instructions by my parents today, so this one day I'll allow this to slide." I swallow. Okay, then. Seems I avoided a minor catastrophe. "And I'll speak to them of this privately as well."

"Yes, sir." I don't know what else to say. "I do enjoy your mother."

He smiles but he's distracted. "Aye. And she enjoys you as well. In fact, I think she—"

But his phone rings. He groans, his brows snap together, and he whips his phone out of his pocket as if it's betrayed him, glaring at the screen. He answers it, listens, then shakes his head. "I've got to answer this call," he says. "Stay here and behave yourself. Eat your food."

He leaves. He just leaves, that quickly. That suddenly. I busy myself with eating. I'm not lonely, but I miss him. And I felt as if he had something important to say to me.

Does a man like him ever settle down? Or is he destined to always answer the call, whenever he's bidden.

I expect him back that evening, but he doesn't return until the sun is rising on a new day. When he comes back, he's weary but not drunk this time. I watch from my cocoon of covers as he undresses and prepares for bed, slides in next to me, and is fast asleep before he's barely touched the pillow. He rises a few hours later and is gone again.

This goes on for two more days, me occupying myself in his room, food brought on trays. He's had to postpone his trip to the school that he mentioned, but he doesn't tell me why. His absence doesn't bother me as it might bother others. I'm used to confinement and my own company. But I do miss him. I wish for something, anything at all that would give me some kind of morsel of his attention, but there's nothing but his utter exhaustion and pervading absence. He replaces my phone that broke. I'm not very interested in using it, though.

When he finally comes back to me, I rise from where I'm reading to greet him, but when he steps into the room, his phone rings. He curses. Someone comes in behind him and slides a tray of food onto the table.

"What is it?" he snaps. He listens, and within seconds his brows draw closer together, and his gaze darkness. My heartbeat quickens watching the rapid, terrifying transformation. I must never forget that this man does wicked things I don't know the half of. Not yet.

Here we go again.

"Mother*fucker.* I'll kill the motherfucking *bastards,*" he growls. He clenches his phone so tightly his knuckles whiten, before he goes deadly calm. "Tell me everything."

He stares at me, but doesn't see me, his focus cast afar as he listens to the details. I watch his lips thin and his body tighten, and for that one brief moment, he looks like a man possessed. I don't want to ever incite anger in him like this. I shiver in fear, wondering what horror that's being relayed to draw out such rage in him.

"I'll go now." Then his gaze snaps to me. "Bloody *hell,*" he mutters. "Can't leave the girl here, she isn't safe. *No.* I don't trust them. I don't fucking trust anyone. I'll take her tonight. Bring in our strongest guard and order them to arrive by nightfall."

He hangs up his phone, curses again, and runs his hand through his dark brown hair. I want to soothe him, to somehow bring calm to the storm that rages within him. But I don't speak. I don't move. I wait for instruction.

I wonder if waiting on him helps or hinders. Does he need to know that I won't leave? I couldn't if I wanted to, but right now, that doesn't matter.

He turns to me, as if just seeing me.

I'm not allowed to ask him what happened or what happens next, this much I know. He doesn't speak at first, then runs his fingers on his phone, and I see words appearing. Texting, I think he calls it. He's done this before, summoning someone who works for him. Pointing distractedly at the table, he waves an impatient hand at the tray.

"Eat. We're leaving here within the hour and won't have time to eat again until this evening."

Trembling, I pull out a chair and eat without thinking, not tasting any of the food. It's hard to swallow, my mouth is that dry, but I do what he says until my belly's full. He opens the door to his room a moment later when someone knocks, and several servants come in with luggage bags. They rifle through the things that Maeve bought me, and I watch in fascination as they pack my clothing and the items I've stored in the bathroom efficiently. Next they pack his things.

I want to ask him questions, but I know he doesn't want to speak right now, and he's asked me not to question him before. Whatever he heard on the phone troubles him, and he's doing what he thinks best. He walks up behind me and drapes his arms around me from behind, before he leans down and whispers in my ear. "You're a good lass. You've not asked questions. I'll remember this. It shows you trust me, or at the very least you're learning your place. I'll explain on the way."

"Are you going to eat?" I ask him, pointing to the half tray of food that remains. He looks at the tray of food as if he's surprised it's there, before he leans in and kisses my forehead. Does my concern touch him?

"I'll eat later."

We leave and head to a car that waits, our bags in the back of the car. Keenan meets with Cormac and Nolan on the front steps, both men carrying bags as well. "More news?" Nolan asks. He's as sober as I've ever seen him, which troubles me, the jovial, boyish look gone, his lips thinned, pinched together.

Keenan relays information to them in a hushed whisper, so I don't hear. Cormac's eyes darken, and Nolan's hands clench into fists. Nolan curses, and Cormac looks ready to murder someone. I'm dying to know what happened that got them in such a rage. It's hard not to ask questions. What would cause such anger in them?

He's gone on errands, one after the other, and I've never seen him behave like this before.

All around us, men are getting into cars and on motorbikes, and Keenan's shouting directions. They're moving en masse, not even bothering to hide the fact that they're holding weapons of every shape and size. I catch glimpses of guns and knives, tucked into harnesses and belts and boots, when Maeve trots down the flight of stairs and joins her sons on the stairs. I look up to see Keenan's father at the very top.

"You'll stay here, then," Keenan shouts to his father, and I realize it's an order, not a question. His father doesn't answer at first, and Keenan continues. "You'll need to be here in case it's a decoy."

His father nods. "Aye. You bringing the lass?"

Keenan's eyes swing to me. "Absolutely."

His father holds his gaze for a moment before he nods, and I know once more it's a concession of sorts. Keenan said he doesn't trust me to be safe here. He wants to keep me safe himself. Are we going into danger, then?

Maeve hugs her boys and bids them farewell, then turns quickly as if she doesn't trust herself not to cry. I feel as if she's sending them off to war, as if they've enlisted in the military and may not return home. I wonder what it's like for her, knowing the dangerous lives they lead. Bidding them farewell.

And then he's coming to me, sliding into the car, and we're peeling off with the crew of his men surrounding us. One man on either side of the car rides a motorbike, and I realize we're being led by a brigade of sorts, flanked on all sides.

Keenan sighs, and shakes his head. "Even now," he says, "Even now, you don't ask questions." But his tone tells me he's pleased.

"I assume you'll tell me when it's time," I say softly. Do I trust him so soon?

"We've a finishing school," he says. "A boarding school at the foot of the mountains we all attended. The school is run mostly by women who're affiliated with our Clan."

"I don't know who your Clan is, Keenan," I remind him. "You haven't told me."

For some reason, he doesn't hesitate. "We're one of the largest organized crime rings in all of Ireland," he says. I don't flinch or act in surprise, for I knew something like this had to be the case.

"Okay," I say hesitantly. "I figured as much."

He smiles. "Just when I think you can't surprise me anymore," he mutters, shaking his head. "Alright, so we've got a school to prepare our boys to become vowed brothers in our Clan."

I nod. "Aye."

That makes him grin, "You've learned our trick of speech," he says on a chuckle.

My cheeks heat. "Well. It's hard not to," I say, feeling my brows knit together. Is it okay that I sometimes speak like he or Maeve does?

He only gives my cheek a quick pinch. "You're sweet, lass." My heart flutters. "Anyhow, I was planning on bringing you with me here sooner, but I had business to tend to that took precedence." His eyes cloud over, and he doesn't tell me what that business is. "But something's made our visit to St. Albert's much more pressing."

I nod. "Can you tell me what that is, or no?"

He takes my hand. "There've been attacks on the teachers who run our school," he says. "Several. We think it's likely retaliation of some sort, but we don't know yet why or how they've gotten there."

"Oh." My stomach twists with nausea. I don't like the sound of this at all, not one bit.

"Has anyone been hurt?"

He nods gravely. "Very much so."

"Oh," I repeat sadly. "Any of the children?"

"No," he says, shaking his head. "But several of our female teachers have been hurt, and it's our job to find out who did this."

I finish for him. "And retaliate."

He holds my gaze for long minutes before he squeezes my hand. "Aye."

It takes us only about half an hour to arrive at the school. Similar to the mansion where they reside, this school is encircled with a large, heavy gate, and security cameras, but this building isn't as opulent as their residence.

"How did anyone unwelcome penetrate a place like this?" I ask curiously.

He wags a finger in my direction. "Good question. Very good question, indeed."

"Had to have been someone inside, then?" I suggest.

He nods. "I think the same. Someone got into the knickers of a teacher, who let someone in. Someone untrustworthy,"

I frown. "That would be terrible," I tell him. "Why would anyone do such a thing?"

"Why indeed," he mutters, and his eyes shutter. "Now no more questions, lass." He's answered more than I expected.

I sit quietly, easily falling into silence that I'm comfortable with. When we arrive, it's unlike it is at his home. There are no servants come to take our things, but rather guards at the gate. The men take their own bags and traipse up the hill to what looks like a big entryway door. As we arrive, young men watch from afar as we enter, sturdy, fearless teenaged boys with the look of both youth and responsibility lining their faces. One boy looks like the clear leader of the rest, tall, with a barrel-like chest and a booming voice.

"What's the craic?" he says to Nolan, jerking his chin in greeting. "Come to investigate, have you?"

Nolan nods soberly, and I think the most disconcerting part of all of this is how serious Nolan is. I've never seen him look like that.

Keenan turns to the tallest boy and nods. The boy looks a bit abashed, as if he knows who Keenan is and doesn't quite know how to respond.

"Grady," Keenan greets. "Alert Malachy we've arrived, will you?"

The boy nods eagerly. "Yessir," he says, taking off a trot. Keenan gestures for another boy. I watch, mesmerized, as they all obey his command. "Lachlan, I'd be remiss if we didn't chat while I'm here. Be prepared to come when I summon you, aye?"

"Aye, sir," the boy says, looking both proud and a bit nervous. He swallows.

Keenan commands this small army as well.

We enter the building and go to a vacant room on the first floor, a small room with a queen-sized bed, a toilet behind a small door, and a tiny sitting area. Keenan smirks. "And this is the largest of the lot."

"It's big enough," I say with a shrug. To my surprise, he spins me around and pulls me to his chest, burying his face in my hair and breathing in deeply. He does this sometimes, as if breathing me in cleanses, or somehow gives him strength. I don't know how. I don't know why. But I easily meld to his embrace and lay my head on his chest.

He doesn't speak at first, just holding me. I hold him back, wrapping my arms around his sturdy body and allowing him to breathe me in.

"I've missed you," I whisper truthfully.

He nods. "Thank you for that. You've no idea what it's like to come home to you. You breathe life back into me when the day's drained it from my very limbs."

I look up at him, at the bright intensity of his eyes, and rest my hand against the stubble on his cheek.

"That might be the most beautiful thing anyone's ever said to me."

He smiles at that, his eyes crinkling at the edges and the corners of his beautiful mouth quirking up. "I can do better than *that*," he says. "I've a question for you, Caitlin. Something that's been pressing on me since that day I found you in the garden."

I hold his eyes, preparing myself for whatever it may be. In this short span of time, I've grown to love the honesty between us, the unquenchable flame that flares to life when we draw near to one another. I feel it now, the pull in my gut that consumes me when he's near.

"Alright, then," I say simply. "Have at it. But I'll have you answer a question for me as well."

"That isn't how we play this game," he says, but his eyes are twinkling for a moment before he sobers. "My question, lass. If you knew that your safety and the safety of others was contingent on your being my wife, would you do it?"

I'm so astounded at the monumental question; I stare at him in stunned silence.

Marry this beautiful, brutal, vicious man?

"Would I... would I have a choice?" I ask. Though he's tender with me, I'm still his prisoner, and I can't forget that.

I watch his eyes grow cloudy for a moment, and a muscle ticks in his jaw before he responds.

"No."

"Well, then, why ask? You have your answer," I say, my heart sinking at his response. "But it wouldn't be for love," I say stoutly. I try to pull away, but he won't allow it, his grip on me tightening. He pulls me closer to him, so that my body is flush against his, and I can see the little flecks of gold in the intensity of his eyes. I'm reminded immediately of how strong he is, how easily he could hurt me.

"It never is," he says tightly. "Never."

"Is that right? You're the expert on this?" I throw back at him, unable to stop myself.

"A naïve, innocent virgin like you is?" he says. The barb stings more than it should, more than I like to admit. "You watch that smart mouth of yours."

"Let me go," I say, suddenly angry. "I don't want to—" but he silences me when his mouth slams down on mine. It's the first time he's kissed me in days, and I'm instantly swooning. I hate that I am. I try to fight against it, to tell myself not to let him sway me, but

205

when I feel the soft, insistent, brutal clash of his lips on mine, my body revolts against my mind and begins the slow surrender.

Tears of anger and hurt blur my vision. I try to push him away, try to resist the enigmatic pull of his body to mine, but it's impossible. He's got an impenetrable grip on me I can't break, and no matter how hard I push against him, it's no use.

"Mmmph," I say, trying to pull away, but he only holds me tighter and backpedals until my legs hit the bed and we fall in a heap. Holding himself on one arm, he braces himself above me with the other, effectively caging me in. He pulls his mouth off mine long enough to glare at me, his face all lines and angles, the brutally, savagely beautiful face of a fallen angel.

I know he could rape me. He could force himself on me or break my bones with one casual swipe of his massive hand. It'd be laughably easy for him to over-power me, with those muscles and strength and the biological advantage of being a man. But that doesn't mean I have to cave to him, give into his every whim like I'm some spineless woman. I've submitted to him. I've trusted him. Against all logic and reason, I've even *fallen* for him. But marriage? He won't get that so easily from me.

He holds my jaw in his huge hand, as if to keep my gaze from straying. Well, that's simple enough. I close my eyes.

"Caitlin," he warns. I turn my head to the side.

"Open those eyes and look at me, or I'll take you straight across my knee." He would, too, and I know it. I flush at the thought of being spanked in this room, likely overheard by any others nearby. With a reluctant sigh, I open my eyes, but I glare right back at him.

"Listen to me," he says. "It isn't just for fun or show. But we—"

A knock sounds at the door. "Always *fucking* interrupted." He curses angrily, pushing himself off me but pointing a finger in my direction as if to remind me, we aren't finished yet. I sit up with as much dignity as I can muster and try to smooth my skirt, when he opens the door.

"Malachy," Keenan growls with a sigh.

A large, tall man with short, iron-gray hair and matching steely gray eyes enters the room. Unlike most of the men Keenan spends time with, this one's clean shaven and a bit older. Keenan shows him respect like he does his dad, inclining his head to welcome him, though his jaw tightens. He sighs and gestures toward me. "Meet Caitlin."

The man enters the room, his gray eyes twinkling, and bows his head toward me. His eyes quickly take in my tousled hair and rumpled dress, but he only says, "Pleased to meet you, Miss Caitlin." I have the distinct impression this man's not often gentle or quiet, and this is a stretch for him.

"Caitlin, meet Malachy," Keenan says tightly. We were interrupted and he's none too pleased about it.

"Was I interrupting something?" Malachy asks, and the amused twitch of his lips makes me think for a moment he either knows he did or wishes he had. He's like an overgrown, stern leprechaun, full of mischief and mayhem.

"You did," Keenan says, his gaze swinging back toward me. "But we'll resume our discussion later."

"Will we, then," I say quietly, meeting his gaze with conviction. I've gone along with more than I should have, and this time, I'm not acquiescing as easily. I don't know what I expected but being married to a man like him wasn't it.

Malachy's gaze swings from Keenan to me, then back again, and he gives a quick nod before turning back to Keenan. "We've cleared a meeting space in the main community room to bring you all up to date," he says, and the jovial look he had in his eyes just moments ago vanishes. He looks suddenly older, when he brings his hand to his nose and pinches the bridge as if to ward off a headache.

"Aye," Keenan says. He turns to me and crooks a finger, snapping out an order. "Caitlin, come here."

I know I'm already pushing him with my reluctant obedience, that the promise of punishment hovers. I further know that disobeying him in front of Malachy would be a serious infraction. Still, I'm angry with him. So I push myself off the bed and stomp over to him, letting my steps slap on the hardwood floor. To my shock, he takes me by the arm, swings me out in front of him, and cracks his hand hard against my backside. My cheeks flame, and I gasp, turning away so I don't have to look at the other man.

"Keenan," I say in a mortified whisper.

"Drop the attitude, lass," he says sternly. "I'll have none of it. We're to meet with my men, and after, the boys under my charge. You can check the surly attitude at the door and show obedience, if you know what's good for you."

"Is that a threat?" I ask, still angry with him.

Pulling close enough to gather my hair in his fist, he tugs my ear to his mouth, his voice low and seductive but laden with steel. "It's an oath, sweet girl. A pledge. It would make my day to have an excuse to punish you in front of my brothers."

I. Am. *Mortified.*

Malachy walks ahead of us to open the door, and *my God,* the corners of his mouth twitch, but he's noted every detail, I've no doubt. I will never be able to look the man in the eye again. I open my mouth to speak, but my tongue is tied, and I don't know what I would say anyway.

Keenan tugs. A reminder. A promise.

"Yes, sir," I manage to whisper. The *jerk.*

At that, he softens, the tightness at his mouth slackens, and he kisses my temple. "Good girl," he approves, and even though I'm angry, even though I'm embarrassed, even though I still want to smack his beautiful face, my chest warms with the praise.

This place is nothing like the opulent rooms at his home. Though impeccably clean and well built, it's simpler. Instead of uniformed servants ready to do what he says, there are students mulling about, and women who look like they could be teachers or administrators talking to the students and giving instructions. I catch the eye of one, a younger woman with wide blue eyes and a freckled nose, glasses perched on the very end. She sees Keenan and grows still, her eyes growing as large as dinner plates as her eyes go from me to him.

"Mr. McCarthy," she greets in a soft, high-pitched voice. "Welcome."

Keenan looks surprised to see her there, as if he's never noticed her before. "Thank you," he says, but he doesn't know her name. It's funny what women notice. He has not a clue who she is, yet it's clear to me she's smitten with him. She clutches papers to her chest, watching him walk by, and something in her deflates when her eyes drop to his hand holding mine.

"Caira," Malachy says. She looks flustered and blushes pink when Malachy greets her. "We're having a meeting in the main hall, and I'll speak to the staff this evening. Please send out an email to alert everyone, will you?"

"Certainly, sir." Her eyes go once more to Keenan, who still looks oblivious that she's watching him.

Do they all admire him, this powerful leader of The Clan? And somehow, watching the men and women and children who clearly revere him, I can't help but look at him with new eyes. Tall and muscled, his dark brown hair cut short and swept to the side, those vivid eyes of his the only angelic part of him. He's the epitome of power, handsome enough to be a prince from a far-off land. But if he's earned the respect of others around him, there's more than stunning good looks about him.

The teenaged boys that mull about know him, too. Several nod in greeting, and a few have the nerve to speak to him, the older ones. "Lachlan," Keenan calls across the corridor, when the boy we saw on arrival walks by. "I want a word this evening. Seven o'clock."

The boy maintains eye contact, an act of bravery, no doubt. "Yes, sir."

I think of what Keenan asked me earlier.

Would I marry him if the safety of others and my own depended on it?

Would that boy's safety be at risk as well?

Maybe I shouldn't be so stubborn. Maybe I should hear him out.

What choice do I have?

Chapter Seventeen

Keenan

I hate that so much is out of my control. I know I have to marry Caitlin, and I know I'm not giving her a choice, but damn if I don't want the girl not to fight me so.

I've taken the lives of men who threatened to undermine The Clan without regret, without remorse even. Why does it seem so difficult to force the woman's hand in marriage? I'm preoccupied when we go to our meeting, Caitlin's hand in mine. I'm dimly aware of those hovering about us, noticing our presence. It's not unusual for any of us to come here at the weekend, but it is for us to come in such large numbers.

I'm a million miles away, when I realize Malachy's ushering us into the large meeting room. There's an electric kettle and paper cups in one corner of the room, a small table set up with scones and biscuits, and folding chairs. Nolan and Boner were sent here before us, fulfilling the orders I gave last week. They sit beside each other, stonily angry. The assault came while they were here, and I've no doubt they feel the weight of that. Tully sits beside them.

Malachy stands before the group. All of us know him, as every one of us was trained by him. He greets everyone cordially. I pull out a chair for Caitlin and point for her to sit beside me. She's the only woman present, and isn't part of The Clan, but I won't allow her to be anywhere but right here. Some of my men look at her curiously, but no one questions.

"Fill us in, brother," I tell Malachy.

The room grows silent.

"Thursday evening, one of our teachers, Caira's sister Monica, went out on what was supposed to be a date," Malachy says. "At least that's what Caira tells us now. She didn't come home that night, and the next morning, Caira found her beaten and raped, and left by the entrance to the school."

The men around me curse, and Cormac's on his feet, pacing, his fists clenched. There's nothing that brings out his most vicious side than a woman in distress.

I feel my body tighten with Caitlin's as she sits up straighter, her eyes wide and scared.

"She can't speak, can't tell us what happened, but has managed to write a few things out. It seems she met a man at the pub last weekend who asked her out. No idea who he was or what his plan was, but that's the story thus far."

"Go on," I tell him. "There's more."

He recounts half a dozen transgressions against the teachers on staff since then. Tires slashed. Another assault. Threats, and a theft. My men simmer with anger as the news is relayed. These women are our sisters, cousins, and friends.

"Cowards," Cormac says, his dark eyes glowering. "Fucking cowards."

"And why? Do we have any word about who or why?"

Malachy turns to me. "I've my suspicions, but we have no proof yet. Have you angered anyone?"

I look to Caitlin. Have the Martins already gotten word that she's been taken by us? Has anyone seen her, and deciphered where she came from?

I shrug. "I anger lots of people, Malachy. You know this."

He nods. "I do. But these acts aren't accidental."

"The information you found," Caitlin says, her eyes on the room around her. Her clear, musical voice immediately captures everyone's attention. "The details you thought I stole from you. Were they due to anyone? Do the men who were waiting on them know you've retained them?"

It's unheard of for a woman to speak at a meeting, but she makes a fair point, so I allow it.

"They must," Cormac says. "'Tis no secret we went to the lighthouse, and if anyone was waiting on the information, they were sorely disappointed."

"Exactly," Caitlin says. "Could it be they believe you stole something that belongs to them?"

"Likely," I say. "And if they see you, their suspicions will be confirmed."

It has to have been the Martins. *Has* to.

"So we set them up," Nolan says. "Make it look like we've gone back. A few of us remain and wait to ambush. When they strike again, we attack. Interrogate. Get answers."

"Has anyone questioned Monica about identities?" I ask Malachy.

"Aye. Naturally. But the name and details she gave us were shite. The man lied to her."

Not a surprise.

I dislike sending my men home. There's power in numbers. But Nolan has a fair point. If we're to draw them out, we need to make them feel confident enough to do it.

I give out my orders, retaining Nolan, Cormac, and Tully on the premises, and Carson and the rest are instructed to keep me informed when they arrive back home. I give strict orders to Malachy that the staff is not to leave without a guard on them. We disperse, my men leaving, and Caitlin sits primly, waiting for me to finish. In silence, I take her hand and we go to the dining hall, where we eat our meal served by the staff on campus.

I signal for Lachlan to join us. I have to give the boy credit. He's unabashed by being beckoned by me, and though there's a faint flush to his cheeks, he comes bravely.

"Sit, lad," I instruct. I have a chance to observe both Caitlin and Lachlan. I make a bold declaration. "Meet my betrothed."

She doesn't even flinch but stretches her hand out to him to shake it. "Pleased to meet you, Lachlan."

"And you, miss," he says, pulling out a chair and sitting down. He's a large, strapping boy, orphaned at infancy but related to The Clan by blood, his father my cousin. He's got a shock of brown hair and bright hazel eyes, a burly lad who'll serve us well.

I ask him about his studies, and after he's filled me in, I ask him some more pressing questions.

"You were written up many times for your temper early in the term, Lachlan," I admonish. The boy appropriately hangs his head but nods. Caitlin watches both of us carefully. "A man does well to rein in his temper. I've heard you've improved, but not enough."

"Aye, sir. I'm sorry, sir," Lachlan says, his hands flat on his knees while he accepts his chastisement.

"Any man can rail in anger or fury," I continue. "It takes a much stronger man to know how or when to act. Do you understand me?"

He looks up at me and nods. "Aye, sir."

"Good," I tell him. "You continue your studies and I want a full report at the end of the month on your studies and behavior. You have the strength of character and integrity to make a fine leader in our Clan. Understood?"

His eyes are bright with hope as he nods eagerly. "Aye. Yes, sir."

My tone sharpens. "But if I don't get a good report, if I hear of even one instance of you losing your temper again, you'll answer directly to me." He blanches, but to his credit swallows hard and doesn't break eye contact. "Yes, sir. Thank you, sir."

"Good lad," I excuse him. "Go with your mates and remember, Lachlan. You are the only one who has the power to control yourself. That power is not in Malachy's hands, nor mine, nor anyone else's."

I dismiss him, and don't realize Caitlin's listened to every word until she takes my hand in hers.

"You'll make a good father someday, Keenan McCarthy."

I look at her in astonishment, surprised at the warmth in her tone.

"Will I?" I can't think of having children, not now. The sudden image of a babe in Caitlin's arms, tucked to her breast and swaddled in blankets, takes me by surprise. "What makes you say such a thing?"

She shrugs. "Well, you can be stern and unyielding, but there's benefit to that. Children need discipline and structure. But you have a gentle, nurturing side to you as well."

I scoff. "Me? Nurturing? Bollox."

"It's true, Keenan," she insists, her pretty eyes wide and earnest. "A good father both structures and nurtures, and I've seen you do both. With your men. With the boys here."

I smile at her.

"Do you want children, lass?"

Her pretty face illuminates with the radiance of her grin. "Of course," she says. "Loads."

I choke on the tea I'm sipping. *"Loads?"*

"Well," she says, thoughtfully tapping her lip. "At least three or four."

Three or four. *Jesus, Mary, and Joseph.*

"Well that ain't *loads,*" I say, as if to justify it, and for some reason that tickles her. Her pretty, musical laugh rings out in the small room, capturing the attention of several of my men. My heart stirs, and I want to secret her away, just the two of us. I want to kiss her until her breast heaves with want, then make slow, heated, sweet love to her until she moans in pleasure. I want to put my babies inside her and raise them with her. I know now why arranged marriage and the like can work. Why the men of The Clan—my very own parents, even—have made it work, because I'm as confident in my ability to care for her as I am of anything.

I reach for her hand. "I want you alone tonight."

"You've a job to do," she reminds me quietly.

"Don't I know it," I say on a groan. "And do it I will, but when I return…"

She takes my larger hand in both of hers and squeezes, leaning closer to me. "I'll be there."

Does she think differently of what we've discussed, then? Does she realize that she has to marry me, that it's the only way to hold the Martin clan at bay? The only way to solidify me as Clan Chief? No. Of course she doesn't. It's my job to explain to her.

My men leave, except for the few I've instructed to remain. Caitlin goes off with Caira to one of the classrooms but stays within ear shot. She's never seen the inside of a classroom and is adorably fascinated by everything about the school. Caira is fascinated by *her*.

Caitlin is nothing like the women we typically wed, and at the same time she's everything I need. Intelligent and brave, honest and loyal. I realize then, this isn't just convenience, it isn't just what The Clan needs.

I'm falling for this woman.

Hard.

When night falls, we take our positions. Caitlin's in the room with me, sitting meditatively in a chair by the window, the book she borrowed from Caira momentarily forgotten.

"Keenan," she begins, her index finger tracing the raised, golden title on the cover.

"Yes?" I'm assembling my weapons, tucking them into the harness I wear, checking my ammunition.

"I've made a decision."

I look to her in surprise. "Have you, lass?"

"I've been thinking about it all day. I've decided not to fight the inevitable."

Her trick of speech makes me smile.

"How so?"

"You said that my marrying you will be for my safety and the safety of others," she says. "Can you explain that?"

219

"I can," I tell her, turning to face her. "Your mother was a Martin. Confirmed by both my mother and uncle. You've a right to Martin's inheritance and a place at his table, as his granddaughter. But the Martins are a ruthless bunch, our greatest rivals. If he knows you exist, your life is forfeit."

Bravely, so bravely, my lass holds my gaze and nods. "He would kill me, because I'm assuming he has another in my place?"

She's a smart girl. "Aye, lass."

"And how does my wedding you prevent any fallout?" she asks, tipping her head to the side adorably, like a little kitten, her long black hair gleaming.

"Clan law," I tell her. "He cannot touch a hair on the head of a Clan Chief," I explain. "If he does, his own life is forfeit. He has no son, so if his life is forfeit, his Clan must join with another."

Her brows furrow, and she nods. "Furthermore, how would my marrying you prevent danger coming to *others*?"

"Inevitable peace between The Clans, lass."

She works her lip, biting down meditatively, her book forgotten. "Even for the boys?"

"Aye. Especially the boys."

She nods, as if accepting this. "Honestly, Keenan," she says. "I have to admit, I don't know what else I would do with myself. The home I knew is no longer. By all intents and purposes, I don't even exist. I can't very well sail away and find a job, or traverse the endless terrain to find a job…"

What on earth is she talking about? I let her go on.

"I've no interest in living the life of a spinster," she says, and I swear the lass is so fetching, I want to gather her to me and kiss every inch of her. "I was lonely in the lighthouse. But with your family… I feel at home. I could… I could grow to love them."

I walk to her and take her hands, drawing her to her feet and close to me. "I wish I had the luxury of time with you right now, sweet Cait," I whisper. "I would show you how thankful I am. You've no idea what it means to be the wife of the Clan Chief, but I promise you. You'll want for nothing. You'll have the protection and respect of The Clan. And as mine, I'll take care of your every need."

I gather her face in my hands, bend, and brush my lips to hers. She closes her eyes and kisses me back, gentle and sweet. She tastes like sugar-dusted shortcake, rich and sweet and decadent.

I love you.

I don't say it. I don't love her, not yet, though I know the tiny seeds of love have been planted. With time and attention, perhaps they'll grow.

Nay. With time and attention, they're sure to grow.

I pull away with reluctance when a knock sounds at the door. Malachy and I will take our positions, prepared to ambush if our women are attacked tonight. Caira and a few others have planned to go to a local pub, to draw out the attackers. Caira's afraid, but Malachy assured her we've got this under control. That we'll keep them safe. The girls are wired, my men armed.

"Take me with you," Caitlin says.

I snort, the very idea preposterous. "Are you out of your mind?" I shake my head.

She doesn't hesitate. "Then let me go with the girls."

I narrow my eyes on her, but I can't help but smile. She knew I wouldn't take her with me, but perhaps thought she could manage another way. I look about the small room. We don't have enough men to do detail inside and out.

"You were hedging your bets, weren't you?"

"Hedging my what?"

I slide my hand up the edge of her dress and cup her bottom. "You were playing me. Manipulating me."

I know I've hit my mark when her cheeks pink, or maybe it's because of the punishing grip on her arse.

"Well. I like to think it was a form of *reason*," she says. "Plus, Keenan, you do know that I've never been with... friends? On a night out like this before?"

"It's hardly a night out, lass. It's to draw out the perpetrators."

"True, but I trust you. You won't let anyone hurt me."

There's no use hiding her from the Martins anymore. I'm going to make this woman mine, and the sooner we do that, the better.

"Of course I won't." I sigh. "Fine, then. You can go with Caira, but you do exactly what I say."

"Yes," she says, pulling away so she can get changed, but I grab her wrist and yank her over.

"Not *yes*," I correct.

She blinks. "Yes, sir. Of course, sir. Will you still have me call you that when we're married?"

"Aye." My dick hardens. I want to fuck this woman so badly I ache, my hunger for her ravenous. "I'll have you do loads of things when we're married."

Her eyes widen momentarily, and she bites her lips. "Well, there's that," she says. I laugh out loud and kiss her pretty mouth, before we prepare to go.

Tonight. Tonight, I'll have this woman, my future wife.

It's with great trepidation I allow Caitlin to go out with Caira, arm in arm. Though they're wired and being watched, I don't like how easily they could be harmed, especially given what's happened to the other girls most recently.

As Captain, I'm the one who should oversee any type of sting, but not tonight. Tonight, I insist on being the man on them, nearby, prepared.

The first half of the night goes off without a hitch. I'm in the cramped black car outside the pub, listening to Caitlin in my earpiece. The other girls enjoy her company. How could they not? She's friendly and kind, intelligent and quirky. She's damn near the cutest fucking thing I've ever seen.

I wonder if we've hit amiss with this sting, when we enter the third hour of the girls' night out without so much as a snare.

"Anything at all, Keenan?" Malachy asks in my ear.

"Nothing."

"Shite."

"Patience," I tell him.

"Fucking grasshopper telling the master, eh?"

I snort. "Something like."

"Listen up, lads." It's Nolan. He's disguised at the bar, and though I've told him to lay off the drink, I've no doubt he's snuck a shot or two in. We go silent. It's then that I hear a man's voice talking to the girls. I have to force myself to stay where I am, not to run in there and yank my lass back to safety and protection.

"He's one of 'em," Nolan says. "I can see his feckin' ink from here, telltale mark of a Martin."

My pulse spikes. We suspected the Martins were at play in this, but if any of them see and recognize Caitlin…

"Caitlin safe?"

"Aye, brother," Nolan says, his tone amused. "You know it."

I don't fucking know it, but she'd better be.

There's the sound of the girls getting up and coming outside. I wait. They're at the door, I can see them from where I am. They're walking to their cars. The man who was speaking to them accompanies them out. My body goes rigid in anticipation, prepared for the ambush. Fucking hell, I hope they give me a reason to strike.

They don't. Not yet. The girls get into their car, and it's when the car pulls away, I see a car begin to follow them. *Not* ours.

My own car purrs along at a safe clip behind them, marking what happens, when another, larger car pulls alongside the first.

"You girls safe?" I say into the mic.

Caitlin's clear voice speaks aloud. "They're following us, Keenan."

"Aye. We've got you covered, lass."

With great reluctance, I allow more distance between my car and the girls', giving the Martins enough rope to hang themselves.

I don't see it coming. Peeling around the corner at a breakneck speed, a car comes straight at the girls. I hear their screams, the squeal of tires. Their car is sideswiped, skidding along until it slams into the guardrail. Six hooded men exit the vehicle.

I'm driving as fast as I can, and Nolan and Cormac are on my tail, but I can't get to them fast enough. They're too far away. Too *fucking* far away.

I peel after them, throw the car in park, open the door, and my gun's in hand, pointed at the perpetrators. They've already got the girls, manhandling them into the waiting cars, when I shout.

"Hands off! Fucking hands off them!"

They move faster.

Caira's shoved into the car despite her fighting back, and a second girl goes in with her. I shoot at the tires, and my mark is solid. The tires deflate. They will not fucking get away. Nolan's at my side and Cormac on my right, and in seconds, we've got them surrounded.

"Fuck!" Nolan screams as a gunshot rings out, narrowly missing him. I get a good aim at one and pull the trigger. The girls scream when glass explodes and blood splashes on the ground. My aim was pure. The man holding Caitlin's shot straight between the eyes. He falls to the ground, and she comes with him, but she's still flanked by men.

"Weapons down," one shouts. "Weapons down or we shoot the girls."

Nolan and Cormac look my way. We're outnumbered. Caitlin meets my eyes, hers filled with trust and bravery. She nods. Christ, she's going to do something, but I don't know what. I open my mouth to tell her no, not to do something reckless and dangerous, but she's already moving. With an ear curdling scream, she falls to the ground and lunges for her assailant's knees. He crumples on top of her, but she doesn't lose her head. She grabs his arm and bites.

He howls, rears back, and whacks her with the butt of his gun across her head. She whimpers but doesn't release him. I'm blind to anything but killing this man, of releasing my woman and ending the man who hit her. In two strides, I've got him by the neck. He's purple, flailing, when I point my gun at his temple and pull the trigger. He slumps to the ground, and I look up to see Nolan and Cormac with guns to the heads of the two remaining men. The others lie dead.

We're panting and silent for a moment.

"All Martins?" I ask.

"Aye," Nolan says.

"Bring them back for questioning."

Chapter Eighteen

CAITLIN

I knew that being with a man like Keenan would mean something like this would happen. I just didn't know it would be... well, quite like *that*. I shudder at the memory of the puddles of crimson blood and vacant eyes of the deceased.

When I close my eyes, I see them. When I open my eyes, I see them. I can still taste the metallic blood of the man I bit.

We're back at the school, and Keenan won't let me go, even as he issues orders like a drill sergeant. "In the meeting room," he says. "And I want Lachlan with us."

"Keenan, he's a child," Cormac begins, but Keenan cuts him off.

"The boy needs to earn his spurs. He's eighteen years old and old enough to drink, old enough to vote. He won't kill, but he'll learn to interrogate. Now get him."

I shudder. I've been to the interrogation room back at their home, and I can only imagine what sort of wicked things they do.

I don't know how I feel about him summoning Lachlan. He's only a boy, and yet... Keenan has a point. They were trained at a young age, and if he's to learn their code of conduct... still, it troubles me, all of it.

I wish I didn't like these men, these fierce, vicious men who flaunt the law and dwell in darkness. But I do. Not only do I like them, I have a strange sense I can't ignore that I'm somehow meant to be here. That I belong. I've never even so much as uttered a curse word or driven a car, I'm as naïve as humanly possible, and yet I feel I belong among this family of criminals.

Maybe I'm going mad.

I watch, under Keenan's protective hold. He's got me pinned against him so tightly it's hard to breathe, and yet I need the weight of his arm and strength of his body at my back. I watch as the men drag their prisoners, bloodied and sulking, through the doors of the hall. Just as they bring the men in, one turns his head sharply to me, his eyes wide as if he's seeing a ghost.

Uh oh.

"Keenan," I say quietly, as they close the door behind their prisoners. "You need to know... the second one. He recognized me."

"Aye," Keenan says, and he seems unperturbed.

"But what if he goes back and—"

He stills, his voice tight and sober, and his stern look darkens. He doesn't meet my eyes when he mutters, "He won't be going back, lass."

Of course not. No, he won't. A chill runs through me at the realization.

"You'll wait for me tonight, Cait," Keenan says, not a question, though there's a hint of a plea in his voice.

"Of course."

"I may be a while." He turns me toward him and kissing the top of my head fiercely.

"Take your time."

He grabs my chin so tightly I gasp, but I know he isn't angry with me. Staring into my eyes, I don't know what he's trying to see, but I don't look away. I don't blink.

"Are y'alright?" he whispers. "You are my brave girl." His men drag their prisoners to where they want him and rouse those they need. There are phone calls and curses, doors opening and closing, and soon, it's just the two of us.

"I'm fine," I lie, my voice tremulous. I'm not fine. I was attacked tonight, I bit a man straight through skin, and the memory makes me want to vomit. But I've agreed to marry into this clan, into this vicious group of warriors who surround me like modern-day Vikings. I've agreed to become his wife, for my safety and for the safety of all. And for the first time since any of this began, as Keenan's eyes meet mine, it dawns on me.

My mother was a Martin. My mother was born into a situation just like this. It's unlike anything I could have ever imagined or wanted, and I know it's disordered and dangerous. But part of me is proud that I've come from sturdy stock, even if her family are rivals to the one I'll become. Something tells me she'd understand. I never knew my mother, but in that one brief moment in time, I feel as if maybe I understand her. Maybe she'd be proud of me for being brave, as Maeve is.

"You're not fine, lass," he says sternly, rubbing his thumb along my cheek. "But you will be. And tonight, when I come back to you, I'll make it better."

I swallow. "I trust that you will," I say with as much courage as I can muster. "Now, go, Keenan. Do what you have to. And come back to me."

He closes his eyes while drawing in a breath, then exhales with a sigh. Bringing his mouth to my ear, he whispers, "I'll make you happy you said yes."

And then his mouth's on mine in a kiss too brief, before he's handing me off to his brothers. It's not lost on me that he doesn't send guards, but his own flesh and blood to watch over me. In these circumstances, he doesn't trust anyone more than Cormac and Nolan, and it pleases me somehow. These men are to be my brothers as well. Cormac stands on my left and Nolan to my right as they walk me back to the bedroom.

I forget how big Cormac is, all burly and bearded, until he has to duck to get into the building. He's a gentle giant, though, this one. I heard him plea for the inno-cence of the boy Keenan's to teach. And though I know he can be firm and unyielding, the man's got a soft spot.

Nolan's got a twinkle in his eyes when he opens the door for me and ushers me in.

"You look a bit shell-shocked," he says. "Could use a bevvie."

"You get her plastered, he'll kick yer ass," Cormac warns.

Oh, dear. They want me to drink with them.

"You get me plastered, he'll kick *my* arse," I retort, which makes both the men burst into raucous laughter.

"There's a world 'a difference between tipsy and banjaxed," Nolan says with a smile.

"And you've got that world in your pocket, aye?" Cormac says.

We're back at the room, and I'm feeling suddenly exhausted. "How long do you think he'll be?"

"Good long while," Nolan says, pulling up a chair and taking a flask out of his pocket. "Drink up, girlie. He won't mind you takin' the edge off." His green eyes twinkle at me, and he pushes the tufts of blond hair off his forehead.

Maybe he has a point. Maybe it'll be good to "take the edge off."

I reach for the flask, open it, and take a long pull. Oh my, I'm not prepared for liquid fire. I gasp and sputter, and in a very unladylike manner, spew the stuff all over the room. My throat burns, and flames lick at my chest.

"Oh!" I cough and wheeze. "Goodness!"

"It's goodness alright." Nolan slaps his leg and guffaws, but Cormac's concerned.

"Christ, Nolan," he says, his dark brows drawing together. "Keenan'll kill you if you hurt her."

"Hurt her? I'm givin' her a taste of drink is all. Didn't know she'd suck it down and near choke."

Cormac pats my back with concern. "Y'alright?"

I try to sit up primly and wipe my hand across the back of my mouth. I'm not going to let one stupid encounter with alcohol dissuade me from learning how to do this right. I'm going to be the wife of the Chief. "Let's try that again."

Nolan grins. "Now easy, girl," he says. "Little goes a long way, aye?"

I nod. "Aye." I take a small sip, letting the slightly sweet, bracing liquid seep into my mouth before I swallow. It travels in a trail of heat down to my chest, and I sigh. It *is* nice. I feel warmed through and invigorated. Nodding, I take another sip, then another.

"Easy, there," Cormac says, gently taking the flask out of my hand. "Remember that line between tipsy and banjaxed? Tiny thing like you'll get knocked on yer arse in minutes, drinking like that."

I nod sagely. I feel somehow braver and more knowledgeable. "Very wise, Cormac. Very wise."

I'm not so sure why both of them are hiding smiles, but I see them.

I sit back on the bed, kick off my shoes, and sigh.

"What will they do with the men they brought back?"

"You don't wanna know that, girl," Nolan says, taking a pull from the flask that would knock me on my backside for a week. He sighs in contentment, leans back, and laces his fingers at the back of his head.

"Aye," Cormac agrees. "What goes on behind closed doors is best staying behind those doors."

"They won't come out," I say, trying to face the truth with bravery. Nolan looks to Cormac, and they don't answer.

"Let's pass the time telling her about Keenan," Nolan says with a grin. Cormac smiles back, pulls a chair out beside his brother, turns it around and straddles it.

"Now yer talkin'."

We talk easily, while they share stories of their youth. They tell me of their travels, their schooling, how Keenan was the star football player and all the girls would pine for him, how he'd have one girl at the front door and one at the back and Nolan would manage to sneak one of them away. How they snuck out of school to party and how Malachy caught them red-handed. How Keenan, as eldest, would boss them around and how they'd play tricks on him in retaliation, how the three of them got into a fight and knocked Maeve's rocking chair straight through the living room window and spent all summer earning money to pay back the repair.

They tell me stories that make me laugh so hard I wipe tears from my eyes, stories that make me wish I knew them all when they were younger. And to think, while all this happened, I was secreted away just miles from their home, drinking tea and reading books and wondering what the world was like outside my window.

These men are to be my brothers, I remind myself again. I like that.

They pass me the flask, and I take a few small sips, and soon I'm pleasantly warm and at ease. I lay on the bed with my hands under my cheek, listening to their deep voices and lilting brogues, and don't realize I've fallen asleep until I feel one of them tuck a blanket around me. I try to open my eyes, but they're too heavy. They shut off the lights, but don't leave. I'm dimly conscious of Cormac's heavier footsteps pacing by the door and Nolan pacing by the window.

Despite the circumstances, despite the raw brutality of the night we've had and will have yet, I feel safe, and warm, and comfortable.

So this is what it's like to have someone care for you. This is what it's like to have family.

I doze in and out, and I'm half asleep when there are footsteps outside the door. Cormac opens it, and the men speak in hushed voices. I hear Keenan's familiar voice, and try to open my eyes, but they're so heavy. A pleasant sort of warmth fills my chest just hearing him speak to his brothers, then the door shuts, and I hear him come to me.

"Let's get you ready for bed, sweet girl," he says, his voice tired but clear as day. He lifts the blanket. "You're still fully clothed."

I turn over toward him and yawn widely. "I didn't want to get changed into those skimpy little night-clothes with your brothers here."

Bending down, he wraps me in his arms and holds me. "Good girl," he whispers in my ear. "That pleases me."

He pauses, then, "Caitlin, have you been drinking?"

I yawn again widely. "Mmm," I tell him. "Loads. I'm very sleepy and warm."

But he isn't amused. He takes my jaw in his large hand and I open my eyes with effort. "Loads?" he repeats.

I shrug. "Well. Loads for *me*," I say. I yawn again. "It just made me sleepy."

His beautiful eyes darken, but a corner of his lips quirks up. He leans in and kisses me questioningly, as if to taste me, his lips gentle and probing. "You taste like whiskey."

"Is that a good thing?"

He snorts with laughter, which pleases me. He can't be that angry, then. "There are worse things."

He lifts my arms, removing my dress, and it isn't until I'm sitting in front of him in my undergarments that I remember. Tonight was the night. How could I have forgotten? But that was before everything else that happened.

"Keenan?" I ask, as he reaches for my bra clasp, and helps me out of it.

"Yes?"

"Do you still... are we... do you want to..."

He slips the silky garment off and lays it at the foot of the bed, then reaches for the elastic waistband of my panties, but doesn't reply or move, his thumbs hooked into the fabric. The feel of his warm, sturdy hands undressing me with confidence, and the way his eyes roam hungrily over my body, makes me shiver.

"Shh, lass," he whispers. And I know then that is a yes. The plan hasn't changed. If anything, he wants to be with me more than ever. He needs me tonight.

"How did everything go tonight?" I ask him politely, even as pressure builds between my thighs and I clench them together. I shake with nerves and anticipation. I'm not sleepy *now*.

"As planned," he says. "We have answers, and tomorrow we'll have to make our move. Now no more questions, Caitlin. I don't wish to talk of anything else. The less you know the better."

There are so many questions I want to ask him, but I want to honor his request. He's had a tough night of it. And I know now it will be like this often, between the two of us, Keenan having a difficult evening, making a challenging decision, seeing the men he cares about hurt or worse, killed. And he'll want to come back to me. He'll need me to be ready for him. He'll need me to *need* him. To let him hold me, to let me absorb the darkness he dwells in and give him a glimpse of light.

I reach my hand out to touch his cheek. Closing his eyes, he holds my hand against him, brings my palm to his lips, and kisses me. A deep, abiding sense of longing pervades me, and I whisper, "Stars, hide your fires; Let not light see my black and deep desires."

His eyes flutter open, and he looks at me.

"Say that again."

I swallow and repeat the line from Macbeth, "Stars, hide your fires; Let not light see my black and deep desires."

"What is it?" he whispers.

"Shakespeare."

"Motherfucker."

I laugh out loud at his reaction, but he isn't laughing, he's dragging my panties down my legs and pulling them off my feet, his gaze fixed on mine. He stands and begins to remove his own clothing. There are specks of blood on his shirt, and a long, angry red scrape along his neck.

"Oh, Keenan," I say, sitting up. "You're hurt."

"I'm fine, lass," he says. "Hush, now."

He shrugs out of his shirt and undresses unhurriedly. I swallow when I note how hard he is, as if he's been waiting for this, as if he's been waiting for me. I have to be honest. I'm nervous about this, too.

But Keenan will be my husband. And he promised he'd take the very best care of me he can. That matters. I repeat the words he vowed to me, *"As mine, I'll take care of your every need."*

I wonder if it's odd, that he's about to take me as his own for the very first time after what he's done today. But I have no social cues or expectations to reference what we're doing, what we're planning to do. This is who he is, and though it might fly in the face of what's proper, I wouldn't know. So I accept him, just as he is. If there's anything I've learned in my limited view of life, from what I've learned in the pages of my books, it's that we need to love each other just as we are, without question or conditions. Just as they are.

I'll do my very best to do that. To love him as he comes to me. To love what he has to offer me. To be the woman he'll love back.

His clothes fall to the floor in a jumbled, forgotten heap, and he stands before me naked. Unblinking. His eyes focused on me as if I'm a puzzle he's trying to sort, and I notice for the first time since I met him, his hands are trembling.

I open my mouth to ask him if he's okay, if he's sure he doesn't need to see a doctor or something, when he puts his finger to his lips to remind me of what he said. A thin sliver of moonlight illuminates his beautiful green eyes, as bright as the depths of the Irish Sea, as he begins to walk toward me.

This is it. Tonight is the night he takes me as his own, and I don't need anyone to explain to me what that means.

"Keenan," I whisper, lacing my fingers together to keep my hands from shaking.

"Yes, lovely?" He kneels on one knee beside me and strokes his fingers through my hair.

I swallow hard. I like that. *Lovely.*

"I don't know what I'm supposed to do."

Leaning down, he laces his fingers at the back of my head and brings my ear to his mouth, the heat and vibration of his voice making me shiver. "Exactly what I tell you."

I close my eyes and nod. He kisses the shell of my ear, and I gasp when his tongue skirts the outer edge. He grasps my earlobe between his teeth and bites, the sharp pain quickly melding into trembling, expectant heat that suffuses my limbs.

238

Pressing one hand to my shoulder, he lays me down. My arms encircle his neck while he kisses his way down my jaw, fluttering, sensual caresses of his lips against my naked skin, down the column of my neck, then back up to my jaw on the other side.

"Tá mo chroí istigh ionat."

I love the sound of the ancient words, though I've no idea what they mean. I want to ask him what he said, what this means, but he's asked me to be quiet. I hold the words in my heart. Maybe I don't need to know what they mean. But he doesn't make me wait.

"Do you know any Gaelic at all, lass?"

I shake my head, running my fingers through his hair, and keen with pleasure when he kisses the valley between my breasts.

"My heart is in you. It means my heart is in you."

I close my eyes, overcome with emotion.

My heart is in you.

"That's beautiful," I whisper, but his finger comes to my lips to silence me.

"*You're* beautiful," he counters, framing my body with his and returning to my breasts. He drags his warm, soft lips under first one breast then the other, before his tongue laves my hardened nipple. I stifle a moan. It feels so good, the heat between my leg intensifies, the pounding need for pressure overtaking me, and it's like he knows this, the way he cups my backside and presses me to his hard length.

"I want you fully ready," he says. "Ready to take me."

"One more question?" I ask, then remembering what he's instructed. "Please?"

He nods. "Aye."

"Will it hurt?"

He holds my gaze, and his hand cups my breast. "It will hurt like this," he says. "Pay attention."

Pay attention? I'm hardly distracted. But I nod.

He brings his mouth to my nipple, clamps the peaked bud between his teeth, and gives a quick, sharp bite. I hiss in pain, but before it's even registered, he's suckling my nipple. The pain quickly shifts to pleasure. My pulse spikes, and I'm trembling beneath him.

"It will hurt, lass," he says, his voice tender but determined. "And then I'll make it better. But before then, I'll ensure you're ready for me."

I wonder what that means, but I've exhausted my limited questions. So I only nod. Holding my gaze, he returns to my breasts, licking and suckling, weighing them in his rough, large palms, until wetness forms between my thighs, and I'm swollen with need. Is this what he means? I'm slick and swollen and aching, though I'm still a little nervous.

He rocks his hips against mine, then kisses me, gently at first before he slides his tongue in my mouth. I shiver at the intimacy, my pulse racing. My eyes close involuntarily as I drown in his kiss, and my heart beats quicker.

He takes his mouth off mine to whisper in my ear, the guttural Gaelic of his homeland, and somehow the words prepare me as much as his ministrations.

"Spread your legs, lass."

I open my legs, welcoming his expert, purposeful touch. While suckling my nipples, he fingers my swollen folds. My hips writhe as ecstasy builds, needing more, so much more, when he dips his fingers lower. It feels so intimate, I duck my head from him, suddenly shy and nervous.

"Look at me, Caitlin," he orders, just as he thrusts two fingers into my core. "Christ, you're sopping."

Does that mean I'm ready?

I feel ready. But how would I know?

He sounds pleased with that, though, so I only nod. His eyes crinkle at the edges and he cups my jaw, bringing his mouth to mine again. My pulse quickens at the softness of his lips and roughness of his whiskers, his masculine scent pervading my senses. There's a hopeless possession in his kiss, as if he's staking his claim with his mouth on mine, and I can tell he's holding himself back, that he doesn't want to hurt me.

While still kissing me, he drags the heel of his hand down my belly, past my pelvis, and gently fingers the curls at my entrance, before he glides his fingers in my core once more. He pumps gently, in and out, sending frissons of heat and awareness through me.

Like that. It'll be like that, only his fingers are... much, much smaller.

All I've learned of human anatomy and biology, I learned from old, hardcover books from the library I read when I hit puberty. The dusty tomes were clinical and detached, and hardly prepared me for what I'm about to do.

He brings his mouth to my ear. "I want to fuck you, sweet girl. I want my cock inside you. *Now.*"

I nod. Even though I'm holding my breath in anxious fear, I want that, too. I want to feel it. I want to own this. I want the togetherness.

"I won't ever forget this, Caitlin," he whispers, his brogue thick with lust and need. "I won't ever forget how you gave this to me. That you trusted me."

"I will love you, Keenan. I may already."

As soon as I say the words, I want to take them back. Is that the least romantic thing any woman on the verge of giving up her virginity has ever said?

"I will love you as well, Caitlin. And I may already."

Then we're laughing and holding each other in this quiet interim before our moment, his forehead touching mine and our breaths mingling like wind and fog.

"Are you ready?"

I don't know. Am I? But trusting him means taking this leap of faith.

So I swallow my fear, and take a deep breath, and whisper the words I know he needs to hear. "Yes, sir."

It was the right choice.

He holds me to him, chest to chest, my naked skin against his hard, firm body. Bracing himself on one arm beside me, he glides the tip of his cock at my entrance, stroking up and down until I tremble with anticipation. I'm holding my breath, bracing for the pain he promised, but he takes it so slowly it's maddening. Just the very tip, then again. I spread my legs further, as if to silently welcome him in, and he takes the invitation. His hands come to mine, our fingers entwine, and he pushes his swollen cock inside me.

I gasp with the pain and sensation. I'm splitting in two, the ache between my thighs growing when he pumps his hips. He said he'd make it better.

"Relax," he breathes. "Don't tense, sweetheart."

I take a breath then let it out. He doesn't move at first, until I take another breath. I can't imagine how this would feel good. All I feel is an ache and fear, like someone's tearing me apart.

And then he shows me. And it's beautiful.

He glides out then in again, the pain still present but abating, the walls of my channel clenching around him. The frissons of pleasure he built earlier return, and I can't help but moan when pain and pleasure become one.

"Jesus, you're tight," he groans. "Christ, that sweet cunt..." his voice trails off. I've never heard these words and I know they're dirty, but it pleases me to know I please *him*. A man like Keenan joins love with possession, and I know as he takes me this means more to him than he can say.

My body aches and throbs with the need for more, and even as it hurts, the pleasure builds. *Pain can heighten pleasure,* he told me. And now, I think I finally understand how.

With perfect, gentle, but purposeful strokes, he glides in and out, his body trembling with the effort of holding himself back, filling me so tightly I'm stretched and aching. My pulse begins to quicken, my breaths shorten, and my skin begins to tingle.

And still he works his slow, deliberate magic, thrusting in and out and fondling my breasts, kissing my lips, my jaw, the column of my neck. I'm panting with desire when his body tightens. "Come with me, Caitlin," he growls in my ear. "Let yourself go." Another firm, glorious thrust, and I'm splitting apart, splintering, my breath caught somewhere between ecstasy and oblivion. He groans, his body tightens, and his hot seed lashes inside me. I close my eyes, hold his neck, and *fly*.

Spasms of pleasure ripple through me, weaving through my body and taking my breath away. He groans again, still pumping his hips, and my hands anchor on his hips, holding onto him for dear life as a second wave of ecstasy washes through me. It's exquisite and mesmerizing, and absolute utter perfection. I don't even realize I'm moaning out loud until he chuckles, but when he looks at me he sobers.

"You're crying. Oh, God, lass. Did I hurt you? I tried not to—"

I shake my head. "No," I say, still riding the aftershocks of bliss, my words coming in pants. "I mean it hurt, but it was perfect. I don't know why I'm crying. It was just... more intimate than I imagined somehow."

He holds my gaze for long seconds before he drops his head to mine and kisses me.

"Christ, woman. *Tá mo chroí istigh ionat.*"

Chapter Nineteen

Keenan

I've done terrible things on this earth. I've commanded an army of criminals without regret. And yet, somehow, somewhere I've done something good in my life to have earned this privilege. This woman. This moment.

Her tight, virgin cunt still tight around my cock, I kiss her in thanksgiving. I make a vow to never forget this, how she trusted me, how she granted me this gift.

My heart is in you.

I'm not a sentimental bloke, but I suppose Caitlin brings it out in me.

She's nearly asleep, still joined together, and I don't wish to hurt her anymore. I brush damp tendrils of hair from her forehead and kiss her gently.

"Let's get you ready for bed," I tell her. But before I take myself out, before I move away, she's wrapping her arms around my neck and squeezing.

"Thank you."

"Thank you? For what, lass?"

"For taking your time and making it memorable. Though I don't have much experience with these things, I suspect that isn't always the case."

Not always the case indeed. My first time was in the back of this very building, with a girl whose name I don't even remember.

"You deserve nothing less, lass," I say simply, and I mean it.

I gently draw myself out, noting there's little blood from her first time. Good. I don't want to frighten her, though I have to admit she's handled everything so far with such bravery. We clean up, dress, and both fall into bed exhausted after all that's happened. Before I sleep, I send a text to Malachy, with strict orders to have no one wake us in the morning. He'll see to it I'm obeyed.

I roll her over beside me, her thick, fragrant hair enveloping my senses. "You're like a black-haired version of Rapunzel," I say with a smile, my eyes too heavy to keep open.

"And you're the prince come to rescue me?"

Hardly. I chuckle just the same. "Naturally."

"The lighthouse would've been—" she yawns widely— "a suitable tower." She sighs, tucking her body closer to mine. "I'm glad you rescued me."

Our breath becomes slower, her body melded to mine, and I wrap my arms around her. I haven't held a woman like this ever, but Christ if I can tear myself away. She's permeating every inch of me, and I'm loathe to be separated. Somehow, miraculously, the horrors we've endured tonight fade into distant memory, as I fade off to sleep.

I wake the next day more rested than I remember being in a great long while, and she's already awake beside me. Her hair's wrapped all up in the sheets and my arms, and we silently laugh as we disentangle ourselves.

"Maybe I should get a haircut," she mutters.

"Don't you dare do such a thing."

She raises her brows. "Oh? Is that an order?"

"You cut this gorgeous hair of yours, and I'll take you straight across my knee." The way she laughs, she thinks I'm joking.

"Well, then. I'll have to remember that."

"And I'll have to show you the fun we can have with that hair."

She flushes a pretty shade of pink. I love when I can make her do that.

But duty calls. I get out of bed and tuck the blanket back around her. Answer my texts and phone calls, issue orders for us to ensure the safety of the women at St. Albert's when we return home, and answer my mother's questions about the wedding.

I take Caitlin's hand and lead her to the shower. She doesn't ask questions, while I mull over what we do next. We get ready for the day and dress, and I'm eager to get back home.

"Keenan?" she asks, drawing a hairbrush through her thick hair.

"Mm?"

"Will you let me come back here sometime? I like the women here. And the boys."

"Yes," I tell her. "But likely not for a while. I'm confident after last night we won't see any more attacks, but I don't want to test that theory. And we've much to do to prepare for the wedding."

She nods, turning away from me as she places the brush back in her bag. "Thank you," she says. "I suppose there's no rush."

I smile. "No."

"One more question, please."

I nod, fastening the buckle of my belt.

"Do you think you got me pregnant last night?"

It's not what I expected her to ask. I discarded the notion of protection, for she was a virgin and to be my wife. We welcome children quickly within Clan unions, to solidify our bond and The Clan itself.

"Don't know," I tell her, wanting to kick myself. "I should've discussed it with you ahead of time."

"Discussed what?"

"Birth control. Babies. Pregnancy."

"I'm assuming the Clan Chief is expected to procreate," she says meditatively, and I can't help but laugh out loud.

"What did I say?" she asks, smiling along with me.

"*Procreate,*" I repeat. "Yes, lass, prepare to *procreate* as often as humanly possible." I take a step toward her, cup the back of her head, and draw her fiercely to me for a kiss. "And you did say you wanted loads of babies."

"Well. Maybe not *today,*" she says, and I laugh out loud again.

"Fortunately, that's not the way it usually works."

My phone rings, and I've exhausted my luxury of silencing it, so I take the call. We make arrangements, head down to get some breakfast. It isn't lost on me how tightly she hugs Caira. I'll have to be sure that she does indeed get a chance to visit her again.

I beckon Lachlan to me. I need a final word before I leave. He looks tired, but a little older this morning, as if the events of the evening before matured him a little. I suppose they did.

"You were brave last night, son," I tell him. "I'm proud of you."

His chest expands, and he lifts his head up high. "Thank you, sir. I'm honored you had me."

I nod. "I was a lad of your age when I began the initiation. I'll be checking with Malachy to ensure you've kept yourself out of trouble. Do you understand me?"

He nods, slightly abashed. "Yes, sir. I will, sir."

"Good. And before I leave, I'm giving instructions to Malachy that you're to come to my wedding. It's my wish that you join The Clan in witnessing our vows. Aye?"

His eyes widen as large as saucers. "Yessir," he breathes. "Thank you, sir."

"Go on, now. Back to your breakfast and studies. Remember my instructions to you. Brave men keep their tempers in check. You've done it before, and you shall again."

"Yes, sir."

Caitlin squeezes my hand when I dismiss him. "You're like a mentor to him. Like an older brother."

I shrug. "It's how we do things with The Clan. We'd be weakened without the strength of the brotherhood."

"Yes," she says. "I can see that. I'm very eager to have your brothers witness our vows."

I kiss the top of her hand as Cormac comes to our table.

"Where's Nolan?" I ask, looking around the room.

He doesn't meet my eyes and mutters when he responds. "He's... a bit under the weather."

"How so?" I snap. I'll have the boy's head. Fucking Nolan.

"Hit the pubs last night after you left, and he—"

"Fucking hell," I mutter. "That's it. I've had it." I've contained my anger too long, withheld repercussions longer than I should have. If he were anyone else, he'd have suffered my wrath long before now. I point a

250

finger at Cormac. "You tell him if he isn't present at the meeting at home this afternoon, I will personally hunt him down and kick his arse from here to the armory. Understood?"

Cormac nods. He knows I mean it, and hell, I do.

"Aye, Keenan. Take it easy on him, though, he—"

"*No.*" I say angrily. "Relay the message."

There will be no more "taking it easy" on him.

Cormac nods and leaves. Nolan and I will have words before the day's out. Caitlin watches in silence.

"He drinks pretty hard, doesn't he?"

"Too hard. Irish men can drink any others under the table, but he takes it to another level altogether."

"He could hurt himself."

"That won't be necessary," I mutter. "Happy to do the job myself." Though I'm angry, I'm concerned above all. This has gone on long enough. No more.

Soon, we're heading back home.

I don't waste any time when we return. I call a meeting of The Clan and bring Caitlin with me. It's time that we told my men what we're planning. My father and mother are on board, but I want everyone to know.

"Keenan," my mother greets us just as we enter the meeting. Her eyes are bright, and she looks as excited as a schoolgirl. I kiss her cheek. She kisses me back, then holds my arm to get my attention.

"Yes?"

"I can begin the preparations, then?"

"Please do," I tell her. "We've no time to waste." Though the Martin men last night did not return home—and they never will—one of them recognized her. It's only a matter of time that Martin finds out who I've got here, and the sooner I stake my claim the better.

"Oh, I'm *so* pleased," my mother says, stifling a little squeal. She lets me go, reaches for Caitlin, and gives her a fierce embrace. "You're to be my daughter, sweet Cait." She kisses first one cheek, then the next, and the two chat excitedly for a brief moment before I pull her away.

"We've got to discuss this with the others," I tell her. "But please, expedite as much as you can, and spare no expense. Notify Father, and be sure we're ready within two days' time, aye?"

"Aye," she agrees, and with another squeal, she leaves.

"She's so happy." Caitlin looks at me with wide, curious eyes. "Does she... is it possible... does she really care so much about *me?*"

"Dear girl," I tell her, amusement laden in my tone. "Do you have any idea how much they love you?"

"Love me?" she says. "How? They hardly know me."

But they will. And simple, innocent women like her don't change their colors. She's already won the hearts of those she touches. She'll make an excellent woman of The Clan.

I shake my head and usher her into the room. "Just trust me, lass. They'll love you more deeply as they get to know you, but you've planted the seeds of devotion already."

She doesn't believe me, but perhaps someday she will.

I'm not prepared for her gasp when we enter the room, and how she draws closer to me, burying her head on my arm.

"Keenan," she whispers. "My God, there are so many. I had no idea."

I forget she isn't used to crowds of people like this. I hold her hand, but I won't coddle her. "Be brave, Caitlin," I tell her. "Face them. They are to be your people, too."

She closes her eyes briefly, before opening them, inhaling, and facing my men. I try to see what she sees, a sea of large, muscled, men of The Clan, their bodies marked with the ink of our people, symbolic Celtic knots and rings that identify us as men of the McCarthy line. They watch her with curiosity and respect.

"Hello," she finally says, her cheeks flushing as if she wonders if she spoke the right words.

A loud welcome greets her, and she falters a little. "Oh, my."

"Sit, lass." I point to a chair beside me.

I face my men and tell them everything. How we found her. What we found. How she's related to the Martins, and why it's essential we wed.

"Was she indeed responsible for spying?" Boner asks. He wants it clarified before all. I look to Caitlin before I answer, conscious of the fact that I haven't exonerated her.

I clear my throat. "No. We know it wasn't her, but the man who called himself her father. Jack Anderson."

Caitlin pales but doesn't speak. I watch her lips thin in a line that spells trouble.

I tell them of the wedding, where and when it will be, and after we've set up surveillance and everything we need, I dismiss them. She sits, her hands in her lap, and doesn't look at me.

"Come, Caitlin," I order, but she doesn't move.

"Caitlin," I warn, not liking that I have to tell her a second time. "You did well, lass. Now come."

Still, she doesn't move.

I step toward her and take her hand, giving her a sharp tug. "You know better than that, lass. When I give you an instruction, you—"

"You didn't tell me."

Gone is my quiet lass, her eyes alight with fire. She's waited until I dismissed my men to have words, and I give her that much credit. But she's furious with me. Her little hands are clenched in fists, and faint splotches of pink paint her cheeks.

She glares at me. "You've never told me I'm not your prisoner. You told me I had no choice but to marry you."

"Watch that smart mouth," I snap. "I'll not tolerate a wife who raises her voice to me. You know what I expect, Caitlin, and I won't warn you again."

But I don't think she's heard a word I've said. "All this time," she says, wagging her finger at me. "When did you *know* I wasn't a spy? I was there when you found out who my father was. I knew that much. But you haven't told me. How long have you known, Keenan? Hmm?"

"'Tis of no consequence," I say, shaking my head at her. "I kept you here for your own good, and I—"

"For my own good!" She throws my words back at me.

"That's twice now you've interrupted me. Do not interrupt me again." The girl's going the right way for a good spanking. "Even if you have a point, even if you've a right to be upset, you may not interrupt me or speak rudely."

I can tell she's warring within herself, her eyes still dancing with fury, when she gets to her feet and tries to stomp off. I reach for her arm to stop her. I won't allow this. We'll talk this through, but when I take hold of her arm, she spins around, rears back, and slaps me across the cheek.

"Don't. *Touch*. Me."

Oh, hell *no*. As she spins to turn around to get away from me, I reach for her again, this time to take hold of her arm and yank her to me. She squeals and fights me, but I'll have none of it. In one swift motion, I swing her up and over my shoulder, and when she kicks her feet in protest and pounds my back, I lace my arms around her scissoring legs and smack my palm against her arse. Hard.

"Let me go!" she fumes. "Let me *go!*"

I'll let her go, after I've taken the fight right out of her with a sound spanking. I don't bother taking her out of the room, but hook a chair with my foot, drag it over, and sit heavily. She squeals when she's sprawled over my knee, fighting as hard as she can, but I won't allow it. The girl's got a good, hard spanking coming whether I have to hold her down every step of the way or not.

And fight me she does. She's smacking at my legs, clearly overpowered but not willing to give in. I hold her in an iron-like grip, one arm anchored around her upper body, while with my other hand, I lift her skirts and yank down her knickers.

"Don't you *ever* raise a hand to me." I slam my palm on her arse, and the breath whooshes straight out of her. She gasps for breath, squealing and howling like I've just branded her. "You will not storm away from me. You will not defy me." I spank her thoroughly, slamming my palm down again and again, when I feel a sharp pain in my leg.

The lass *bit* me. With a growl, I tip her up just long enough to unclasp my belt. I don't let her get away, holding her with one hand while I yank my belt from the loops with my other. I form a loop, hold her down, and whip her with the folded leather. It has the desired effect. Within three sound smacks of my belt, she screams in protest.

"Okay, *okay!*" she says, and I can tell by the sound of her voice she's crying. "Let me *go,* you beast!"

But I'm not done. I won't let her go until I've administered a proper belting she'll feel well into tomorrow. She'll learn her place and calling me a beast certainly isn't helping her arse. Still, she's a little one, and I have to exercise caution, so I keep my head about me while

I punish her. I could easily hurt her, and I don't wish to do that. I wish to punish her, and there's a difference.

I wait between strokes of my belt, letting my words sink in. "I'll not have a wife that talks back to me. I'll have obedience from you." I pause, before I lift my belt again. "I'll listen to you. I'll admit when I'm wrong. Any good leader learns meekness and patience, and I won't fail you in that. But it's too dangerous for you to defy me, young lady. You're safer under my protection, and the sooner you learn that the better."

I spank her until she finally slumps over my lap, swiping at her eyes and sniffling, and her voice has softened. "I'm sorry."

I drop my belt and lift her into my arms, cradling her. Though a part of me loves administering pain, and a part of me longs to wield my power, I have to admit I dislike proper punishment.

"So you want a meek wife, then, do you?" she asks, and I don't miss the note of petulance in her voice. She's feeling sorry for herself. I need to make this right again. Now that I've disciplined, it's time to bring her back, to be sure her heart is in the right place. To be sure she isn't walled up against me.

I take her chin between my fingers and lift her eyes to mine, but she looks away, her eyes shining with unshed tears. I won't lie, it tears my heart in two. I don't like seeing my brave, sweet lass crying. I pull her chin to bring her eyes back to mine.

"Caitlin," I say, trying to gentle my voice but failing. Her name is harsh on my lips, and she flinches. I'll need practice learning to deal with the likes of her. I draw in a deep breath, then let it out again. I try once more. "Caitlin, look at me."

She finally does, and the betrayal in her eyes slays me. "You could have told me," she whispers. "I've given you so much..." her voice cracks. "So much. The least you could give me is truth."

Christ, but she's right. She's fucking right. I wrap my fingers around the back of her neck and knead the tension away, dropping my forehead to hers.

"You're right, sweetheart. And for that, I'm sorry."

But she's tight against me, her feelings walled up inside. She's warring within, and I don't know how to break through her hurt and anger to make things right again. I open my mouth to speak again, when the pounding of footsteps outside the door makes both of us leap to our feet. Something's wrong. Caitlin holds my hand and we face the door, as it opens. Cormac's on the other side, his face pale beneath his whiskers.

"Keenan," he says, in a choked voice. "It's Nolan."

Chapter Twenty

My heartbeat hammers at the sound of Cormac's voice.

It's Nolan.

Even as my heart still aches with the sting of betrayal, and my body still aches from the pain of the stern punishment he inflicted, I squeeze Keenan's hand. It feels as if we're frozen in time, waiting for Cormac to finish what he's come to tell us.

"What is it, brother?" Keenan asks, his bright green eyes clouded with worry.

"He was found a short while ago."

"Where?"

"At the school. Bless him, Lachlan found him and called me. I called Sebastian."

Though I can tell Keenan is angry, as he always is whenever anyone mentions Nolan and his drinking, there's a brightness in his eyes and tightness in his voice that tells me he's concerned.

I don't care I don't care I don't care.

I've made a mistake falling for this family. I can't let myself get pulled any further in.

But when Cormac continues, I can't help myself.

"The nurse at the school said it was acute intoxication. Alcohol poisoning. Confusion, vomiting. He had a fucking seizure."

"*Christ.*"

"Can't rouse him, Keenan. Skin's all blue and pale, and he's shaking."

They're leaving the room, and Keenan's got his phone out. "You called Sebastian?"

"Sebastian's on his way. But fuck it, Keenan, we've got to admit him. 'Tis out of Sebastian's control, this is."

I cover my mouth with my hand.

"Have you told dad?" Keenan asks. His eyes flash at Cormac, but I know by now that what looks like fury is really fear.

"Aye," Cormac says.

"But not mam?"

"Hell no."

Keenan's lips thin. "Fucking keep it that way."

He turns to me. "You'll go to our room," he says. "You're not to come out again without my permission." He signals for a guard. I want to slap his face all over again, I'm that angry with him.

"So I'm your prisoner again, am I?" I say, but when he turns to me, the look on his face makes me close my mouth.

Leaning down toward me, he drops his voice to a whisper and cups my sore, throbbing backside. "Aye," he says. "The Martins could be at large, and for all we know they could've had something to do with this. You're not safe until we're wed, and I can't wed you 'til I see to my brother's wellbeing. I know you're angry. I know we haven't resolved this. But for Christ's sake, Caitlin, use common sense."

I close my eyes, mortified that he's dressing me down and squeezing my backside in front of Cormac. This is what it means to be wed to a man like him, and his highhanded ways will only intensify as he assumes the throne as Chief.

"You will go to our room," he repeats.

Cormac clears his throat. We both look at him.

"Mam'll want to speak with her, Keenan," he says sheepishly, as if he knows he's intruding on a private moment, and it embarrasses him to do so.

Keenan curses. "Aye."

"Perhaps let the lass go only with mam? Keep her under the watch of the guard?"

Keenan's jaw clenches, and his eyes narrow. "Bloody hell," he curses, then, *"Fine.* But only with my mother, and you'll have your phone with you the entire time."

I nod. I'm still angry with him, but this much I can do for my own safety.

And then he's gone. I'm in the room, pacing, wishing there was something I could do to ease the ache from punishment and the ache in my heart. I'm worried about Nolan, and I can't even speak to Maeve about it, for they're not going to tell her.

I pace the room, trying to sort through the thoughts and feelings that flutter through my head like a flock of birds.

Do I still have a say in this?

Does he really have my best interest in mind?

Do I have what it takes to a be a woman of The Clan?

My husband expects obedience and will demand it from me. Can I acquiesce to a man like Keenan?

Have I made a grave mistake?

I have no answers.

No answers.

But what happened just now… I'm not sure if I've got it in me to be the woman he wants, the woman he expects, the woman he needs. And I make up my mind. I can't go along with this. I have to leave. Somehow, I have to get away from the guard he's got watching me like a prisoner, take some food and money, and find my way. Leave this place, and never look back. For once I marry, there will be no escape.

I sit by the window, a book in hand, but I've read the same paragraph three times over. I can't focus, but I can't leave the room either. He told me I could see his mother, though. I lift my phone and frown at it.

I'm ashamed to admit, I don't quite remember how to use it. How do I call her again?

But before I can remember, a knock comes at the door, and I rise to my feet.

"Yes?" I ask.

"It's Maeve, lass. May I come in?"

I put the phone down and rush to the door, so eager to see her I'm slightly embarrassed. I want to tell her everything that happened, what I'm trying to sort, that I'm worried about Nolan. I want her to hug me and ease my worry. But I hold myself together and usher her into the room.

"Caitlin, y'alright, lass?" she asks, stepping into the room. She looks as beautiful as ever, in a lovely emerald green dress that clings to her curves. Her hair's swept up in a graceful up-do, and though she's stunning and graceful, her eyes look so tired, I wonder if she's ill. She's got shiny, glossy books in her hand.

"I'm alright," I tell her. "Are you?" I reach for her hand and squeeze.

She sighs, comes into the room, and shuts the door behind her. Looking about the room, she shakes her head.

"Not in here," she says. "I'm too restless to sit. Walk with me in the garden?"

I look out the window. It's warm and sunny.

"Keenan says we're to have the guard with us," I tell her.

"Yes, of course." She makes a quick call on her phone, and I take note, trying to remember how to do this when I need to. They're right outside the door, so soon we're surrounded by Keenan's small army. I recognize Boner and Tully, and a few others who accompanied us to the church.

"Thank you, boys," Maeve says. "We're only going to the garden."

She takes my hand, and we walk downstairs like that, hand in hand, like friends.

"What are the books you have?" I ask her.

"Oh, they're magazines!" she says. "Bridal magazines. We've no time to order anything, but we can get some ideas about your hair and such." She smiles at me and squeezes the hand she holds. "I've never had a daughter, you know," but her eyes are troubled. We reach the door, and she releases my hand and hands me one of the magazines.

"Have a look, will you?"

"Oooh," I say, when I see the beautiful, elegant bride on the cover. Her hair's swept up gracefully, tendrils of curls on either side, the loops of chestnut curls dotted with pearls. Her dress dips so low in the front it hits her naval, her full breasts barely contained. Tufts of fabric and lace and pearls make up the gathered skirt, and she wears shoes that look as if they came from Cinderella herself.

But though Maeve seems interested, she's distant, and I fear she's troubled.

"Maeve," I ask her, as we reach the garden, and I follow her lead in sitting on one of the benches beneath the swags of greenery.

"Mmm?"

"You seem worried. Is something upsetting you?" I ask. I hate that I know about Nolan.

Sighing, she turns to face me. "They try to shield us, sometimes, Caitlin," she says. "But a mother knows. You'll know yourself, some day."

"Know what?"

She looks over my shoulder, and her brows knit together. "Everything, lass. What they do. Why they do it. Who they bury, and why." She turns back to me. "And most of the time, I allow them to shield me. I let them think I don't know. It's better that way. But I made a mistake with Nolan."

She knows then, at least partly.

"How so?" I want to learn from this beautiful, brave woman. I want her to teach me.

"I protected him. Too much, you see. And it did more harm than good." I wait, for I know intuitively she isn't finished. "When the boys were young, their father took them under his wing. They were taught respect and obedience, and off they went to St. Albert's, where they learned so much more. But when it came to Nolan…" her voice trails off.

"Why was he different?" I ask, keeping my voice gentle. She's opening up to me, but I don't want to push her too hard.

She drags her eyes away from the distant memories and looks back at me. When she answers, her voice cracks, and I'm startled to see her eyes are bright with tears. "He was the one that lived, lass."

A chill runs down my spine, and a lump rises in my throat. I feel as if I'm going to cry. There's a heart-breaking story there.

"The one that lived?"

She nods. "Come for another walk, love? Let's leave the magazines here. We'll return shortly."

I stand, and the guards that held their distance flank our sides again.

She leads me back toward the house, but we don't go inside. Instead, we take the pathway that leads us to the church.

"I've never shown this to the boys, though I'm sure they're familiar."

We walk quietly side by side, the wind rustling the leaves in the trees among the faintest call of goldfinch.

"Thank you for trusting me."

I'm surprised when we walk past the church, rising high above us, the cold gray stones sturdy and unyielding. The cross at the very top glimmers with a hint of sunlight, and the stained-glass windows shine brightly against the backlight of sky.

Maeve opens a small gate, and I realize with a start she's taking me to the graveyard.

Nolan's the one that lived.

I've no superstitions about graveyards, and they don't spook me. But I feel somber and reserved, looking at the stones with carved dates that hearken back centuries. There's history in this graveyard. People have loved and lost, lived and died, and all that remains are their bones, buried beneath the soil, and the marker of tombstones at their graves. Some of the graves have flowers on them, still others greenery, but others have long since been forgotten.

She pauses at a cluster of three. When I read the dates, I close my eyes and swallow hard.

"These were the ones that died," she whispers. "Three of them. Sweet, wee babies that never lived past their first month of life."

"I'm sorry," I whisper.

And she doesn't explain away my apology or tell me it's alright. She only nods, accepting the belated condolences and with a small nod, says, "Thank you."

We stand in silence, but it isn't awkward. It seems we need to keep a moment of silence for the little babies she's buried. After a moment, she speaks again.

"They were born before Keenan," she says. "Each was a girl. I cursed God for taking them from me and convinced myself that it was because my firstborn was meant to be a son."

"I don't blame you," I say in sympathy. "I'd have felt the same."

"It was senseless. By the time we had our third, we had the best care of every doctor we could summon, but it was no use. Hours after birth, she died like her sisters."

I want to cry for the young woman she was, who experienced the tragedy of infant death. I want to cry for her husband, who bore the pain with her, and for her sons, who never met their sisters. "Then Keenan came. And Cormac. And I resigned myself to the fact that they were born to be leaders of The Clan. I allowed Seamus to take them from me, right after they were weaned." Her voice drops, and she fingers the delicate chain at her neck. "But I lost two more after Cormac. And when I gave birth to Nolan, I nursed him at my breast until he was two years old. Seamus railed against me, fought me as hard as he could, but I'll tell you something, Caitlin."

She looks to me, her eyes earnest and stern. "There are times to obey your husband. To allow him the lead in your house, as it were. We're old-fashioned people with old-fashioned notions, and Keenan will expect obedience from you."

I tighten my lips before responding. "Don't I know it."

Her eyes twinkle, then sober again. "But it's not always possible to do so flawlessly. There will be times when you're convinced you're right, of the merit of what you believe. There are times you'll fight against him. And there are even times he may allow it."

It's almost uncanny how well-timed her words are. I can only nod.

"And when Nolan grew to be a toddler... that was my time. I'd given Seamus three sons. I'd withstood so much, taken what I could, upheld the code I was expected to. Lass, I'd even left my home to wed a man I'd never met, all for the good of The Clan."

Her example is powerful. One that I'll remember.

"How did you do it?"

"Leave?" she asks.

I nod. "We all have a purpose, Caitlin. And I knew in my heart my purpose was here. Among them. That I was to be the matriarch of the family."

I sigh. I know what my heart tells me as well, though I don't want to listen or heed the message. My marrying Keenan will bring peace between The Clans. It will secure my own safety as well as the boys at St. Albert's. And joining the McCarthy family means more than that. So much more. Here, I'll have friends. Brothers. A mother. And soon, little ones of my own.

Family.

"There have been times I've gone against Seamus. Times I came to be glad that I did. And times I wished I hadn't. Sheltering Nolan as I did, I came to regret it." She sighs. "I babied him. And he grew to be a good man, loyal and honest, but he lacks the self-control and discipline of his brothers. And it shows." She looks away, back to the church, her gray eyes once more shining with tears. "I well know he's taken to the drink, that he's in a bad way. I know they'll have to do what needs to be done to see to his wellbeing. But God, sometimes it hurts right here." She makes a fist, pounds her fist at her heart, and closes her eyes. Tears leak from her closed eyes.

I can't help myself. I reach for her and hug her. She hugs me back. It's only a brief moment, but we understand each other in that moment. She knows the difficulty I face. I know the pain she holds. I can walk away from this, away from all I've ever had, and seek the great unknown on my own. Or I can stay, in soli-

269

darity with the people I've come to know and dare I say, love.

She wipes her eyes and takes a deep breath. "I could use a stiff drink," she says with a laugh. "But we've got a wedding to plan. Thank you for sharing this with me."

We leave the little graveyard, and I leave a piece of my heart behind me. At the edge of the graveyard, one of the men stiffens and curses, and signals to the other.

Boner looks to Tully and lifts his phone. "We lost the signal. Christ, we missed calls." Boner signals to me and Maeve. "Go. Now. Something's amiss, and we need to find out what."

We walk quicker than we did before. Maeve's eyes are drawn together, and she holds my hand tightly. "I shouldn't have taken you there."

"You didn't mean anything by it. How were we to know they'd lose connection?"

"He wouldn't want me to take you off the grounds, not when so much is at stake." She shakes her head. "*God*."

"Maeve," I begin, when shouts come up in front of us. Men are running, weapons are drawn. We still, both of us, waiting for direction, when a car comes toward us.

"It's Seamus," Maeve says.

Seamus rolls down the window when he approaches and speaks directly to Maeve. "Keenan and Cormac were taking Nolan to the doctor," he says. "They were overtaken. Seems Nolan's sickness was a decoy, likely orchestrated by our rivals. Retaliation for the death of the Martins at St. Albert's."

"Mother of God."

"Cormac says that Keenan was taken into custody. Five masked men, and he couldn't fight them off. He saw the Martin mark."

The Martins. My blood relatives. They took Keenan?

"Where'd they take him?"

Seamus shakes his head. "No idea," he says. "They shot Cormac." Maeve gasps. "He's alright, lass," Seamus says, in a voice that's so familiar to Keenan my heart aches a little. "He will be, anyway. Shot him in the leg. Told him to relay the message. Says we've got something of theirs, and they won't let him go until they have it back."

Maeve's eyes go to mine, and we know. We know exactly what's theirs.

Maeve grabs my hand and tugs me to her.

"Get her into lockdown," Seamus orders his men. "*Now.*"

Chapter Twenty-One

Keenan

I open my eyes, blinking at the dim yellow light that hurts my head. I'm bound, somehow. Rope tied about my body, my mouth gagged. I hear voices all around me, none familiar. I try to remember what happened. What the bloody hell happened?

I try not to move. I'm lying on a bed, my eyes unfocused. I don't want the people who've taken me to know I've woken.

I can't tell where I am, or who I'm with. The voices aren't familiar, nor are the dimly lit surroundings. I try to assess my situation. My head aches. I was struck somewhere. By the feel of my chest, I've broken ribs, and there's something wet and crusty on my lips. I was beaten as well.

Nolan.

With effort, I keep myself from knifing up and demanding answers, calling attention to myself. We'd just gotten Nolan, just brought him to Sebastian, when we were fucking ambushed. Cormac said it was the Martins, but I didn't get a good look before they assaulted me.

Did Cormac get away? Thank Christ Nolan was with Sebastian.

Is Caitlin safe?

"Thought he could tell us where to look for the rest if we brought him here," one says.

"You feckin' *eejit*," a hoarse, raspy voice says, in a thick brogue. "You took the feckin' heir to the throne. You've got no brains in that head of yers, do ya? Could've taken any of the lot, but this feckin' heir's the future Chief."

"Fuckin' shut it," the other snaps. "He's as guilty as the rest."

"Could've gotten retaliation without a fucking *war*," the raspy voice continues. There are several distinct voices, several men in the shadows of this room. I can't quite tell how many are here.

So someone took me without permission. That bodes well for me. Maybe they won't kill me.

Mention of retaliation confirms they're Martins. They know of the men we killed at St. Albert's, and now they've come for vengeance.

They argue among themselves, before they finally realize I've come to.

"Take off his gag," the raspy voice says. He's the leader, it seems.

The light casts across their features. This one's dirty, his hair matted, and he's missing a tooth in the front. My stomach churns. My father's told me they're a manky lot, but I've not had much interaction myself. They're underhanded and conniving, he says. Unprincipled. They're known for seeking easy money and spending it as quickly as they can earn it.

We may be violent ourselves, but I shudder to think of Caitlin among the likes of these.

Someone unfastens my gag. I move my tongue around my mouth. No missing teeth. The few broken bones I have won't keep me from fighting.

"State yer name," the leader says. He knows who I am. He's already chided them for taking me.

"Keenan McCarthy, Captain of the McCarthy Clan" I say, my voice laced with anger. I want them to know exactly who I am. "And you're…" I want to hear them say it. I don't want them to know I know who they are.

"None of your damn business," he snaps, but he looks nervously over his shoulder. Where are we? The blanket beside the bed where I'm sitting is familiar, but I can't place it. Why would a place they take me to look familiar? It doesn't make any sense at all. I look about the place, and realize the light is coming from above us, natural light filtering in through small glass windows. The room is so small, I couldn't stand up straight if I tried, but would smack my head. It's too dark to see much else, the only light cast from an oil-burning lamp on a table.

"Why've you taken me here?" I ask. "Where are we?"

But they don't answer. One of them, a large, burly man with a shaved head and jaw, pulls out his cell phone. He speaks hurriedly into it. "They took the feckin' Captain." He looks over his shoulder at me. "Bloody hell."

He continues to talk, and my mind is churning. They didn't mean to take me, and I have to use that to my advantage. These are the lackeys in the group, not the ones with power. Taking me, or any attack at all, was likely retaliation for the weekend, for the men they lost that we questioned. We're at war with the Martins, and there's only one way we can end what's to be inevitable bloodshed: my marriage to Caitlin. But hell, if they've already seen her, she isn't safe. She's in mortal fucking danger.

He slides his phone back into his pocket and looks to me. I need to decipher two things in this conversation: where I am, and if they know of Caitlin.

It's so dim in here, it's hard for me to get my bearings. I can talk to them, though, maybe even set them up.

"Do you know what it means when you kidnap the Captain?" I ask, my mind racing to come up with something that would scare them. They look at each other. My mark was right.

One swallows. "We were told to take you," he says, the fucking idiot, as if I don't have brains in my head.

"I didn't ask if you were told to take me," I say, letting my head flop back on the pillow as if I'm exhausted, when what I'm really trying to do is move my hand enough to see if I can reach the knife I keep at my belt without them seeing. "I asked if you knew what this meant."

Silence. I speak quickly.

"My father's the head of the firing squad. You're outnumbered, lads, three to one. Soon as my family knows you've taken me, he'll send out his top shooters to go straight for yours. Our best fighters, our heaviest artillery, and you well know we're outfitted better than you lot."

One whispers to the next, "He knows who we are then, bloody hell."

Christ, but they're idiots.

"You have what belongs to us," one says.

"No fucking idea what you're talking about," I say, facing the wall, my fingers on the very edge of the handle. "We did nothing against you."

"You took what's ours!"

If they're talking about Caitlin, I'll kill them. I'll fucking tear their hearts out with my own bare hands.

"And what's that?" I ask, feigning ignorance.

"As if you don't know you've got intel from the keeper that was rightfully ours? Hmm?"

I blink in surprise, truly astounded they're so brainless. "You mean the spying he did on *us*?"

"We paid half a million quid for that intel."

I laugh out loud. "And you think I'm going to hand you back information he stole from *us*?"

One of them grumbles. "We paid for that intel. Furthermore, you killed our men."

"Fair kills," I counter. "They attacked our women and bylaws are clear as fucking day. You attack a woman of The Clan, your life is forfeit."

"We're due retaliation!" one says, getting to his feet. I have to use their stupidity against them.

My hand just barely gets the very edge of the knife. "They're coming now," I say, shaking my head at them. "I hear them. You'll be surrounded. You're outnumbered. And when your Captain or Chief catches word of what you've done, who you've taken…" They look at one another, buying every word of my bluff, and at that very minute the sound of a motorbike goes by the window. I doubt my men know I'm here or that they've come, but it's to my advantage to distract them while I cut my bonds.

"Go look," the bald man says to the manky one. "Fucking look."

He rushes to the center of the room, and I blink, my eyes finally adjusting to the darkness. I watch as he descends a spiral staircase to the floor below.

Bloody hell. I know where we are.

They took me to the lighthouse. *The lighthouse.* Why are we here?

A second man ascends to the top floor, and I'm left with the bald guy, who paces around, looking out the window below. I'm not going to be left alone. I use the momentary distraction to draw my blade up. It slices through my finger and I brace against the pain, fumble with it, my back my captor. Thank Christ the blade is sharp and my bonds makeshift and weak. My hands spring free. I pretend I'm still bound and tuck the blade under my body.

"There's no one here, boss. He's either delusional or lying," one yells from above.

"Anything below?" he asks. "We need to—"

But he doesn't get any further than that when I lunge and strike. He isn't prepared for me, as I vault across the small room. My knife meets its mark, and he screams in pain. I hear the sound of the others coming, but I have an advantage. In seconds, I incapacitate the one beside me, and knock him out. The manky one's on the stairs, but I kick him swiftly and send him flying, and the second becomes victim to my blade. Now that my hands are free, I can reach for my pistol that the idiots didn't even realize I had on me.

The man beside me launches himself at me, and in his haste, he knocks over the oil lamp. It crashes to the floor,, the oil leaking onto the hardwood, and flames begin licking at the oil. It flames like a match to tinder, and the bald man howls when the flames hit him. I reach for him, drag him into the heart of the flames, and he screams as the fire meets its mark.

In seconds, the small interior's filled with smoke and flame, and I can't stop it. I drag him to the edge of the fire and leave him, howling in rage and pain, unable to escape the flames. I assess my situation. I'm too high to jump, and I've got two barely incapacitated men after me. I cover my face against the heat and flames, everything igniting so quickly I fear I won't make it out.

I run to the stairs, but one of them's after me. I kick his face, and he screams, falling to the floor. I leap off the stairs, crouch on the ground beside him, and when he attacks, I roll with him. I've still got my knife in hand and use it to my advantage. I slash his chest, and he howls, rears back, and decks me so hard I see stars, but I keep my head about me. I slice at his neck, and when crimson blood spurts out and he gasps for air, I whip out my handgun and shoot. My mark is certain, and he slumps to the ground with a bullet through his temple. I toss the dead body to the side and run for the exit.

Chapter Twenty-Two

I go with the men Seamus hands me to.

"Do exactly what they say, lass. Your safety is of the utmost importance. Do you understand?" It surprises me this is the man from day one, the vicious man who tried to slap my face. He's concerned about me, concerned for my safety.

I'm one of them now.

I sit in the back of the car, but when I do, I see something up ahead on the cliff.

"Stop the car!" I shout. The men look at each other, but I pound on the seats. "Stop the car!"

They do, and I reach for the door handle. I need to tell Seamus and Maeve.

"Bloody hell!" one of the men shouts when I tumble out of the car, waving my hands at the car behind us.

But it isn't Maeve. It isn't Seamus. They're… men I don't recognize. Tires squeal as they come to a stop, and an older man, younger than Seamus but older than Keenan, rolls his window down. He stares at me as if he's seen a ghost.

No.

He recognizes me. I scream when strong arms come around me, dragging me back to the car.

"Don't fight me, lass. Get into the car or yer man'll beat the shite outta me."

He lifts me in his arms and carries me back to the car. I'm out of my mind, I'm fighting against him. Keenan's in danger. The other man saw me. We're all in danger.

I hear deafening gun shots but can't see what's happening, as he climbs into the back of the car with me and manhandles me inside. I haven't seen this man before. He's thinner than the rest, wears wire-rimmed glasses, but he's got the same ink and sternness about him as the others. "You don't fucking pull that shite again," he says. "Seamus ordered you taken to the bunker, and we're fucking doing what he tells us."

"The lighthouse," I tell him, trying to keep my nerves in check while the men in the front shoot their guns at our assailants. "They've got him at the lighthouse!"

He nods. "What'd you see, lass?"

"Flames," I say, my voice choked, when the realization hits me. The lighthouse is on fire. My home. My child-hood home is on fire.

He pulls out his phone and makes a few calls. I hear the blast of a gunshot and squeal of tires.

"Lost them," a voice in the front says.

"The lass saw flames at the lighthouse. Thinks Keenan's there."

"Taking her in now."

It's a jumble of confusion as we race faster than I knew cars could even go, and we're driving down, away from the lighthouse, away from the shore, deep into the heart of the city. We pass the church and the grave-yard, the armory and the castle, as we drive further and further away. I swallow hard, kneading my hands.

They have to find Keenan. They have to save him. They have to save the lighthouse.

Why do I care?

God, what I've gone through since they took me... I don't even know when it was. It feels like it was yester-day, and it feels like it's been forever. I can't imagine myself not surrounded by this family, by these men, by *Keenan.*

The thought of him being hurt, or worse, killed, makes me want to scream. He can't die. He can't.

We're going downhill now, and my stomach swoops as they drive into what looks like a cave. What on earth? We're surrounded by darkness when the car screeches to a halt.

"Nothing foolish, lass," the man beside me says. "You're under our protection, and it's crucial you do as we say. It's what Keenan would've wanted. Aye?"

Would've wanted? Why is he talking about him in the past tense? What? I nod dumbly, not sure what else I can do.

He holds my gaze as if gauging my reaction, when he finally opens the door. "Alright, then. Out you go." He gets out first and takes me out, then holds my elbow as if I'm a child who might run.

"I'm not going to run away."

He doesn't respond, his jaw tight and his grip on my arm even tighter. There's a door in front of us, barely visible, but another one of the men opens it. I step inside, the air instantly cooler. It isn't used very much, that I can tell, by the musty, damp smell that clings to the air.

When all of us have entered the small room, I hear the heavy clanging of a door being shut, and someone flicks the light switch. I shade my eyes, not used to the light, and look around us. It's a tiny apartment, windowless, with a door so thick and heavy, it looks as if it's made of solid iron. There's a refrigerator, a small, utilitarian toilet and sink, a sofa, and a cot.

"Sit, lass," one of the men says, pointing to an ancient-looking loveseat in the corner of the room.

"Get us some drink, Tully, will you?"

"Aye."

I sit and look at the two men. Tully I recognize from the day we went to the church. I blink in surprise when I realize the third man with me isn't a man at all, but the boy called Lachlan.

"What's your name?" I ask the man with the glasses.

"Name's Carson."

"And your role here?"

His lips twitch before he answers, and I'm not sure why. "Clan bookkeeper," he says, holding my gaze.

I turn to Lachlan. "Lachlan, what are you doing here?"

The boy also holds my gaze without turning away. "Brought word to Cormac of his brother's illness," he says. "Keenan told me to shadow the men for the day, see what happens." A corner of his lips quirks up. "Got lucky. Seems I came on a good day."

Carson cuffs him good-naturedly. "'Tis about time we induct Lachlan anyway," he says. "Once Keenan signs off."

I exhale in relief. "He's alright, then?" I ask. "Keenan?"

"Aye," Carson says, his eye gentling, though he looks away this time. "Don't you worry about Keenan, lass. The best of The Clan are onto the extraction right now."

"Extraction?" I say, my voice oddly high-pitched. "That sounds painful."

Why do I care so much? This is a man I wasn't going to stay with. He's highhanded and domineering, and, and...

I love him. I sigh.

"Sounds painful," Tully repeats, not bothering to hide his booming laugh or the fact that he's amused by me. "Aye, lass, it very well may be, but yer Keenan's a champ. He'll come out of this just fine, you'll see."

Still, I pace the small area back and forth, and every second that ticks by feels like hours. The men don't do much more than guard the door, and after some time find food.

"Eat," Tully says, handing me a plastic cup with soup in it. I frown at it.

"Where'd you get that?" I ask. I've never eaten anything out of a plastic cup, and I don't trust it.

He snorts. "We keep rations here," he says. "You add water, and you're good to go. I trust you've never seen such a thing?"

"No," I say, "and I have no appetite anyway."

"You best eat, ma'am," Lachlan says, almost apologetically. "Keenan won't be pleased if you don't."

I furrow my brow at him and frown. "How do you know what Keenan wishes for me?" I'm feeling petulant and moody. I want out of here. I want to know Keenan's okay.

To his credit, Lachlan looks a bit abashed, but his voice and gaze don't waver when he looks at me. "They sent you to the bunker, miss," he says, as if that explains anything at all. When I look at him blankly, he continues.

"She don't know what it is," Tully says, slurping soup from the cup.

"I do so," I protest. "It's a safe place, where we are now."

"Aye," Tully says. "But you don't know the purpose, lass. The bunker's meant for the Chief only. In the entire history of The Clan, we've never had a woman in here. The Chief's sent here if his life is endangered. Notice only one bed?"

I nod, looking around the dark interior a second time.

"That's for the Chief. The others who accompany him are his watch. There's no way in, except through the guard, sent here to watch the Chief. And yet here you are, the one under the deepest protection we can muster. Guard with you in a veritable fortress, and guards stationed outside as well. Absolute iron clad protection."

I finally realize what he's telling me. "Oh," I say in a little voice.

Seamus sent me here for a reason. They don't take this level of protection lightly. For some reason, my nose feels all tingly, and a lump forms in my throat. Maeve loves me like a daughter, and Seamus has given me the highest level of protection.

I... mean something to them. To all of them. To the man I'm betrothed to and the men in front of me now.

"I see," I say finally.

"Eat, lass," Carson suggests, pointing to the cup, though there's a note of steel in his voice I recognize. He's trying to be polite, but they want me to take care of myself. So I do. I frown at the cup and raise an eyebrow at the little square-shaped vegetables I recognize as peas and carrots. I take a tentative sip. It's hot and salty, and surprisingly tasty. I finish it, hand the cup to Tully, then go to lay on the bed.

"Good girl," Carson says gently. "Get some rest. We shouldn't have to be here much longer." He sits and takes out his phone. Lachlan paces by the door and Tully stands guard nearby.

I close my eyes, praying that Keenan's okay, that Nolan's alright as well. That Maeve and Seamus aren't injured in whatever happens and trying not to think about the lighthouse on fire. It was my home, but it was also a prison. I don't know how I feel about it. I must fall asleep, for I wake with a start when I hear Carson talking on the phone.

"Yes, sir. She's here, sir."

I sit up, brushing sleep from my eyes, when Carson hands me his phone.

"Someone wants to speak to you."

"Hello?"

"Caitlin."

The sound of his voice floods me. "Keenan." I breathe out a sigh of relief that feels as if it comes from my very toes. "Where are you? Are you okay?"

"I'm fine," he says. "I'm with Sebastian."

"Are you injured? Did they hurt you? Did you have to kill them?"

His chuckle is like balm to my soul, deep and reassuring. "Easy, lass," he says. "I'm really and truly fine. Yes, I've sustained injuries, but none that won't heal. Soon as he finishes bandaging me up, I'll be there."

He doesn't answer my question about killing anyone. I don't know what came over me. He's told me not to ask too many questions, and it's best this time if I heed that.

"You alright, sweetheart?" he asks. "Were you hurt at all?"

"No," I tell him. "I'm fine. Just... worried about... everyone." Why is it so hard to tell him it's *him* I'm worried about?

"Where are you?"

I smile to myself. He was so eager to talk to me he didn't even ask them where I was.

"In the bunker."

"Bloody hell," he mutters. "Dad sent you to the bunker? Good call." His voice pitches off, and I can tell he's not talking to me. "Let it go. I want to go to her, and I'm fucking fine. You can shove concussions up yer arse, Sebastian, I'm telling you what—"

They have a heated discussion, but Keenan wins. He always does.

"I'm on my way," he says. "Be a good lass, now, and do what they tell you, aye?"

I sigh. He's on his way. My heart swells with anticipation, eager to see him. I give him what I know he wants. "Yes, sir."

I hand the phone back to Carson, who puts it in his pocket. I get out of bed. I want to look presentable for Keenan, but when I go to the bathroom, I frown. That isn't going to happen. There's a scratch along one cheek, and my long, thick hair's in crazy waves about me. My dress is torn, and I look pale as a mermaid.

"I look like Medusa," I mutter.

"Well, you don't act like her, so you're good," Lachlan says, making the men laugh.

A few minutes later, the door swings open. I see Cormac, Boner, and then I get to my feet.

"Keenan," I breathe. He crosses the room to me in three quick strides, pulls me to him, and holds me so tightly I wheeze, gasping for air.

"*Jesus, Mary, and Joseph,*" he mutters. "Bloody hell, lass. Y'alright?"

I nod. "*I'm* fine," I tell him. "How about *you?*"

But he ignores my question. He's running his thumb gingerly along the scrape at my cheek, frowning. He's a mess. One eye's swollen shut, his lip's twice it's normal size, and there's a bandage along the side of his head. His arm's in a sling, and he's got something wrapped around his torso. He's got broken bones, no doubt.

"They were looking for the notes from Jack Anderson," he says, first to me, then he turns to the room. "And they didn't know about Caitlin, not at first. Seems one of the men who attacked saw and recognized her, though." He turns to me. "We have to get married. Tomorrow. There's no time to waste, lass."

I nod. I can't leave this brotherhood of fierce warriors, the found family that's accepted me and welcomed me as their own. I will do what's right, marry Keenan, become his wife, and ensure the safety of all those around us.

"Aye," I whisper. "I agree. Just put your mom on the job, and she'll help me get ready. Too bad you'll be all banged up for the wedding, but it's of no consequence. You'll heal up soon."

His beautiful green eyes twinkle. "Let's get you out of here."

Chapter Twenty-Three

Keenan

We ensure that no one's tracked us, and that the Martins have been suitably punished. There will be no retaliation this time. Clan laws are clear on an attack like theirs: they apprehended the Captain. The loss of a few of their soldiers in self-defense evens the score. Though I've no doubt Mack Martin himself is fuming, he has only himself to blame. It was a grave mistake apprehending me.

But I still worry for Caitlin. Word's out now that she's mine, that she's the spitting image of her mother. She isn't safe until she's wed to me, until she bears my name and my ring upon her finger. I even contemplate bringing Finn into the bunker and marrying her here, but my mother loses her mind and won't allow it.

So I secret her back to the mansion under the watchful eye of my guard.

I've got Caitlin in my room, sitting on my lap. Her head rests on my shoulder, and her arms encircle my neck. We don't speak for long minutes, both of us lost in our thoughts after what's happened. The last time I was with her, she'd walled herself away from me.

"Caitlin," I begin, my eyes roaming out the window to where my guard stands watch outside. We're safe here. Still, I won't settle until she's got my ring on her finger.

"Yes?"

I place my knuckle under her chin to bring her eyes to me. "The last time we were together, you were still angry." I pause. "I punished you."

She nods. "I've forgiven you," she says simply. "I wasn't very happy with you."

"You had reason," I tell her with a nod. "And I'll tell you once more, that I'm sorry. I should've told you that you weren't my prisoner and given you the choice."

She worries her lip, but still looks in my eyes. "If you... if you had it to do over, Keenan," she says. "Would you do anything differently?"

I think about it for a moment before answering. "I told you I wouldn't lie, lass. So I'll have to be honest."

"Please."

"No."

Her musical, ringing laughter takes me by surprise. She takes my fingers from her chin and brings them to her lip, kissing them.

"I'm going to make a bold declaration, Keenan McCarthy," she says. It's the first time she's ever said my full name and God, but I like it.

"Aye?"

"I love you. I love your fierce loyalty and honesty. I love your determination and spirit. And I… I love how you love *me*. I don't understand so much, and I know that. I vow that I'm going to do my very best to ensure I learn everything I can. My *very* best. And I know that love can still grow, and that what I feel now is only… what did we say before… the very *seed* of love."

I nod, pulling her to my chest. "Sometimes, sweet Caitlin, circumstances change. People do, too. A month ago, I didn't know you existed, and now…" his voice trails off, and he weaves his fingers through my hair, playing with a stray strand. "Now I can't imagine not having you with me. For I love you, too, my sweet fae."

C *aitlin*

I know in my heart that this gentler side of him… this fierce, protective side of him that calls me his sweet fae, that holds me to his chest, that promises to slay my dragons and take the very best care of me that a man could… is only for my eyes. No one else sees the fullness of Keenan McCarthy. No one else knows his heart.

"So tell me, Caitlin," he asks, reaching for my hand. "Up with you a moment, will you?"

I stand in confusion, not sure why he's gently pushing me off his lap. But when he drops to one knee, I stare in disbelief. He's ordered me to marry him. He told me I had no choice. Is he… is he doing what I think he is?

Taking my hand, he looks straight into my eyes. He works his jaw and I watch his Adam's apple bob up and down as he swallows hard. My fierce warrior is overcome with emotion. I swallow hard, my own emotions mirroring his.

"Sweet Cait, will you have me? I've no ring, but I promise you I'll remedy that."

"You're giving me a choice?"

His eyes darken, but there's a twinkle in them. "Aye," he says. "A choice, but if you don't say yes…"

I laugh out loud. He doesn't need to complete the threat. "Yes," I say. "I'll marry you. In fact, why don't we go ahead and make that happen *tomorrow*?"

He kisses the back of my hand and gets to his feet.

"An excellent plan," he says, as if he only just thought it. "One I can absolutely get behind."

And then he's stripping my clothes and his and leading me to the bathroom. His mouth is on mine, and his firm hand at the small of my back.

"Please, be careful," I whisper. "I don't want you injured anymore."

"I'll be careful," he says. "So careful."

He turns the stream of water on, and billows of steam quickly fill the room.

"No washing my hair!" I tell him, with a laugh.

"Why not?"

"It's too thick," I tell him. "It won't dry until after the wedding. I'll braid it."

"They have things to speed that up, you know," he says. "Though dammit if I can't remember what they're called."

I laugh, and he spins me around, gathering my hair up. I close my eyes at the feel of him plaiting my hair for me.

"Where'd you learn that trick?" I ask him.

"I've many tricks," he says, with mock offense. "You've only seen a few."

"I'm eager to see the rest," I say with a coy smile.

"You shall." He kisses the back of my head and leads me into the shower. We lather each other up, and he takes his time massaging the fullness of my breasts, the swell of my backside, between my thighs. I lather him up as well, careful not to touch his ribs, all wrapped in waterproof bandages.

"I'll have you again, lass," he says.

His mouth comes to mine, and I go up on my toes when he kisses me, sighing into his mouth as one of his hands travels between my legs.

"Let's wait," I whisper. "Let's wait until we're married."

"Wait?"

"We're both exhausted after the day, and I want our wedding day to be special," I tell him. I hate telling him this, for my body's already in flames, the pulse of desire between my legs relentless.

"I can grant you that," he says. "But know that once you're mine, I won't be holding back."

I grin. "I'm counting on it."

"I'll want you often."

I nod. "Well, then, that goes both ways, doesn't it?"

He smiles.

We head back to the room, and I'm surprised to see a silver tray with two fluted glasses and a bottle of wine.

"It's got a cork," I say. "How do you open it?"

He spins me around and faces the bottle of wine, his naked chest against my back. "Like this," he whispers in my ear. The way he holds me to him, his body flush against mine, makes my heart beat faster. I'm hyper aware of his raw, masculine strength, and his hardness pressed up against me. I feel small and quiet, and I'm eager to learn from him.

I watch as he uses a metal contraption to open the bottle of wine and places the cork on the little tray before pouring me a glass.

"Here you go, sweet girl," he says. "It'll help you sleep."

I'm pleasantly sleepy and warmed through with the wine when he leads me to bed, tucks me in, and kisses my cheek before taking another call.

"Sleep, lass," he whispers. "And tomorrow, we wed."

I wake the next day to no Keenan. I look about the room, and the only remnants of his being here are the dirty clothes hanging off the side of the clothes hamper, and his empty wine glass next to mine on the tray. I yawn widely, when I notice a note on the

295

bedside table. I can almost hear him reading it in his thick brogue.

Good morning, sweet fae. I won't see you until we take our vows. I want to ensure your safety today, but my mother will be up shortly to help you prepare.

Tá mo chroí istigh ionat.

Though I feel a sense of loss at his absence, I know today is a special day. I trust that if he has something to do, it's worth it, and I know beyond question that he's left me with a sturdy guard in his absence.

A knock comes at the door.

"Hello?"

"It's Maeve."

I quickly don my robe and let her in. She's carrying a silver tray laden with a teapot and scones. Leaning in, she kisses my cheek. She's dressed in a beautiful navy blue gown that hugs her curves and graces the floor, and when she walks, she swishes.

"You look lovely," I tell her. "And I'm still in my robe!"

"Tsk," she says, waving aside my concerns. "I've come to get you ready. Now have your breakfast and we'll get started." Behind her come several of their servants, and a tall, much younger woman I've never met before who's dressed as impeccably as Maeve. They carry a variety of things, including a dress, that make me quickly lose my taste for my breakfast.

"Caitlin, meet Megan," she says. "My niece."

"You're Keenan's cousin, then?"

"Aye," the girl says, grinning at me. She's got the same eyes as he does, and she's lovely with her dark, wavy curls and bright pink lips.

"You're so pretty," I tell her, not knowing if it's an appropriate thing to say or not. "Pretty as a picture."

She grins and turns to Maeve. "You're right. She's a charming little thing, isn't she, though?"

"I—I'm sorry, I don't know the right thing to say sometimes," I begin, but Megan shakes her head.

"Aw, no. Don't you go apologizing for being who you are. It's why my cousin loves you, you know. And please don't ever apologize for paying me a compliment!"

"Oh, Maeve," I say, looking with concern at the dress, my appetite for the scones I normally love evaporating.

"What is it, lass?" she asks.

"I can't... how am I... what am I supposed to do? How can I do this?"

She smiles at me and reaches for my hand. "It's very simple, sweetheart. You just say *I do.*"

"You make it sound easy," I mutter, pulling my hand away and beginning to pace. "And I—there's so much... I mean I—"

She suddenly goes wide-eyed and brings her hand to her mouth. "Oh, sweet Jesus," she says, and I look at her in surprise. "Are you afraid of giving him virginity, lass? I can't believe I didn't think of it before. Locked away in the lighthouse like that, you've never even—"

I shake my head, my cheeks on *fire*.

"I… um… oh, goodness," I squeak. "No, I'm not worried about that. We've, um, well I—" how am I supposed to tell his mother I'm not a virgin anymore?

She takes one look at my flustered face, throws her head back, and laughs so hard I can't help but join her.

"Seems you've got nothing to worry about, then."

"Please, God, no," I tell her. "He's your son, so if there's anything else I need to know—"

"You ask *me*," Megan says, giving me a wink and cracking her gum. "Alright?"

"Alright," I agree. I take in a deep breath.

"Now," Megan says. "On with your dress."

I keep my back to the wall and quickly undress, slipping into my undergarments. If they notice the marks he left, they don't bat an eyelash. I'm grateful for the women of The Clan who know what these men are like. Something tells me I'll be glad of their company soon enough.

I stand like a mannequin, letting them dress me, fix my hair, and slide on the prettiest glossy shoes I've ever seen.

"Mother of God, if she isn't the prettiest bride that ever *lived*," Megan says enthusiastically, clapping her hands with glee. "She's *gorgeous*."

I look at myself in the mirror, not recognizing the woman who stares back at me. My hair's plaited and woven onto my head, pinned up with little flowers and gems. A gauzy veil hangs down to my elbows. They've

298

done my makeup, and my eyes look brighter, my cheeks flushed, my lips full and pink. But the *dress.* The satin white dress is simple but elegant, the top of the bodice held up with thin straps. The bodice itself glitters with rhinestones, sequins, and iridescent beads to a high waist, and full skirt.

"I love this dress," Megan says. "'Tis a Georgette maxi skirt and hand-beaded bodice. It makes you look like a princess."

"How did you get this so quickly?"

Megan giggles. "We've connections, you know."

Don't I know it.

I spin around in front of the mirror, when Megan hands me a bouquet of white roses.

"We've no time to waste, Caitlin," she says.

Maeve is on her phone, waving us along. "We do have to go," she says. "He's going to lose his mind, that son of mine."

"My goodness," is all I can reply. But I know that time is of the essence, that I'm to marry him quickly if we're to secure the safety of all. They open the door to the bedroom and usher me out, and half a dozen armed men stand outside my door. Gone are the friendly expressions, every one of these men wearing the stern, hardened faces of soldiers.

Our procession is a somber one with our guard marching beside us, but Megan tries to make small talk. Maeve laughs at her jokes, but I can tell she's concerned as well.

"Where are we taking our vows?"

"By the garden," Maeve says. "It's a beautiful spring morning, and we want your vows to be publicly witnessed. They must be, to spread the word far and wide, and quickly. Father Finn's there, as well as Keenan, and the rest of The Clan."

"Is it safe out there?"

"They'll see that it is. It's our best bet, since the wedding must be on record and witnesses present. We've got all our men prepared, Caitlin."

Still, foreboding gathers in my stomach, and I try to dismiss it. Is it because I'm about to take permanent vows to a man like Keenan? Or because my intuition is alerted to something else? I can't tell. But I have no choice. With the guard flanking me on all sides, I leave the mansion.

My heart twangs like the long-forgotten strings of a violin when I see, far beyond the mansion, the burnt remains of the lighthouse. They put out the fire, but little could be saved. I'm pleased, though, somehow, even as I ache for the home I knew. It signifies the end of an era, and the beginning of a new one.

The start of *family*.

Mine, where I'm to be the mother and Keenan the head. Hope blooms in my heart, and I'm filled with a sense of awe and wonder. Down by the garden, where the archways blossom, lay miles of white flowers. They've done magic overnight, it seems. There's a flower-lined trellis, and every man of The Clan's dressed in black suits. Beneath the trellis stands the priest, and—is that him? My future husband. He's dressed in black, his hair slicked back, as large as life standing before his uncle. He turns and freezes when he sees me.

It's as if someone's waved a wand and frozen that moment in time, when his eyes meet mine. I smile, lift a finger off my bouquet, and give him a little wave. He grins in return. A sparrow twitters overhead, the clouds break free, and sun beams down on the small gathering. I see Seamus and Cormac, Boner and Tully, Carson and Lachlan. The rest of the men as well line like soldiers bedecked for a banquet. I ignore the drawn weapons and the guard that escorts me toward the trellis.

I take in a deep breath and remember what Maeve said.

All I have to do is say, "I do."

But as I walk toward Keenan, the foreboding I felt earlier returns. I look to my left and to my right. I'm surrounded by armed, stern soldiers, ready to protect me, ready to lay down their lives if necessary. Then why do I feel a sense of dread in my stomach? I force myself to look at Keenan. He stands under the trellis, the early morning sun casting its light before him, and I'm reminded of the time I thought him a fallen angel. Do fallen angels get a chance at redemption? Even recovering from his injuries, he's so handsome waiting for me. Sebastian's doctored him up well.

I'm paces away from him, nearing the men who stand by Keenan: Cormac and Lachlan and Seamus. Everything's quiet, everything's still, when Lachlan suddenly starts. He jerks his head up and stares beyond. Lachlan suddenly tackles me, shoving me into Keenan. I scream.

"Sniper!" Lachlan shouts.

It all happens so fast, it's a blur of screams and confusion. I'm thrown to the ground, the damp grass in front of me saturating the lovely dress. Keenan's full body's over me. Gunshots ring out. Footsteps sound, and then more. Keenan's issuing orders, but I can hardly hear for the ringing in my ears.

"Fucking sniper!"

"Someone get him!"

"The boy's after him, fast as a shot."

"I don't think I got him."

"Go see if there's more!"

There's a tumult of voices and sounds, and then I'm dragged to my feet beside Keenan. He's shaking me, grasping my arms. "Y'alright? Are you, lass? Christ, woman, tell me you're alright." Keenan is kneeling in front of me, holding me to him, his eyes roving my body for any signs of injury. "Are you?"

"I'm fine," I whisper, but he rubs his finger on my cheek and it comes back red.

I raise my hand to my face, my heart pounding. Was I shot? I don't feel anything at all. I look, and even Keenan isn't shot. He pulls me to him as if to shield me from more bullets, to keep me from further danger, when a loud wail goes up. I look with horror to see Maeve, on her knees, holding Seamus to her. My body grows stiff, my pulse cold. His bright white shirt is stained with blood. Seamus was shot.

Keenan stills, but he won't let me go. He looks to his mother, and I tell him to go to her, that it's okay, but he shakes his head.

Sebastian's kneeling beside her and issuing commands. "Call an ambulance," he shouts, and Cormac pulls his phone out with trembling hands. "He's still alive!"

"Keenan," Maeve says through tears, her gaze as fierce as I've ever seen it. "Do it. He would want you to. *Do it.*" She's crying freely now. "No more bloodshed, son. Take her as your wife."

Keenan takes my hand and turns to Father Finn. The priest is white as a sheet, the book he holds shaking in his trembling hands, but I know. We have to do this. We have to take our vows now. We have to prevent any more injuries, any more violence.

We utter our vows in whispers, repeating what Father says. We take our rings, and place them on our fingers, as an ambulance drives up the path. It's surreal and painful and beautiful, the way the men stand and watch their leader taken onto a stretcher.

"He still may live," Sebastian says to Maeve, as she climbs into the ambulance.

She turns to Keenan. "I'll tell him," she says. "You did the right thing."

There is no party, no celebration. Keenan holds my hand up and faces everyone. It's then that I notice people with cameras. He's invited reporters here. They've seen everything. They heard us take our vows.

"Welcome Caitlin McCarthy," he says, his voice loud with victory and twinged with pain. "The newest member of The Clan."

Chapter Twenty-Four

Keenan

We pace the hospital waiting room, still dressed in our wedding garments. We make quite a sight, grass-stained and bloodied. I get as much intel as I can, from where I am.

Lachlan's quick eye and speed paid off. He caught our sniper, hauled him in for questioning. I've left Boner and Tully to deal with him, as Cormac's with me.

The news of our wedding made headlines. We've an in with the reporters, and made it abundantly clear my father being shot at the wedding was not to make the headlines. The pictures show my wife, lovely as a lark. Mrs. Keenan McCarthy.

There's no mention of the bloodshed, no mention of the war between The Clans. Just my beautiful bride. My wife.

She sits beside me in the waiting room, holding my hand.

"Shit luck for a honeymoon," I quip, smiling at her. Christ, but I'm glad to have her. My father was shot near his heart, and he might make it through surgery.

I have to face what may happen.

If he doesn't make it... I'm Clan Chief. I've a wife, now.

"I don't need a honeymoon," Caitlin says in her quiet way. "We'll find a way to celebrate."

I lean in and kiss her cheek. "I have *many* ideas."

My mother dozes in a chair beside Caitlin. I'll never forget the way Caitlin's handled her tonight. She's held her when she cried, fetched her tea and food, and talked to her in her soft, soothing way.

"Will he make it, Keenan?" Caitlin asks, her troubled eyes looking at my mother.

"Dunno, lass," I whisper. My throat tightens. My father's heart is weak. I don't know if he will.

The doctor comes to us late in the night, exhausted. He knows who we are. Everyone in Ballyhock does. He scrubs a hand across his brow and speaks aloud for anyone to hear.

"He's pulled through, but he isn't doing well. The... accident took a toll on his heart."

"Can I go to him?" Mam is on her feet, her eyes rimmed with black mascara. She's had her cry and now she's doing what she always does: facing what she needs to bravely.

"Of course," the doctor says.

I join her, and the doctor puts a hand on my shoulder as mam walks by.

"He may not wake from this, sir," he says. I nod. I know it.

We go to my father, and it scares me a little to see him stretched on the bed, his eyes closed shut, so white he looks like vapor. There are machines stretched out beside him, all around him, regulating his heartbeat and breathing. We're not supposed to be in here, not so soon, but the doctor's waived protocol to let us in.

My mother stands on one side and I on the other.

"He'd be pleased to see you wed," she says, her eyes shining brightly at us. She reaches for my father's hand, and squeezes. Caitlin, the brave, sweet lass that she is, reaches for my father's second hand.

"Mister McCarthy," she says in her clear, pretty voice. "If you can hear me... I want to thank you. For raising this son of yours. For allowing me into your family. And for taking such very good care of me."

I love this woman and will spend the rest of my days seeing to her every need. She's so brave. Unencumbered with the ways of the world, she faces everything —life and death, marriage and circumstance, the violence and loyalty that forges our brotherhood— with steadfast loyalty and honesty.

We stay by my father's bed until the wee hours of the morning.

And when the sun rises on a new day, my father's gone.

Chapter Twenty-Five

Keenan

O*ne week later*

W e're assembled in our meeting room. Every
one of us. Caitlin's with my mother. They're
picking out furniture for the new bedroom, and I
think packing a bag. We're going to the school at the
weekend.

My father was buried with the highest honors, and the
men of nearly every clan came to pay their respects.
Martin sent a letter to me, asking for permission to
speak to me. He didn't come to the funeral. He wasn't
welcome.

Today's the day he's to come.

But we have business to attend to, first.

Lachlan, standing bravely before me, holds his hand on mine, taking his vows. We've followed the rules of induction, the ceremony. My father would be proud. We've gone over the rules of The Clan, then Sebastian slit his hand. Lachlan didn't even flinch. I did the same, and our blood joined as one in the first initiation shake. Cormac followed suit, and when Nolan returns home next month, he will as well.

He'll have to undergo final training. But it won't break him. He'll do well. It's because of him my bride survived.

"Keenan?" Carson stands by the door, gesturing for me. "Mack Martin's arrived."

I nod. "See him to the study, please."

Lachlan's taken under Cormac's wing. Tonight, he'll be brought to the pub, they'll drink to his honor, and get him a woman for the night. And tomorrow, I'll give him his first assignment. He'll get his Clan ink at the weekend. I'm proud of the boy and pleased that we've welcomed him into the fold. He's my first inductee as Chief. He'll serve us well.

I steel myself for what I have to do next. Mack Martin, the man who ordered a hit on my wife, the man responsible for my father's death. I want nothing more than to make him hurt, but he's here to speak to me, and it's in everyone's best interest if I keep the peace. So I go.

The short, fat, beady-eyed man waits in my office, flanked by his soldiers. As if I'd kill him right here.

He nods his greeting to me, his voice oily and thick when he speaks.

"Keenan, my condolences for your loss, and congratulations on your wedding."

"Thank you," I tell him, gesturing for him to sit.

I sit on the other side of the table.

"I want you to know that the sniper who arrived the day of your wedding was not sanctioned by me."

Bollox. But I let him go on.

"We were not trying to hurt you or any of your Clan."

"But he bore the ink of the Martins," I counter.

Martin nods. "Quite right. And I know the laws state that if one clan is responsible for the death of a Clan Chief…"

"We go to war. Aye."

"…*unless,*" he continues. "Unless a tribute's brought forth."

The son of a bitch. My marriage to Caitlin's solidified my Clan and prevented any of them from attacking her. What fresh, insidious plan does he have now? Still, I want to know.

"Tell me more."

"In exchange for peace between us, I'll offer you a daughter of The Martin Clan. No relation to your wife."

I feel my eyes go wide. A Martin daughter? *Christ.*

"The laws of our founders state such a tribute wipes all debt," he says. "No more bloodshed, my boy. The future of Ballyhock lies with us."

I don't know what his plan is, what he's trying to gain by this, but it seems a fair trade.

"How old is she?"

"Twenty."

"A virgin?"

"Aye."

"Show me a picture."

He gestures for one of his men to hand over a folder. He opens it, and shows me a picture of a beautiful lass, blonde-haired and blue-eyed. Christ, but she's young, though.

"When?"

"When she graduates uni. Next year. She's betrothed to no one, the youngest of six."

The son of a bitch sells them like chattel. I shudder.

"We'll talk more of this another time. I wish to speak to my brothers before I make this promise."

"Grant me temporary immunity?"

I grunt. "Aye."

He leaves, but I keep the folder. My men and I will have a talk.

I stand, looking out the window that overlooks the graveyard. It's hard to believe the weight of responsibility's fallen on me, that now I've assumed this role as clan leader. I knew it was coming. I wasn't prepared for it coming so soon.

I tuck the folder under my arm, weary of the day I had, and head upstairs to my wife.

My wife.

She's the balm to my wounds, the salve to my soul. Caitlin McCarthy wears my ring, bears my name, and soon will bear my children.

I take the steps two at a time, a buoyancy in my step I haven't felt since we buried my father. I want to see her. I want to hold her. I need to.

I open the door, and hear her laughing with my mother, before I see them.

"Oh, hello, there, husband!" she says, grinning at me. "We were just looking at these..."

She holds a tiny little romper thing in her hand. I feel my brows draw together.

"Whatever for?" I ask.

My mother looks tired, but there's hope in her voice when she says, "For my *grandchild.*"

"You're pregnant?" I ask Caitlin, and she only laughs.

"Not yet," she says. "But your mother's decided it's time to preemptively shop."

The elation and fear I felt quickly leaves me, and I give Caitlin a sharp look. "How about you don't give me a heart attack, wife?"

Caitlin gives me a knowing look, and mam gathers up her things. "I'll leave you two lovebirds."

As is tradition, we've moved into the larger rooms on the third floor. Mam's pleased that Caitlin's here now, and though she's mourning the loss of my father, she seeks comfort in the presence of another woman.

"That was very naughty of you," I say, shaking my finger at her.

"What?" Caitlin asks. "Soon, I'll bear you children. For all I know, I could be bearing them now."

"Perhaps we can wait another day or two? There've been so many changes I'm not sure I'm ready for a child."

She sighs and places her hand on my chest. "I don't know a lot of the ways of the world, but I'm fairly certain children don't arrive *overnight*. And Keenan, it would please your mother very much. It's been hard on her, losing your father."

It's been hard on all of us.

"Aye," I say to her. "I agree. But honestly, lass, you've made it so much better."

"Now, Keenan," she begins. "I know what you're thinking when you get that look."

"Oh? Tell me what I'm thinking," I say, reaching for my belt and unfastening it.

"You're *either* of thinking of dominating the life out of me *or* having your way with me."

"Quite right." I snap off my belt and give her a teasing swat. She yelps, squeals, and tries to run away, but I'm faster. I catch her with the tail end a second time, and the silly girl seeks refuge belly down on the bed.

I don't want to punish her, though. No. I want more than that tonight.

"You're a very dirty man, you know that?" she says over her shoulder.

"You weren't saying that last night when you came on my tongue," I remind her.

She flushes. "Keenan!"

"Nor when I clamped your nipples and ripped three orgasms from your pretty little body."

"Mmmm."

I'm tearing her clothes off, eager to have her naked beneath me. She's so responsive, so eager, and *all mine.*

"Take off your knickers," I order. The silly, lacy things are tricky to maneuver.

"Impatient, are we?"

I give her a teasing slap to the ass.

"Tonight, sweet girl, I'm taking you from behind," I tell her. "*Now.*"

Like the good lass she is, she strips what remains of her clothing and kneels, facing away from me. Tossing her hair over her shoulder, she shoots me a fetching grin.

"I love you, even if you're one of the Neanderthals."

"You love me *because* I'm a Neanderthal," I quip, raking off my own clothes and positioning myself behind her. I've waited for this. She's used to me now, so I don't have to ease myself in her. I can take her the way I want to, and tonight, I'm impatient.

I finger between her legs, pleased to see she's ready for me. "That's my girl. Good girl, so ready already, are you?"

She moans in response, already gripping the headrail for support like I've taught her. My cock's already hard, and I'm so eager for her I'm shaking a little. Every time she yields to me, every time she takes me, she soothes a little of the beast that rages inside me. I love this woman.

I line myself up behind her, and anchor myself on her hips. "Good girl," I approve. "Just like that, lass." Without preamble, I impale her with my cock. She groans and shifts, taking all of me, welcoming my firm, unhurried thrusts.

"That's it, sweetheart," I encourage. "Just like that, sweetness."

I rock my hips and she rocks hers, moaning and panting as she chases her own pleasure.

"I love how easily you respond," I tell her.

"Hard"—*pant*—"not"—*gasp*—"to."

I slap her ass in approval, pull out, then thrust back in to the hilt. She keens with pleasure and rocks her hips with me.

I unleash myself on her, thrusting in and out without pausing, no words needed. I know she's on the verge of coming when she throws her head back and pants my name. "Keenan *oooohhhh*."

"Come, sweet girl," I order, my own release ripping through me. We ride the spasms of pleasure until we're spent, panting and sated. Her head falls to the head-board and I drop my forehead to her shoulder.

"I love you, sweet fae," I whisper. "And I love that you're mine."

"And I love you, Keenan."

We clean up in silence and I lead her to bed. It's my favorite part of the night, when she snuggles up onto my chest and rests on me, her body folded up to mine as if she's meant to be right here, just like that.

I brush my fingers through her hair and hold her, rocking her tonight, though I think it's more for me than her.

"Do you really think we'll have a baby soon?" I ask her.

"I do," she says. "And I hope we do. It'll please your mother so."

It pleases me that she cares about this at all.

"We should take a honeymoon first," I say to her. "Don't you think?"

"Paris!"

I pause. "Have you rehearsed this?" I ask warningly.

She giggles and hides her head beneath my chin. "Mayyybe."

"With whom?"

"Megan may have suggested it."

I love how easily she's become one of them. One of us.

"Paris is doable," I say. "In fact, I'd love that. I've got business to tend to there. We need to see Nolan home as well, and there's other Clan business, but once we're settled we can do it.

"And to think…" her voice trails off.

"Aye? Go on."

"A few months ago, I sat alone in the tower. Overlooking the sea, but I didn't even know who you are. And now… and now I'm part of the family."

I kiss her forehead and hold her to me. "One of the family," I tell her. "And a gift of my heart."

She reaches for my hand and entwines her fingers with mine.

"Tá mo chroí istigh ionat, Keenan," she says. "My heart is in you. My everything is in you."

I hold her to my heart and squeeze. "And I in you, sweet lass. Thank you. I love you, Caitlin McCarthy."

She closes her eyes and smiles. How a woman like her can be pleased with a man like me, I may never know. But as the sun sets on today and rises on another, I give thanks for this woman. My beautiful, sweet wife.

My heart.

Epilogue

CAITLIN

Six months later

A brisk wind stirs my hair as I walk to the top of the cliff, the very edge that overlooks the Irish Sea. Keenan's had the lighthouse taken down, and in its place, there's now a garden.

"New life will bloom here," he said. It made me smile, how my stern, fearless leader of criminals has a romantic edge. The earth where the lighthouse once stood is surrounded by dark, rich soil, the seeds of the future garden planted only last week. But new life *will* bloom. Of that I'm certain.

Keenan sits on the cliff's edge, looking out at the sea. He does this early in the morning, and it's become our tradition. Many mornings, fog rises, or a fine mist. It's often windy and a bit chilly, but it doesn't deter him. A part of me wonders if he likes when the weather's inclement. He's certain to be alone then. While he overlooks the ocean, I bring him morning tea.

He doesn't look up when I approach, but when I sit, he smiles at me.

"Good morning," I say simply. My heart flutters when his green eyes meet mine, and his deep, husky voice greets me.

"Morning, lass."

I sit beside him, with my own steaming mug of tea.

"I sat right here," he said. "The morning of the day I found you."

"Did you?"

"Aye. I knew something was brewing but didn't know what."

"I was starving to death and friendless," I say. I don't need to tell him how drastically that's changed. I now have a family, friends who love me, and my needs are met in spades. I shiver when a brisk wind picks up, tinged with the salt of the sea. I breathe it in. My chest expands when my lungs fill. Keenan reaches his arm out and stretches it across my shoulders, pulling me closer to him. I put my head on his shoulder, shielded from the cold.

We stop talking for a few minutes. I don't know what he's thinking, but I'm marveling at the changes we've seen in such a short time. Nolan, bless him, my new-found brother and secretly my favorite of the lot, has been released from rehab. He hasn't touched a drink and swears he won't again. There's a crease on Keenan's forehead I swear Nolan put there, but Keenan's been patient with him. We all have. Nolan's family. As of yesterday, though, Keenan's put him to work. I'm intentionally kept out of the inner dealings of The Clan, but I know that Nolan's latest personal mission has been keeping the nosy reporter who *will* keep trailing The Clan in check.

My husband leads his fierce group of soldiers with fearlessness, bravery, and honesty. Though I know they skirt the law, and that old Father Finn shakes his head at what they do, I love this brotherhood of men. They live by a code unique to them, symbolized by the Celtic knot tattooed on their bodies. Keenan's too humble to talk of it, but Maeve explained the knot they wear.

"'Tis the Dara. It symbolizes wisdom, strength, leadership, and power," she said. "A reminder that they're bound by blood, honor, and loyalty."

And they are. They fight like brothers do. They tease, they drive each other crazy. But they'd lay down their lives for each other.

We visit the school sometimes, and Keenan's allowed me to befriend the women who teach there. His cousin Megan's taken a liking to me. She's bold and fearless, and in many ways my opposite. But she's got a good heart and a ready laugh. Keenan's possessive of my time, though.

Keenan squeezes my shoulder.

"A question, Caitlin."

"Yes?"

His eyes still watch the endless waves as he clears his throat. "Are you happy, lass?"

319

My only hesitation comes from the lump that's suddenly formed in my throat. I swallow hard a few times before answering.

"Keenan, I'm happier than I ever thought possible."

His lips tip up in a rare grin, laugh lines crinkling around his eyes. "That pleases me, sweetheart."

"Keenan?"

"Mmm?"

"Are *you*?"

He thinks for long minutes before he speaks, and I wonder if he's going to answer at all. Finally, he nods. "Aye. I carry responsibility, and you know that. For my men. My brothers. My mother. For you, and the little one you carry." He places his hand thoughtfully on my swollen belly. "But every night, I come home to you. You're a precious gift to me. I don't know what I've done to deserve you, but I will spend the rest of my days honoring that privilege." He cups my jaw and kisses my cheek.

He's introduced me to so much. The world outside my door, from the highest mountain peaks of Dublin to the lowliest pub in the valleys. He's shown me sunsets from the peak of Cold Stone Castle, and held my hand when I dipped my toes in the Irish Sea. He gave me my first kiss. My first taste of what it means to make love. My first earth-shattering orgasm. He even took me to a club his brothers frequent, and shown me just how much pain can heighten pleasure.

"I've got something for you," he says, and he dips his head almost shyly as he reaches into his pocket.

320

"Do you?"

He gives me a boyish smile. "Aye."

His hands shake a little when he draws a slim, narrow box from his pocket.

"Keenan… what is it?"

"Open it, then." He hands me the box. "Our wedding wasn't a memory I want you to keep," he says, his brows furrowed. "It was pragmatic and had a violent end. I want to give you something more. Something to remind you that you belong to me."

I open the lid with trembling fingers. I'm not sure why this makes me nervous. Keenan isn't a sentimental man, so gestures like this bear greater weight. In the box is a slim golden necklace, and at the very center, the Dara knot.

"It's beautiful," I breathe, drawing the slender, delicate piece of jewelry out of the box.

He takes the necklace from my palm and unfastens the clasp. "It locks, lass. Won't come off unless I remove it myself."

"A collar, then?"

His brows rise in surprise. "You know?"

I nod. "You collared me once with a thicker, clumsier sort of thing. But Megan told me about them."

He snorts. "Of course she did." Then he sobers, and his face once more takes on a bit of a boyish look. "Will you wear it, Caitlin?"

He botched the proposal and the Martins botched our wedding. This feels like a chance at redemption, a chance to make our union right.

I lift my chin and look him straight in the eyes. "Absolutely. Put it on."

His booming laugh startles me, echoing off the cliffs that overlook the sea.

"I love you," he says softly when he's finished laughing. He yanks me to his chest so hard I can hardly breathe. "I love you."

"And I love you. Now please stop squashing me to death," I say, my grinning face smashed up against his hard chest.

He lets me go, but not before he kisses my forehead. "Let's go," he says, getting to his feet and taking my hand. I rise with him, and he gives me a playful smack on the butt.

"So how will you take this off if necessary?" I ask him.

"I've got the key."

I smile to myself. He does. He owns the key to my collar and the key to my heart.

We walk hand in hand back to the house, the sea at our backs, and a lifetime before us.

F*rom the author: I hope you've enjoyed reading* Keenan: A Dark Irish Mafia Romance.

. . .

I am so grateful for your support! Please read on for previews of my other books you may enjoy. If you enjoyed Keenan: A Dark Irish Mafia Romance, you might also enjoy book two in the Dangerous Doms series, Cormac.

R ead on for a preview.

Previews

CHAPTER ONE

Cormac: A Dark Irish Mafia Romance

My mouth waters when the bartender places three large, frothy pints of Guinness in front of us. Christ, I need a pint like a newborn calf needs her mother's titties.

"Anything else I can get you boys?" Rafferty Kelly asks with a ready grin. The oldest son of a dirt poor family of ten, he's scrapped his way from the dank hovel he grew up in the Midlands to Ballyhock. A stone mason by day and bartender by night, word has it he still supports his mam and the little ones back at home. Rafferty runs a hand through his short, ruddy hair, and folds his arms on his chest. I down my pint in long, thirsty gulps, slam it back down on the counter and give him a chin lift. He grins in approval.

I tap the empty glass. "Another one, lad." He clucks his tongue and takes my empty pint with a wink. When his back's turned, I fold a tenner into the tip jar.

"Y'alright, Cormac?" Keenan asks, nursing his pint. His tone's casual, but I don't miss the way he drums his fingers on the table, or the ramrod stiffness in his spine. He knows I've been wrestling with what I have to do all week. Hell, he was the one that threw the fucking gauntlet.

"I'm alright," I mutter. I'm in the mood to drink, not talk.

The door to the pub section of the club swings open, and Nolan ambles in. I snicker to myself as every damn girl in the pub takes note. One girl tosses her hair back, and another straighten her shoulders to show off her tits. One even takes out a golden tube of lipstick and smears red on her pouty lips. Some whisper and point, and one even walks his way, but he walks past her without a second glance.

Nolan's single, and every damn girl in Ballyhock knows it. They don't care that he's the youngest McCarthy son. They don't care that he's the heart and soul of the Irish mafia closest to Dublin. How he gets his money or spends his time is of no consequence to them. He's rich, he's easy on the eyes, and he's a fucking charmer.

He walks past each of them and stalks straight toward us. Rafferty wordlessly slides a pint of Rock Shandy in front of him, the yellowish orange drink good enough without a drop of alcoholic. A year ago Nolan would've have scoffed at a virgin drink and called the manhood of any bloke who drank one into question, but now, Nolan doesn't even flinch. I'm proud of him. He's been nearly a year sober, and it's only been in recent weeks he's even come near a bar. Takes fucking bollox to face your weaknesses and stay strong.

"What's the story, brother?" I ask him, tapping my pint to his in greeting.

He swigs his drink before speaking, places it on the bar top, and sighs.

"Christ, but it feels good to be back here."

Nolan was the first of the McCarthy brothers to frequent The Craic, the dual-purpose club now under new management and aptly named.

Rafferty wipes the counter in front of Nolan and nods. "Good to have you back."

Nolan was the one who recruited us all here to begin with. Beyond the bar is a members-only exclusive section of the club, reserved for those who've got what Nolan calls, "tastes of a particular nature." In Ireland, we hide our sex clubs well. I suppose we have to reconcile the ghosts of our Christian forefathers by keeping up appearances, or some such shite. But we have our demons, too, behind closed doors.

Keenan looks to Nolan with concern. He knows how Nolan's bout with alcoholism nearly destroyed him, and as the older McCarthy brother and Clan Chief, it's his job to be sure Nolan's alright.

"All good, lads," Nolan says with his signature grin. "I figure now that I've got control of myself, time to control some tits and arse."

I snort, and even Keenan's lips tip up.

"Sounds about right," he approves. "You're heading to the back, then."

"Aye." Nolan takes another long pull from his drink.

"Any word on the bitch you're trackin'?" Keenan asks.

Keenan assigned Nolan to tag the nosy reporter who's had her head up our arses, and it seems he's making headway with her.

"She's hot onto the Martins, it seems," Nolan says.

"Will you need to teach her a lesson?" Keenan quirks a brow, his pint to his lips.

Nolan grins, his voice lowering an octave to a lust-filled groan. "Christ, brother, I hope so."

I laugh out loud. I know exactly what he means.

Keenan shakes his head, but he smiles, his eyes crinkling around the edges, and for one moment, my heart squeezes. God but he looks like my father when he smiles like that. Seamus McCarthy, father to the three of us, has been dead now for nearly a year. He was a hard-headed son of a bitch, but a loyal man. I wouldn't be the man I am today if it hadn't been for him.

"Cormac, we said we'd talk about your decision this weekend. What will it be, brother?" Keenan shoots straight and is ready to move ahead with our plans. It's rare we discuss Clan business in a pub instead of one of the more private meeting rooms, but sometimes if we can talk discreetly enough, it's worth it.

I don't answer at first, but take another long pull from the cold, frothy Guinness. I welcome the thick, slightly bitter taste, my belly warming with the gulps I take. Up until now, we could've been any three brothers sitting at a pub with a cold drink. But few people have to wrestle the decision before me now.

My father was killed by a Martin clan sniper, an act of war according to the iron-clad code we follow. But shortly after my father's death, our rival, Mack Martin, offered a virgin tribute to Keenan, to be given to one of our men. Marrying the Martin girl would ensure peace between the Clans. We agreed she wouldn't marry until she'd graduated, but now that she has, it's time.

As the second eldest McCarthy brother, I'm next in line to the throne. There's no escape. If anything were to happen to Keenan, I'd have to take his role and by clan law, I'm not allowed unless I take a wife.

The thought of marrying a Martin makes me sick. Fucking Martins. I've little choice when it comes to marriage, though. The men of The Clan rarely date for sport. A Clan marriage should solidify bonds, and rarely take place because of love. Sometimes we take captives in payment for a crime .Sometimes marriage is an act of retribution, and sometimes we agree to arranged marriage. Often, we're betrothed. If I decline the Martin girl, what other chance will I have? But more importantly, what will happen to our Clan?

"She's fucking gorgeous," Nolan says to me. We've been given pictures, and I've done a fair bit of social media stalking myself.

"Aye." But what if the girl's looks are only a mask? "She may be spoiled. Her father's one of the wealthiest in the Martin clan."

Keenan smiles. "You could fix spoiled."

Nolan groans. "I'd fucking love a chance to fix spoiled. Put that little girl right over my knee and teach her the lessons her dad forgot, aye?"

Despite my reservations, I shift on the bar stool, the instant image of the pretty blonde I've been poring over strewn on my lap temping as hell. I don't like the more violent line of work we do at times, but I do like what Nolan's introduced me to at the club, deliberate pain laced with raw sexual power.

"Agreed," Keenan says. "Spoiled is an easy fix, and one you'd handle well."

I grunt and take another swig. "Could be a nag." I grimace at the very thought.

Nolan snickers. "Also quickly remedied with a firm hand. Hell, the first thing you ought to teach a woman's to watch a smart mouth."

Keenan rolls his eyes. "For a jovial fuck-up, you're a dominant son-of-a-bitch."

Nolan clinks his drink against Keenan's, smiling. "Why thank you," he says, as if he's just been paid the highest compliment. "And anyway, you should talk. You think I didn't notice the crop and cuffs you nicked from the club, or at slender collar your own wife wears? You might be private, Keenan, but I'm no *eejit*."

Keenan smiles wordlessly as he takes another sip from his pint. He enjoys the finer tastes of domination, but would cut off his own bollox before he brought his wife in the presence of other men. He may have taken her here once or twice, but he's a possessive bastard, and saves his escapades for the privacy of his bedroom.

"You are not," Keenan says. "And Cormac, I agree with Nolan. Both spoiled and nagging are easily remedied."

"Not everything can be fixed with a crop or a firm hand," I tell them, barely tempering the need to roll my eyes.

"No," Keenan agrees. "But you're McCarthy stock. You'll know how to handle her."

"Aye," Nolan says, his bright blue eyes widening in earnest. "'Tis easy to train a woman. When she's naughty, you take her across her lap, teach her manners and to watch her mouth. Then you show her just how nice it can be when she obeys you. If you catch the right sort, she might even be wet between the legs after you punish her."

Keenan chuckles. "Aye."

"Then when she's good and well tamed, you reward her for being a good girl. Take care of her, and her heart will be yours."

"You act as if training a woman's a simple as training a feckin' filly."

"Aye, lad," Nolan says sagely. "But it is."

Keenan shakes his head. "Not hardly."

"You ought to talk," I say, shaking my head at him. "You ended up with Caitlin."

His eyes darken, and he places his pint on the table. "Come again?" The dangerous tone of his voice warns me, but I'm not afraid of Keenan, and I say what I mean.

"Oh come off it, Keenan. All I mean is that she was neither a nag nor spoiled," I tell him. "She was sweet from the day we found her."

"Did you forget she nearly clocked us with a trowel? I had to carry her away, kicking and screaming like a banshee."

"In self-defense," I remind him. "Hardly a banshee."

"No," he admits with a smile, his eyes getting that faraway look when he speaks of his beloved. "Caitlin is a sweet lass."

Sweet lass indeed. He fucking worships her.

"The more pressing question isn't her temperament, lads," Nolan says. "But what our choices are. If you don't marry her, Cormac, she'll have to go to another of the Clan, at the very least. Rejection of a tribute's serious business, a luxury we can't afford. I'd take her myself if you won't, Cormac. It's our duty."

"Aye." Don't I know it. I feel the weight of responsibility to make the right choice. The livelihood of the Clan's on my shoulders. Keenan's wife's heavy with child, ready to burst at any moment, and though he'll have a nanny and help, he'll be occupied for a time. And if we don't take the tribute offered by the Martins, our clans will war. Someone has to marry her.

"Honestly, brother, it isn't hesitation," I admit. "I'll take the Martin girl. I just want to be prepared to deal with her."

Nolan leans forward, a shock of blond hair falling across his forehead. "I've met her, you know."

"Have you?" It's news to me.

"Aye," he says. "Banged one of her roomies."

Keenan's lips thin, but he doesn't speak.

"Course you did. And what'd you find?"

I'm suddenly curious. I need to know everything about the girl I'm to marry.

"I wasn't joking when I said she's gorgeous," Nolan begins, when Keenan's phone rings. He answers, and a few seconds later, drops his pint. It clatters to the floor. Nolan and I look to each other in astonishment. Keenan never loses self-control.

"It's Caitlin," Keenan says. He's on his feet, his eyes wide, hands trembling on the phone he holds.

"She alright?" I ask him.

"Aye. Water's broke. She says her contractions are two minutes apart."

"Christ, man, *go!*" I tell him. "You want me to drive you?"

"No, I'm good," he says, already at the door.

"Good luck, brother!" I shout after him.

He waves, and he's gone.

Nolan and I sit for a moment, stunned. He polishes off his Shandy with a flourish, and slams it on the countertop.

"Brother, it's time we pay a visit to the real part of this club, aye?"

The real part of the club, where women are aplenty, and the air is ripe with the sweet, seductive scent of sex.

"Hell yes."

I pay our tab and head to the back with Nolan. We move past the dimly-lit front room, past the idle chatter and clink of glass, to the thick black door guarded at the back.

"Tell me more," I say to Nolan when we enter the members-only section of the club.

"First," he says with a roll of the eyes, "her name's Aileen, not 'the Martin girl.'"

I punch his shoulder, which only makes him grin while he rubs it out.

Aileen. Have to admit, I love that name.

"Second," he says, smiling and waving to a girl dressed in black latex in the corner of the room. He snaps his fingers and points to the floor. She drops to her knees and begins to crawl toward him, her ready grin revealing this is not a hardship. "She sings like a lark."

He freezes when a man steps toward the little kitten heading his way, lumbering toward her with the grace of a troll. He's masked and wearing all black. He reaches down, blocking the girl's path, and grabs a fistful of her hair. My pulse spikes. I'm used to all manner of manhandling at the club, but the tone of her scream and shocked expression tells me she didn't authorize this.

"Son of a bitch," Nolan growls, and takes off. I groan but follow. If there's a throw-down, I'm his backup. I see Tully and Boner with a few girls nearby, and catch their attention as we go.

By the time we get to the girl, the bastard's got her on the tips of her toes, her hair entwined in his meaty fist. She's beating at his hand, tears streaming down her cheeks. "Flagon!" she screams. *"Flagon!"* It's the goddamn club safe word. He doesn't stop.

Nolan doesn't hesitate but tackles the man full on. The girl topples to the floor, and Tully catches her.

The man's mask falls off, hanging around his neck like an executioner's noose, but he doesn't bother fixing it. His beady black eyes are infuriated. With a savage growl, he lunges at Nolan. They fall to the floor, fists flying. Tully, Boner, and I watch, ready to defend Nolan if we need to, but we let him fight it out, our own bodyguards about the place as well. No one comes to aid his opponent.

"You fucking asshole," Nolan fumes, landing a solid punch to the guy's nose. We've all been trained in martial arts, and will easily take this guy out. His aim is solid, his fist connecting. Blood spurts everywhere, and the guy covers his face with his hand. In a flash, he reaches to his foot, and the light catches a gleaming silver blade in the light.

"Fuck!" I growl, and in one reflexive motion, kick the blade from his hand. The knife clatters to the floor. Nolan decks him again. He's on his knees, grabbing at his broken nose, when uniformed security guards grab both of them.

"He assaulted her," Nolan says, pointing an irate finger at the guy, who still looks ready to kill. "She safe-worded and he wouldn't stop."

"She fucking likes it," he growls. He's missing teeth, and his bloodied face is contorted in anger. His thick, heavy eyebrows draw together over black eyes that are too-small for his puffy face, like buttons sewn too tightly on a throw pillow.

"I know what she fucking likes," Nolan fairly spits back.

"He pulled a goddamn blade," I say to security, my voice thick with anger. For half a pound I'd slice the man's throat with his own blade.

He growls and tries to lunge back at Nolan, but the guard holds him back. His shirt rips, revealing pasty white skin and ink I know on sight.

"Shite," I mutter, when I recognize the mark of a Martin.

"Son of a bitch," Boner groans beside me. "Mother of *God*. I know him."

I turn to him. "You know him?"

He sighs. "Yeah, brother." He shakes his head. "Meet your future brother-in-law."

READ MORE

Previews

Beyond Measure

Chapter One

T*omas*

. . .

I scowl at the computer screen in front of me. As *pakhan,* the weight of everything falls onto my shoulders, and today is one day when I wish I could shrug it off.

A knock comes at my office door.

"Who is it?" I snap. I don't want to see or hear anything right now. I'm pissed off, and I haven't had time to compose myself. As the leader of the Boston Bratva, it's imperative that I maintain composure.

"Nicolai."

"Come in."

Nicolai can withstand my anger and rage. Over the past few months, he's become my most trusted advisor. My friend.

The door swings open and Nicolai enters, bowing his head politely to greet me.

"Brother."

I nod. "Welcome. Have a seat."

When I first met Nicolai, he wore the face of a much older man. Troubled and anguished, he was in the throes of fighting for his woman. The woman who now bears his name and his baby. But I've watched the worry lines around his eyes diminish, his smile become more ready. While every bit as fierce and determined to dutifully fill his role as ever, he's grown softer because of Marissa, more devoted to her.

"You look thrilled," he says, quirking a brow at me. Unlike my other men, who often quake in my presence, having been taught by my father before me that men in authority are to be feared and obeyed, Nicolai is more relaxed. He's earned the title of *brother* more readily than even my most trusted allies.

"Fucking pissed," I tell him, pushing up from my desk and heading to the sideboard. I pour myself a shot of vodka. It's eleven o'clock in the fucking morning, but it doesn't matter. I've been up all night. "Drink?"

He nods silently and takes the proffered shot glass. We raise our drinks and toss them back together. I take in a deep breath and place the glass back on the sideboard before I go back to my desk.

"Want to tell Uncle Nicolai your troubles?" he asks, his eyes twinkling.

I roll my eyes at him.

I made an unconventional decision when I inducted Nicolai into our brotherhood. The son of another *pakhan,* Nicolai came here under an alias, but I knew he had the integrity of a brother I wanted in my order. I offered him dual enrollment in both groups, under both the authority of his father and me, and he readily agreed. We've come to be good friends, and I would trust the man with my life.

"Uncle Nicolai," I snort, shaking my head. None of my other brothers take liberties like Nicolai does, but none are as trustworthy and loyal as him, so he gets away with giving me shit unlike anyone else. "It's fucking Aren Koslov."

Nicolai grimaces. "Fucking Aren Koslov," he mutters in commiseration. "What'd the bastard do now?" He shakes his head. "Give me one good reason to beat his ass and I'll take the next red-eye to San Diego."

He would, too. Nicolai inspires fear in our enemies and respect in our contemporaries. Aren falls into both categories.

"Owed me a fucking mint a month ago, and hasn't paid up," I tell him. I spin my monitor around to show him the number in red. "And you don't need me to tell you we need that money." As my most trusted advisor, Nicolai knows we're right on the cusp of securing the next alliance with the Spanish drug cartel. Our location in Boston, near the wharf and airport, puts us in the perfect position to manage imports, but the buy-in is fucking huge. We have the upfront money, but the payout from San Diego would put us in a moderately better financial position.

Nicolai leans back in his chair, rubbing his hand across his jawline.

"And you have meeting after meeting coming up with politicians, leaders, and the like."

I eye him warily. Where's he going with this?

"It's easy to say you need money. But that isn't what you need, brother."

I roll my eyes. "I suppose you're going to tell me what I need."

"Of course."

"Go on."

"You know what you need more than the money?" he asks. I'm growing impatient. He needs to come out with it already.

I give him a look that says *spill*.

"You need a wife," he says.

A wife?

I roll my eyes and shake my head. "Sometimes I think your father dropped you on your head as a child," I tell him. What bullshit. I look back at the computer screen, but Nicolai presses on.

"Tomas, listen to me," he says, insistent. "Money comes and goes, and you know that. Tomorrow you could seal a deal with the arms trade you've been working, and you know our investments have been paying off in spades. But a good wife is beyond measure, and Aren has a sister."

"You've been married, for what, two fucking days and you're giving me this shit?" I reply, but my mind is already spinning with what he's saying. I never dismiss Nicolai's suggestions without really weighing my options. Aren is one of the youngest brigadiers in America and has a reputation that precedes him everywhere he goes. He commands men under him, and I'm grateful he hasn't risen higher in power.

He grunts at me and narrows his eyes. "I've loved Marissa for a lot longer than we've had rings on our fingers."

"I know it, brother," I tell him. "Just giving you shit. Go on."

"Aren's sister is single, lives with him on their compound. Young. I don't know much about her, and haven't seen a recent picture, but I met her years ago when I first came to America. And she was a beauty then. I imagine she's only grown more beautiful."

Seconds ago, this idea seemed preposterous, but now that I'm beginning to think about it, I'm warming to the idea.

"You think he'd let her go to pay off his debt?"

"With enough persuasion? Hell yeah. And a good leader needs a wife. You've seen it yourself. There's something to be said for having a woman to come home to. The most powerful men in the brotherhood are all married."

He's right. Just last week, I met with Demyan from Moscow and his wife Larissa. He brings her everywhere with him. The two are inseparable. And he's risen to be one of the most powerful men the Bratva has ever known.

"And face it, Tomas. You're not exactly in the position to meet a pretty girl at church."

I huff out a laugh. The men of the Bratva rarely obtain women by traditional means.

I lift my phone and dial Lev.

"Boss?"

"Get me a picture of Aren Kosolov's sister," I tell him. Our resident hacker and computer genius, Lev works quickly and efficiently.

"Give me five minutes," he says.

"Done."

I hang up the phone and turn to Nicolai. "I want to see her first," I tell him.

"Of course."

"How's Marissa?"

He fills me in about home, his voice growing softer as he talks about Marissa, but I'm only half-listening to him. I'm thinking about the way a woman changes a man, and how he's changed because of her.

Do I need a wife?

The better question is, do I want Aren Kosolov's sister to be the one?

My phone buzzes, and Nicolai gestures for me to answer it. A text from Lev with a grainy picture pops up on the screen, followed by a text.

There are no recent pictures. This was from a few years ago, but it should give you a good idea.

Still, it's a full profile picture. I murmur appreciatively. Wavy, unruly chestnut hair pulled back at the nape of her neck, with fetching tendrils curling around her forehead. Haunting hazel colored eyes below dark brows. High cheekbones, her skin flushed pink, and full, pink lips. She's thin and graceful, though if I'm honest, a little too thin for me. The women I bed tend to be sturdier and curvy, able to withstand the way I like to fuck.

I don't want to have this conversation via text. I call him and he answers right away.

"Background?" I ask.

"Never went to college. Under her brother's watchful eye since her father died."

"Lovely," I mutter. He might not give her up easily.

"Temperament?" I ask, aware that I sound like I'm asking about adopting a puppy, but it fucking matters.

"Not sure, but she has no record on file at school or legally. Perfect record. Graduated top of her class in high school." He snorts. "Volunteers in a soup kitchen in San Diego and attends the Orthodox Church on the weekend."

Ah. A good girl. Points in her favor. Sometimes the good girls fall hard, and sometimes they're tougher to break, but they intrigue me.

"Boyfriend?"

"None."

"Name?"

"Caroline."

"Caroline?" I repeat. "That isn't a Russian name."

"Her mother was American."

I nod thoughtfully. Caroline Koslov.

She would take my name.

Caroline Dobrynin.

I drum my fingers on my desk, contemplating. I nod to Nicolai when I instruct Lev. "Get Aren on the phone."

READ MORE

The Bratva's Baby (Wicked Doms)

The wrought iron park bench I sit on is ice cold, but I hardly feel it. I'm too intent on waiting for the girl to arrive. The Americans think this weather is freezing, but I grew up in the bitter cold of northern Russia. The cold doesn't touch me. The ill-prepared people around me pull their coats tighter around their bodies and tighten their scarves around their necks. For a minute, I wonder if they're shielding themselves from me, and not the icy wind.

If they knew what I've done... what I'm capable of... what I'm planning to do... they'd do more than cover their necks with scarves.

I scowl into the wind. I hate cowardice.

But this girl... this girl I've been commissioned to take as mine. Despite outward appearances, she's no coward. And that intrigues me.

Sadie Ann Warren. Twenty-one years old. Fine brown hair, plain and mousy but fetching in the way it hangs in haphazard waves around her round face. Light brown eyes, pink cheeks, and full lips.

I wonder what she looks like when she cries. When she smiles. I've never seen her smile.

She's five-foot-one and curvy, though you wouldn't know it from the way she dresses in thick, bulky, black and gray muted clothing. I know her dress size, her shoe size, her bra size, and I've already ordered the type of clothing she'll wear for me. I smile to myself, and a woman passing by catches the smile. It must look predatory, for her step quickens.

Sadie's nondescript appearance makes her easily meld into the masses as a nobody, which is perhaps exactly what she wants.

She has no friends. No relatives. And she has no idea that she's worth millions.

Her boss, the ancient and somewhat senile head librarian of the small-town library where she works won't even realize she hasn't shown up for work for several days. My men will make sure her boss is well distracted yet unharmed. Sadie's abduction, unlike the ones I've orchestrated in the past, will be an easy one. If trouble arises eventually, we'll fake her death.

It's almost as if it was meant to be. No one will know she's gone. No one will miss her. She's the perfect target.

I sip my bitter, steaming black coffee and watch as she makes her way up to the entrance of the library. It's eight-thirty a.m. precisely, as it is every other day she goes to work. She arrives half an hour early, prepares for the day, then opens the doors at nine. Sadie is predictable and routinized, and I like that. The trademark of a woman who responds well to structure and expectations. She'll easily conform to my standards... eventually.

To my left, a small cluster of girls giggles but quiets when they draw closer to me. They're college-aged, or so. I normally like women much younger than I am. They're more easily influenced, less jaded to the ways of men. These women, though, are barely women. Compared to Sadie's maturity, they're barely more than girls. I look away, but can feel their eyes taking me in, as if they think I'm stupid enough to not know they're staring. I'm wearing a tan work jacket, worn jeans, and boots, the ones I let stay scuffed and marked as if I'm a construction worker taking a break. With my large stature, I attract attention of the female variety wherever I go. It's better I look like a worker, an easy role to assume. No one would ever suspect what my real work entails.

The girls pass me and it grates on my nerves how they resume their giggling. Brats. Their fathers shouldn't let them out of the house dressed the way they are, especially with the likes of me and my brothers prowling the streets. It's freezing cold and yet they're dressed in thin skirts, their legs bare, open jackets revealing cleavage and tight little nipples showing straight through the thin fabric of their slutty tops. My palm itches to spank some sense into their little asses. I flex my hand.

It's been way, way too long since I've had a woman to punish.

Control.

Master.

These girls are too young and silly for a man like me.

Sadie is perfect.

My cock hardens with anticipation, and I shift on my seat.

I know everything about her. She pays her meager bills on time, and despite her paltry wage, contributes to the local food pantry with items bought with coupons she clips and sale items she purchases. Money will never be a concern for her again, but I like that she's fastidious. She reads books during every free moment of time she has, some non-fiction, but most historical romance books. That amuses me about her. She dresses like an amateur nun, but her heroines dress in swaths of silk and jewels. She carries a hard-covered book with her in the bag she holds by her side, and guards it with her life. During her break time, before bed, and when she first wakes up in the morning, she writes in it. I don't know yet what she writes, but I will. She does something with needles and yarn, knitting or something. I enjoy watching her weave fabric with the vibrant threads.

She fidgets when she's near a man, especially attractive, powerful men. Men like me.

I've never seen her pick up a cell phone or talk to a friend. She's a loner in every sense of the word.

I went over the plan again this morning with Dimitri.

Capture the girl.

Marry her.

Take her inheritance.

Get rid of her.

I swallow another sip of coffee and watch Sadie through the sliding glass doors of the library. Today she's wearing an ankle-length navy skirt that hits the tops of her shoes, and she's wrapped in a bulky gray cardigan the color of dirty dishwater. I imagine stripping the clothes off of her and revealing her creamy, bare, unblemished skin. My dick gets hard when I imagine marking her pretty pale skin. Teeth marks. Rope marks. Reddened skin and puckered flesh, christened with hot wax and my palm. I'll punish her for the sin of hiding a body like hers. She won't be allowed to with me.

She's so little. So virginal. An unsullied canvas.

"Enjoy your last taste of freedom, little girl," I whisper to myself before I finish my coffee. I push myself to my feet and cross the street.

It's time she met her future master.

R EAD MORE

Get your freebie!

Don't forget to grab your copy of *Island Captive*!

https://BookHip.com/QGLGGJ

About the Author

USA Today bestselling author Jane Henry pens stern but loving alpha heroes, feisty heroines, and emotion-driven happily-ever-afters. She writes what she loves to read: kink with a tender touch. Jane is a hopeless romantic who lives on the East Coast with a houseful of children and her very own Prince Charming.

What to read next? Here are some other titles by Jane you may enjoy.

CONTEMPORARY ROMANCE

Dangerous Doms

Cormac

Nolan

Carson

Lachlan

Dark romance

Island Captive: A Dark Romance

Ruthless Doms

King's Ransom

Priceless

Beyond Measure

Wicked Doms

The Bratva's Baby

The Bratva's Bride

The Bratva's Captive

The Savage Island Duet

Savage Dom & Savage Love

Undercover Doms standalones

Criminal by Jane Henry and Loki Renard

Hard Time by Jane Henry and Loki Renard

NYC Doms standalones

Deliverance

Safeguard

Conviction

Salvation

Schooled

Opposition

NYC Doms Boxset

The Billionaire Daddies

Beauty's Daddy: A Beauty and the Beast Adult Fairy Tale

Mafia Daddy: A Cinderella Adult Fairy Tale

Dungeon Daddy: A Rapunzel Adult Fairy Tale

The Billionaire Daddies boxset

The Boston Doms

My Dom (Boston Doms Book 1)

His Submissive (Boston Doms Book 2)

Her Protector (Boston Doms Book 3)

His Babygirl (Boston Doms Book 4)

His Lady (Boston Doms Book 5)

Her Hero (Boston Doms Book 6)

My Redemption (Boston Doms Book 7)

And more! Check out my Amazon author page.

You can find Jane here!

The Club (Jane Henry's fan page)

Website

Made in the USA
Monee, IL
31 January 2021